OOBE

To Mike & Sylvia

OOBE

by

Andrew E. Haughton

Best Wishes

ISBN: 1-58820-475-8

1stBooks - rev. 10/9/00

BACKGROUND

OOBE (pronounced Oobee) is an abbreviation for **Out Of Body Experience**. For those who have not yet encountered this phenomenon, the late U.S. businessman and author, Robert Monroe, founder of The Monroe Institute, who experienced many **OOBE**'s first hand and wrote three books on the subject, defined the **OOBE** as follows:

*"What is the Out Of Body Experience? An **OOBE** is a condition where you find yourself outside of your physical body, fully conscious and able to perceive and act as though you were functioning physically, with several exceptions. You can move through space (and time?) slowly or apparently somewhere beyond the speed of light. You can observe, participate in events, make wilful decisions based upon what you perceive and do. You can move through physical matter such as walls, steel plates, concrete, earth, oceans, air, and even atomic radiation without effort or effect. You can go into an adjoining room without bothering to open the door. You can visit a friend three thousand miles away. You can explore the moon, the solar system and the galaxy if these interest you. Or, you can enter other reality systems only dimly perceived and theorised by our time/space consciousness.*

The OOBE has also been linked to the more frequently documented Near Death Experience but without the implied threat of damage or death to the physical body. According to a 1998 MORI® poll, thirty per cent of British adults believe in OOBE's; and of those, more than one in five says they have actually experienced them!

OVERVIEW

This plainly written story is centred on the busy lives of Diane and Alan Harris, an average thirty-something professional couple who have just moved from the hustle and bustle of London into their new home; an old stone-built farmhouse in the countryside of West Yorkshire, England. When out exploring their new village for the first time they buy a book on the OOBE at a garage sale held by two young boys; and from that moment on their lives are irreversibly transformed.

Halfway into the story the main characters experience their first joint OOBE but due to an unexpectedly hasty return, their spirits enter the wrong physical bodies! This apparent catastrophe requires the couple to, literally, step into each other's shoes for a few days, and many dramatic, comedic and touching scenes unfold, including:

- Wife and husband make passionate unfettered love from each other's physical body
- They both learn, first-hand, the pros and cons of being the opposite sex
- Each experiences their partner's working day with quite unexpected results
- Many other remarkable role-reversal scenarios

During her many OOBE's, Diane Harris, the main character in the story, experiences global travel, a sojourn into outer space, time travel back to 55BC and several visits to the Ether, a spiritual place on another plane. OOBE makes for easy yet compulsive reading as it roams between village life in rural Yorkshire, the business dealings of a North-of-England law firm and the day-to-day lives of … ordinary people?

"Yorkshireism's" & Other Unusual Words

This book is written in "British" English and is set in the county of West Yorkshire, in the North of England. Therefore, some readers – especially those from outside the British Isles – may find some words, phrases and abbreviations of the small amount of local dialect within OOBE, strange, to say the least! So to assist readers a list of some of the more unusual Yorkshire anomalies has been compiled.

- T' / t' – Are frequently used and can mean several things but most commonly: e.g. "A'm off *t' t'* shops." Translation: "I'm going *to the* shops."
- A and A' – are again frequently used: e.g. "*A* do't know; *A'm* not really shuwer." Translation: "*I* don't know; *I'm* not really sure."
- 'e – Can sometimes find itself as a lower case letter at the beginning of a sentence: e.g. "*'e* allas did stuff wi' me an' mi bruvver an' *'e* nivver lerrus down." Translation: "*He* always did things with me and my brother and *he* never let us down."
- O' / o' – Another commoner: e.g. "*O'* course 'e wa' one *o'* us." Translation: "*Of* course he was one *of* us."

- Y' / y' – e.g. "*Y'* know, *y'*ve bin there." Translation: "*You* know, *you'*ve been there."
- All words that are clipped in normal Yorkshire dialogue are treated thus:
  - Livin' = Living – Showin' = Showing – Comin' = Coming – 'ello = Hello
- Anyroad = Anyway
- 'ave = Have / I have
- Bruvver = Brother
- Cum = Come – as in "come on"
- Eyup / 'ow do = Slang greeting terms
- Knackered = Worn out – tired out – spent
- Lerrus = Let us / Let's
- Mi = My / Me
- Nivver = Never
- Pillock = Commonly-used derogatory comment
- Plonker = Slang for Penis – e.g. "Don't be a plonker."
- Reight / Alreight = Right / Alright
- Sez = Says
- Shuwer = Sure
- Todger = UK vernacular for Penis
- Wi / Wi' = We / With

In the majority of the county of Yorkshire, words such as "Pub" and "Bus", and other words with a "u" near the beginning, are nearly always pronounced with the "u" stressed, sounding more like the "oo" sound in "good". As you can probably guess from this somewhat abysmal attempt, the sound of the Yorkshire accent is extremely difficult to articulate!

If readers of OOBE use the above as a rough guide, then reading and understanding the smattering of Yorkshire dialect within should be somewhat easier, and hopefully give at least a flavour of the real, rich sounds of Yorkshire. Alternatively, seek out an "Audio Book" version of OOBE, or, find a Yorkshire pen pal!

I sincerely hope that you enjoy reading OOBE as much as I did writing it.

Andrew E. Haughton

1

It was one of those uncommonly bright and clear early-autumn Yorkshire mornings. One of those days when the air was so clear you could see Blackpool Tower from the Cow and Calf rocks atop Ilkley Moor, if it weren't for the Pennine Hills of course!

A herd of sheep was grazing in the shaded stone-walled fields on the other side of the small valley, quietly cropping the dew-covered grass; but the old Yorkshire-stone farmhouse situated on the south-facing slope of the same valley was bathed in bright sunlight. Until its latest refurbishment the farmhouse, and all other structures made of the local porous stone, had been blackened with the grime of decades of belching smoke; which up until the mid-to-late 1960's had emanated from the woollen-mill chimneys that surrounded the city of Bradford, just a few miles to the south east. But with its exterior cleaned, the large rough-hewn stone tiles of its roof restored and the two stumpy chimneystacks rebuilt, the old house now looked much as it must have in 1785, when first built. The access drive, which dropped gently down a small incline from the main road, swept back on itself in an arc around a small copse of oak and beech trees before terminating at the cobbled courtyard of the house. Although it hadn't been re-gravelled for years the driveway was relatively free of potholes and didn't pose any problems for the removal van that was just pulling away from the house.

The couple, framed by the large wooden porch that protected the front door from the cold and wet of winter, waved at the departing vehicle; and as the van disappeared from view behind the trees they kissed and went inside.

The kitchen was large, which was not unusual for this type of farmhouse, where in years gone by the whole family would eat together before tending the farm's needs. Now, newly fitted-out with an array of light-oak cabinets and Hi-Tec work-surfaces, it had as its centrepiece an enormous welsh-dresser, situated directly opposite the brand-new, bright-red, four-oven Aga. A stout oak table, which came with the house when it was purchased and had been renovated along with several other large pieces of furniture, stood exactly in the centre of the room, encircled by ten locally purchased sturdy oak chairs. However, today, rather than brimming with food, the table was laden with numerous cardboard boxes from that morning's move.

Diane walked over to the sink and turned on the tap, filling the shiny chrome kettle to the brim.

"Alan, is it true that the water here's the best in the country?"

Alan looked up from a box he was burrowing into and shook his head, blowing a piece if paper off the end his nose.

"Yes, it's something to do with the porous nature of the limestone around these parts; it filters the water, making it extremely soft. That's why they centred the woollen industry down the road in Bradford all those years back. Just add a bucket of lanolin and it brings the fleeces up a treat. Your hair will be squeaky-clean and silky with just one wash up here! Not like that hard water down south. You had to use nearly half a bottle of shampoo to get a decent lather down there."

He grinned at Diane like a young schoolboy and delved back into the box like a Jack Russell terrier down a rabbit hole.

Diane laughed as she switched on the kettle and retrieved two mugs out of a large box marked 'Kitchin China'; a small spelling mistake for such a big box! As she walked back to the sink she gave a little shiver and wrapped her arms around herself, gazing around the kitchen as if she expected to see something. She looked over at Alan with a puzzled expression on her face.

"Ooh, I just had a strange feeling, like a cool breeze; no, not a breeze, more like a presence or something. Weird!"

Alan clumsily extricated himself from his box again and wiped his brow.

"It's probably just a draught from one of the upstairs windows. The removal men were dripping grimy-sweat all over the new stair-carpet so I cracked a few open for them, to cool them down. I probably forgot to close one of them when they'd finished. Still, it'll help clear that manly aroma they left behind! You know, one of those guys' overalls smelled like a hooker's jock strap; a rugby hooker that is!

Diane frowned at Alan's locker-room humour but he continued nonetheless:

"I'm not exaggerating love, I've had first-hand experience of these things. Remember, I spent most of my rugby-playing life in a scrum, with my head stuck up a hooker's arse!"

He gave Diane another quick grin and burrowed back into his box.

With a shake of her head at her husband's tawdry comments and with another quick scan of the room, Diane shrugged her shoulders and finished making the tea; putting the pot on one of the Aga's hotplates to keep it warm.

The couple, both thirty-somethings, were dressed casually for the day's move, with both of them wearing jeans, sweatshirt and training shoes. Diane, a sub-editor for a national women's magazine, is a happy, resourceful and compassionate person. Standing a little over five feet six tall, she has thick shoulder-length auburn hair, hazel eyes and a very pretty face. Her figure is the envy of most of the women who know her, and the desire of virtually every man who lays eyes on her.

Diane was born into a South-of-England middle-class family and privately educated from the age of four until leaving school for higher education at eighteen. She was, throughout her whole school life, an excellent all-round athlete and academically above average. Having grown into a very bright and creative woman, she ended up in journalism, her first career choice.

Diane met Alan when she was twenty and studying at the London Polytechnic. Immediately after their meeting she finished a two-month relationship with John, Alan's best friend; having found John's goal in life, to be an eternal bachelor, not to her liking. However, as it was this brief relationship with John that brought her and Alan together, she doesn't view it as a total waste of time!

Diane and Alan went out together for the better part of three years before getting engaged, and, due to career moves and pressures, didn't trade-in their engagement for marriage for another two years.

Once married the couple moved into a jointly purchased apartment in the then up-and-coming Docklands area of London, on the river Thames. An area which although not their first choice, was close enough to both their places of work and much cheaper than the more established areas of London. They lived there until recently when Alan was offered a position with the Leeds office of his law-firm. Fortunately, Diane's employers also had a Leeds office, and she managed to swing – what she still views as a sideways move career-wise – a position as a sub-editor for things national.

Although they have no children yet and rarely discuss the subject, Diane feels privately that she and Alan must make that very important decision soon, or it will be made for them by default.

Alan, a corporate lawyer, is more of an academic with a sporting bent. At six-feet-one tall and weighing around 220 pounds, and with the physique of a recently retired second-row rugby player – which position he played as an amateur for many years – Alan doesn't personally think he is good looking. However, his looks are the kind that attract the majority of women; more rugged than handsome, with a hint of naughty schoolboy when he laughs.

Alan was born into a working-class Yorkshire family. His father died when he was ten and his mother struggled to bring up him and his two brothers. However, being an extremely talented and conscientious boy he won a free scholarship to Bradford Grammar School, where he attained above average grades in most subjects, particularly excelling at English and Rugby.

Alan met Diane at a party that his best friend, John, had invited him to at the time that he and John were studying law at University in London. Although Diane was with John that particular night, it was love at first sight as far as Alan was concerned; and when John and Diane split up shortly thereafter, Alan made sure that she didn't escape.

After graduating he got a job at a medium-sized London law firm that within two years was eaten up by one of its bigger rivals who had offices throughout the whole country. Alan was promoted to junior partner status quite recently, just prior to his firm announcing a vacancy for a junior partner position in their Yorkshire office, based in Leeds. After much discussion with Diane they decided that they would give Yorkshire a try, but with the caveat that if things didn't work out within two years, they would look to return to London or maybe even consider jobs overseas. Alan likes reading, eating, rugby and rugby.

Alan played rugby union at Bradford Grammar School and developed into a very good player. Good enough in fact to earn a trial for the England schoolboy team. But his greatest love was rugby league, a predominantly northern game with working-class roots that his father had avidly followed; being a supporter of the local professional club, Bradford Northern. Now renamed the Bradford Bulls, Alan follows this top Super League rugby club as enthusiastically today as his father followed Bradford Northern in the past, sometimes to the chagrin of Diane!

Alan came up for air, giving up on his search for … whatever!

"At least we won't have to buy a water filter up here," he glibly remarked.

"That's true," agreed Diane, "we can offset the saving against the deposit on a Range Rover."

"What Range Rover?" asked Alan, casting a quizzical look at his wife.

Diane turned from the sink and put her hands on her hips.

"The one we're going to have to buy if we want to be mobile up here in winter."

Alan looked across at Diane again, this time with a scant frown.

"Oh come on love, it's not that bad. Once we've had the drive re-gravelled it'll be okay."

Diane wasn't at all convinced and she pressed him further:

"But I heard it can snow like mad up here in winter and I don't think this area's a priority for the local highways department. Just look at the potholes in the lane, and you can't re-surface that now, can you?"

"Look love," said Alan, sighing loudly. "I know that you weren't keen on this move initially but we've made the commitment now. I mean, God knows how but we managed to convince the bank to buy us ninety-five percent of this place. Although kidnapping the bank manager's wife probably helped," he joked. "And we've both moved our jobs here for at least two years."

This time Diane didn't laugh at Alan's attempt at diversionary humour.

"Hang on, let's be absolutely precise about this," she replied somewhat caustically, putting the two china mugs she was carrying down on the Aga just a little too heavily, chipping the base of one. Swearing delicately under her breath she continued her discourse: "You've moved back to your beloved Yorkshire and I've moved my job up from bustling cosmopolitan London to the ... crappy Leeds office."

Alan groaned at Diane's newly acquired dislike of anything northern. Up until they'd started to pack for the move Diane had always loved visiting the north.

"I know that love," he said desperately, "but you'll be working from home most of the time, thanks to that very expensive all-singing-and-dancing super-computer the Magazine provided. You can edit articles all day long, in peace and tranquillity; and surf the world-wide-whatever-dotcom-net to your hearts content!"

He walked over to the kitchen window and stared out over the green hillside that gently rolled away into the distance, periodically broken into an uneven patchwork by blackened dry-stone walls with weathered wooden gates.

"Just look at the views from here," he said, sighing audibly. "Aren't they just wonderful?"

Diane sensed her husband's deep affection for their surroundings and yielded.

"You're right, I'm sorry darling. I'm just feeling a little isolated that's all. I'm not used to being this far from civilisation."

Alan laughed, more from relief than anything.

"City gal," he said, ambling over and giving Diane a friendly bear hug. "I know it's not London but you've seen Bradford and Leeds, they can be pretty lively places. In fact Leeds is the envy of most UK cities since it revitalised its business and shopping areas. I heard that it's now ranked as the north's top financial, accounting and legal centre. It's a pity Bradford isn't," he said, shaking his head slowly.

Diane smiled putting on a mock Yorkshire accent:

"Aye lad, 'ave seen it all. Cultural centre o' t' North this part o' Yorkshire."

Alan feigned a miffed look.

"Oh come on love, don't take the piss! There's a lot of culture up here, not to mention good restaurants and theatres. The Alhambra in

Bradford is renowned for its plays and shows; and the National Museum of Photography, Film and Television pulls in masses of people every year. And Bradford's got some of the best Indian restaurants in the western world."

He smirked and raised his eyebrows before continuing with gusto:

"Then there's the great Yorkshire beer and both types of professional rugby; and don't forget the Bronte's just up the road in Howarth, that's a great place..."

Diane cut across his outpourings with raised arms.

"I know, I know; if it was good enough for Charlotte, Emily and Anne..."

Alan went over to the Aga and picked up the teapot, pouring the steaming brew into the two mugs.

"Look, we've been on the go since six this morning and we're both a bit edgy, so let's have this tea and take a break. We could go for a walk in the village and have a good old nosey around."

"Okay, I'm up for that," agreed Diane, sounding a little more enthusiastic.

2

The couple walked arm-in-arm down the quiet main street, taking in the scenery. The village was, in the main, made up of short terraces of modest stone cottages with slate roofs, originally built for the mill-workers; interspersed here and there with the odd, large Victorian-built detached house, originally built for the mill owners and managers. The few small streets that branched off the main thoroughfare were narrow and steep, cutting deeply into the hillside above the village; and surprisingly, most still had their original cobblestone surface.

At one end of the village was a small Norman-built church, surrounded on three sides by a well-populated graveyard, bristling with large weathered tombstones. At the other end stood the old mill, a large four-storey redbrick building, which although derelict looked quite picturesque with its thick covering of ivy turning reddish-brown.

The focal point of the village during the day was the combined shop and Post Office, which most of the elderly female inhabitants visited on a daily basis; meeting up with friends and neighbours for a welcome gossip.

At night, however, the local pub, an old coaching stop – which stood slightly back from the main street and was also covered in the same turning ivy as the mill – was the main meeting place, predominantly for the older male populous! Most evenings' talk was of the good old days, when the mill was functioning to capacity and was the main employer for the majority of the villagers, both men and women.

As they walked on Alan soaked up the scenery and with a big grin took in a chest-full of air.

"Wow, isn't it great around here?"

"Yes it is," said Diane, snuggling up closely to Alan's shoulder, "especially at this time of year, with the trees just on the turn. Oh that reminds me, we must sort out that lawn mower and get a yard brush, we don't want our new neighbours thinking we're lazy Southerners."

Alan grimaced at this, the ultimate insult for any Northerner.

"Eyup lass," he said gruffly in his old native tongue, "who a' you callin' a S'uthner."

Diane stopped suddenly, tightening her grip on Alan's arm; then smiling warmly stroked his lightly bristled cheek with her forefinger.

"I'm sorry I had a go at you earlier darling, I'm sure we'll be just fine here. It's a very pretty village and the house is fabulous now the refurbishment's finished."

Alan kissed Diane's forehead and gently brushed away a few loose strands of hair from her brow.

"It's okay love," he said compassionately, "I know it can be a wrench. I felt it when I first moved away from these parts. And we will be fine here, I just know it."

The couple kissed warmly and continued their stroll in silence, and as they turned the corner by the small lichen-encrusted stone church they saw a garage sale set up in the driveway of one of the larger houses and stopped for a look. At the entrance to the drive was a large wooden trestle table, groaning under the weight of a multitude of books. Two young boys, who looked about twelve and fourteen respectively, were leaning against the large weathered-stone gateposts, gently throwing a rugby ball to each other, feigning a lack of interest in the couple. Diane started to browse the books.

"Oh, look at all these wonderful books darling."

Alan picked up books one-by-one, briefly reading their back covers.

"There's a lot of science fiction and new-age learning stuff here."

Diane's hand wandered along the rows of books and abruptly stopped over one particular paperback that she picked up and started to flick through.

"This one looks interesting darling, it's all about Out Of Body Experiences."

The older of the two boys looked up and spoke with a slightly mocking tone:

"Yeah, our Dad used t' read everythin' 'e could lay 'is 'ands on if it wa' weird."

The younger boy tossed the ball at his brother a little harder than previously and chipped in defensively.

"It's not weird, our Dad really believed in all that stuff. Anyroad, a've read some o' these an' they art that weird. It's all down t' whether o' not you find that sort o' thin' interestin'. Our dad did."

Alan addressed the older boy:

"You said your Dad used to read all these books. Doesn't he want them any more, or at least want to keep some of them?"

The boy twirled the ball in his hands a few times before answering:

"No, 'e died last summer an' our mum said wi' could sell 'em," he remarked without looking up.

Alan glanced briefly at Diane before responding sympathetically to the boy.

"Oh, I'm sorry."

"It's alreight mister," said the older boy with a slight shrug of his shoulders.

He then looked up at Alan and stared square into his eyes, slightly narrowing his own.

"Anyroad, who a' you? Mi mum ses wi' not supposed t' talk t' strangers."

Diane answered him with a sympathetic smile:

"And she's right, you shouldn't. So let's properly introduce ourselves. We're the Harris's, I'm Diane and this is Alan; we've just moved into the old farmhouse at the other end of the village."

The younger boy responded to Diane's amiable nature.

"Ow do Missis Arris," he said congenially, dropping the "H" in Harris as is customary in that part of Yorkshire. "A'm Matt Ayres an' this is mi bruvver Mark.

"Ave yer moved int' t' house where t' Ryan's used ter live?" enquired Mark somewhat brusquely.

Matt looked up longingly and let out a wistful sigh.

"Missis Ryan med great cakes," said the young lad affectionately. "She all'as give us a big un every 'alloween. But A think the've moved down south now. Shame really, the' wa' reight nice; well for old folk!"

"Yes they did move south," said Diane, nodding in agreement with the young boys words but smiling inwardly at his delivery. "Mister Ryan moved to a new job, a bit like us I suppose but in reverse. They've moved south and we've moved north."

There was a pregnant pause as the couple looked at the books and then Diane broke the silence:

"Anyway, good luck with the sale but we must get back and crack on getting the house sorted out; but if you ever want to call around we'd be glad to see you. Although I don't bake very good cakes I'm afraid," she concluded with a laugh.

Alan was still scanning the mass of books on the trestle table.

"We should buy something before we go," he said, turning to Diane. "Would you like one love?"

She looked down at the many rows of both old and new-looking books, pondering a possible selection.

"Yes I would but there's so much choice."

Then, quite unconsciously, she reached over and picked up the first book she'd looked at.

"How about this one on Out-Of-Body Experiences?"

Young Matt looked straight into Diane's eyes.

"Y'll enjoy that book missis, especially if y' read it wiy an open mind. Well, that's what mi Dad used t' say anyroad."

Diane perceived the young boy's grief at the loss of his father and felt a tug on her heartstrings.

"I'll do that," she said softly.

Alan paid for the book and saying their goodbyes, the couple walked off, leaving the boys arguing about the custody of the cash!

Diane and Alan sauntered around most of the village that afternoon, striking-up conversations here and there when they saw people in their gardens or out walking the dog, and eventually arrived back home quite weary.

Alan tossed the book they'd just bought onto a pile of magazines stacked on the coffee table in the lounge, and after a quick snack they got on with their unpacking, which lasted all weekend!

3

It was an overcast Monday morning and Diane was working in the upstairs study. Originally a large bedroom, this light and airy room was now fitted-out as an office, with a reproduction antique oak desk – currently the home for the computer – a secretary's chair, a two drawer filing cabinet and a sofa bed; for those creative moments and visiting-guest-overflow. Originally, the idea was that Diane and Alan would share this room but Diane had quickly claimed it as her home-office; enforcing that claim by adding brightly coloured curtains, a large vase of matching silk flowers and a myriad of little feminine touches scattered here and there.

Diane was reading a copy of a competitor's magazine – a part of her job that she found quite enjoyable – when the silence was momentarily broken as the computer beeped. A synthetic female voice – sounding very much like the British actress Joanna Lumley – softly said: 'You have E-mail', signifying that Diane had received a message. She got up from the sofa and went over to the desk to check it out.

It was an article for editing from her office and it read:

"INTERNATIONAL MOVIE STAR, JOHNNY BIZARRE, HAS NEAR DEATH EXPERIENCE. BIZARRE HAS REPORTED THAT WHILST ON THE OPERATING TABLE HE SEEMED TO LEAVE HIS PHYSICAL BODY AND ACTUALLY WATCH THE SURGEONS AS THEY WORKED ON HIS LIFELESS CORPSE..."

Diane stopped reading and looked up from the computer, her brow furrowed in thought.

"That book we bought from the two boys..."

The article had jogged her memory about the book on out-of-body experiences that they'd bought from the garage sale last Saturday. She bounded down the stairs to find it and while down there made herself a fresh mug of coffee. Sitting down at the kitchen table with her back to the warm Aga oven, Diane began to read the book and soon became deeply engrossed. She read:

"... AROUND TWENTY-FIVE PERCENT OF PEOPLE REMEMBER HAVING HAD AN OUT OF BODY EXPERIENCE (OOBE) AT SOME TIME IN THEIR LIVES BUT MOST OF THOSE INTERVIEWED BELIEVED IT WAS JUST A VIVID DREAM..."

She read on eagerly, becoming so absorbed she was almost halfway through the book before realising it was nearly five-thirty.

She jumped up from her chair and started to prepare dinner and was still at the Aga cooking when she heard Alan enter through the front door.

"Hi love, I'm home," he bellowed from the hallway.

Diane returned his greeting cheerily:

"Hi darling, have a good day at the office?"

"Not bad," he shouted, "considering we nearly lost one of our largest clients. It wasn't anything to do with me of course but everyone got a hell of a rocket," he said, walking into the kitchen.

"Never mind," said Diane, looking up from her cooking with a dazzling smile and kissing Alan sloppily on the lips. "You go sit down in the lounge and I'll bring you a long, cool drink. I've had an interesting day too!"

Diane carried the drinks into the spacious but warm and cosy lounge – with it's heavily beamed ceiling, large stone inglenook-fireplace and thick cream-coloured fitted carpet – and gave Alan another more lingering kiss as she handed him his drink. She sat down next to him on one of three copious primrose-coloured couches that surrounded a low stained-glass-topped coffee table set slightly back from the fireplace. Alan nodded his thanks for the drink and smiled.

"Thanks love," he said as he took a large gulp from his glass.

"I got an interesting article to edit today," said Diane. "The first one via my new computer's e-mail system. It was about Johnny Bizarre, the movie star. You remember, there was an article in the papers, about him being taken to hospital after a car crash on the M25 motorway last week?"

"Yes," said Alan, nodding his recollection. "Wasn't there a rumour that he'd been drinking, or taking drugs or something? Our London office represents one of his companies; not that they encourage that type of client you understand, but I suppose it pays good money."

"Hypocrite!" squealed Diane. "You lawyers will do anything for money."

Alan looked at her with raised eyebrows.

"Yes, I suppose we will, as long as it's legal that is. Anyway it's a good job we are overpaid," he said, overtly puffing himself up, "otherwise we wouldn't be sat in this fabulous house, sipping drinks in front of this roaring fire. I told you it would stay in all day," he added as an afterthought, taking another drink from his glass. "Anyway, what was it that you were saying love, about Johnny Bizarre?"

Diane bit her tongue over Alan's inference at being the only wage earner in the house. He could be a bit of a male chauvinist when he wasn't thinking. In fact, he could be one even when he was thinking!

"The article I was sent today claims that Bizarre had a near death experience, so I started to read that book on OOBE's; you remember, the one we bought from the Ayres boy's garage sale last Saturday?"

Alan nodded.

"Well apparently the word's pronounced OOBEE."

"It sounds like a baby that's just seen a bee," chuckled Alan. "Ooh, Bee," he repeated in a chipmunk-type baby voice.

Diane laughed at his antics and continued a little more excitedly:

"But you wouldn't believe the research that's been done on this whole out-of-body thing, going way back; and I mean way, way back. Apparently the ancient Egyptians believed in travelling out of their bodies when they died, that's why they stuffed their tombs with all sorts of things they might need on a long journey. And they say that Tibetan monks have been practising OOBE's for thousands of years, something to do with their meditation process. And for the past thirty years or so really in-depth hi-tech studies have been undertaken on the subject, in controlled surroundings in America."

"Oh yes, whereabouts?" cut in Alan inquisitively.

Perceiving a flicker of interest from her husband, who could sometimes be less than attentive when the subject matter of their discussions involved anything ethereal, Diane continued enthusiastically:

"There's an Institute somewhere in Virginia that's been researching OOBE's since the sixties, and hundreds, or it might even be thousands of people there, have been monitored actually leaving their physical bodies. OOBE's have been around for ... well ... forever. In fact, surveys done here in England suggest that twenty-five percent of the population believe they have experienced an OOBE at some time in their life. But most people who have similar experiences think they've just had a vivid dream about flying."

Alan looked askance at Diane.

"Hold on there a minute love! Are you trying to tell me that you believe in all this stuff? I mean, I know that you've always had an open mind for these sorts of thing, it kind of goes with your job; but doesn't this stretch even your fertile imagination just a little?"

Diane, now on something of a roll, brushed aside Alan's downbeat comments.

"No, it's truly amazing, and I intend to do some more research on the subject. I might even consider writing an article myself, for the Magazine."

Alan shook his head and exhaled loudly through pursed lips.

"You really mean it don't you? I know you've always had a hankering to write features but I thought it would be about something more down-to-earth, if you'll forgive the pun!"

He laughed loudly at his own joke but this time Diane didn't reciprocate, becoming just a little frustrated with Alan's enduring lack of regard.

"But I'm really interested in all this," she said resolutely. "When I started reading that book on OOBE's, I got this strange feeling creeping all over my body, it was really weird, but at the same time compelling. Anyway, I just have to understand more."

Alan laughed again.

"Oh Di."

Diane's face instantly reflected her hurt and she responded quite bluntly:

"Don't make fun of me, I'm serious. I really believe that we can do this if we learn more about it."

Alan sat up straight at Diane's implied assumption.

"What do you mean, we?" he exclaimed, casting an eye over the book that Diane had been holding since they first started the conversation. "Anyway," he said more calmly, finally realising that Diane was serious about the topic; "you haven't read the whole book yet, in fact you can't have even read half that book in one afternoon."

"Exactly! Don't you see darling," she said, still uncompromising in her own defence, "if I've been motivated to this extent by just reading a part of it, then just think what reading the whole book will do?"

Alan threw his hands in the air in defeat.

"Okay, you win. Read the whole book and then tell me that you're still convinced and I'll take a look at it too."

He stood up and adopted a pacifying smile, patting his stomach.

"Now, what's for dinner?"

"Italiano," quipped Diane, accepting Alan's unspoken apology. "You open de wine and I'll drain de pasta."

Over the next few days Diane blitzed the local research library in Bradford and read everything she could obtain on the OOBE phenomenon. She even used her computer to surf the Internet in her quest for knowledge and was amazed at the huge amount of information out there. Wherever 'there' was!

At the same time and unbeknownst to Diane, Alan was sneaking the odd book from her study and reading it on the train on those days he didn't take his car to the office. It seems he was as curious about OOBE's as his wife but not yet as ready to admit that interest. After all, lawyers are supposed to be logical, structured professionals and all this OOBE stuff was, at least in Alan's voiced-opinion, just a bunch of ghostly supposition. Wasn't it?

4

Alan was sitting behind his desk in his new office, located in a swish up-market block in central Leeds. He had just finished a phone call with one of his clients when his close friend, John Sagar – who was also a corporate lawyer with the same firm – dropped in for a chat.

John was raised in a similar working-class environment to Alan and although very bright at school, not quite up to the same standard as Alan. This was primarily due to his pre-pubescent preoccupation with the opposite sex; something that he still suffers from. A confirmed bachelor from the age of about sixteen he never had time for participating in sports – girls again – but is now quite fit for someone who eats out most nights and is not averse to the odd drink!

John still rues the day that Diane left him, but has to admit to himself that it's probably more a macho thing; that he wouldn't necessarily feel that way if she hadn't immediately taken up with his closest friend. Of course it's even more difficult now, as Alan and Diane have moved back to Yorkshire and he sees Diane quite regularly.

After graduating John went straight back to his beloved Yorkshire, even though Alan had secured a position for him at the firm he'd joined in London. But when informed of this great opportunity John had said: 'Absolutely no way Al old buddy.

I've spent five years down here and that's five years more than any self-respecting Yorkshireman should spend away from home. The beer and the women are better in Yorkshire and I'm off back on the first train from Kings Cross station!'

Joining a small Leeds law-firm on his return from London John climbed the corporate-law ladder quite quickly, becoming head of his department in only three years. And even when the London practice that Alan worked for acquired the smaller Leeds-based practice, John managed to keep his position; which now made him head of IPOs (Initial Public Offerings) dealing with private companies that want to move into the public sector for the first time. Apart from corporate law, the only things that Alan and John have in common are rugby league and Diane.

John likes girls, women, cars and money. The latter two because it helps him to attract the former two!

"So, how's it going?" asked Alan.

"Great thanks," said John, slumping into one of Alan's client-chairs.

"How are you old-buddy?"

Alan groaned loudly and rubbed the back of his neck, mainly for effect!

"Oh I'm not too bad but I could do with a week off to rest. This moving job's nearly killed me. Diane's had me unpacking boxes and moving furniture since we moved in. I wouldn't mind so much if we put things in their place and left them there but she seems to want to 'experiment', as she calls it. So I've moved the same furniture around the same rooms about ten times already."

John smirked openly at his friend's tale of woe.

"So how is the delightful Diane?" he enquired. "You know I should never have let you take her off me when we were at University in London. She's a great gal."

"If I remember correctly," said Alan with a frown, "she dumped you for me. Anyway she doesn't fit your criteria; she's a southerner and intelligent!"

"Cheeky bastard," cursed John amiably.

Alan got up from his desk and walked to the window, looking out over the bustle of Leeds City centre. He paused for a second, taking in the view, and then turned to look at John with a half-smile on his face.

"So," he said, diplomatically changing the subject, "how's the Mega-Software floatation going? I heard a rumour it was getting just a little bit sticky."

John sat up in his chair and wagged his finger at Alan in mock warning.

"I've told you before, you shouldn't listen to rumours. Anyway, It's been a real push but we'll be ready according to schedule."

Then he shook his head and sighed, rubbing his eyes with his clenched fists.

"Actually, we've been working eighteen hours a bloody day for the past two weeks and I can tell you, I'll be glad when it's all over. I'm fucking knackered!"

"Ah yes, the price of fame and fortune," said Alan with a grin. "So, how much cash are they hoping to raise now?"

John revived at the mention of money and smiled greedily.

"They increased the offering to five billion quid last month."

Alan let out a long, low whistle.

"Five billion pounds! Wow, these hi-tech computer companies are just incredibly priced right now. But isn't it a bit of a lottery the way the markets are playing up at the moment?"

"Between you, me and the gatepost," said John, looking around melodramatically and lowering his voice to a near whisper, "it's a fucking nightmare. If we've got our timing wrong we'll be bum-shagged by everyone down the other end of the M1 motorway, and we'll never get another hi-tech client again, that's for sure."

He sighed deeply, reflecting for a moment before continuing:

"I wish I had a bloody crystal ball so I could see what the markets will be doing on floatation day. This uncertainty's giving my ulcers too much gyp."

Alan looked at him thoughtfully.

"It's funny you should say that, about a crystal ball that is. Diane's been reading up on out-of-body experiences for some article she's doing on the infamous Johnny Bizarre. She believes, having diligently undertaken all the relevant research of course, that it's possible to leave ones physical body and travel anywhere in the world; and one of the books she has on the subject reckons that you can even travel in time and space as well. Once you become experienced that is," he added as an afterthought.

"Fuck off!" exclaimed John loudly. "You don't believe all that crap, do you?"

Alan was momentarily taken aback by his friend's overt demonstration of scepticism.

"Well, not at first," he said a shade defensively, "but I've been reading some of her research books, and I can tell you, there's a lot of compelling evidence out there to suggest otherwise."

John shook his head and frowned, adopting a more earnest tone:

"Well don't let any of the senior partners hear you talking about it," he cautioned, "or they'll have you working on sodding house-conveyancing for the rest of your career."

He got up from his seat and walked around the desk to Alan, who was still standing by the window.

"Seriously though Al, people can get the wrong idea about that kind of thing."

Alan wished he hadn't said anything on the subject but nevertheless kept up his defensive stance.

"Okay take it easy, it's only something I'm reading up on because of Diane," he said testily, walking back over to his desk and sitting down. "All I'm saying is that if these books were half-right it'd be better than your crystal ball, wouldn't it?"

Noticing his friend's discomfort and with his next meeting just minutes away, John decided it was time to leave.

"Sure would," he promptly agreed, laughing as he did. "Let me know when you've cracked it and we'll make a fortune in the City!"

He looked at his watch, mainly for effect.

"Oops, must go, I've got a meeting in five. See you around."

He made to leave but as he reached the door he turned.

"Oh, by the way, don't forget the Bulls' game on Saturday. It's a big one, they're playing those bloody Wigan Warriors from over the Pennines."

And with that he walked jauntily out the door, closing it heavily behind him. Alan sat there for a moment reflecting, then with a little shake of his head went back to his paperwork.

Later that day, back at the farmhouse, Alan and Diane were sitting watching the television news in what Alan called the TV room but which Diane had mentally demarcated as the family room. However, with just a television, CD sound system and a matching sofa and two chairs, Alan's classification of the room was presently nearer the mark.

Drinking his after-dinner coffee with one eye on the television, Alan turned to Diane, giving her a smile.

"Great meal love."

"Thank you darling but it wasn't much."

There was a short pause in the conversation as Alan watched the local business news.

"Oh, by the way," he said, as the dulcet tones of the theme tune for Emmerdale Farm, a nationally popular Yorkshire-based TV soap cranked up; "John dropped in for a chat this morning."

Diane picked up the TV listings book and feigned disinterest, lowering the sound on the TV with the remote control.

"Oh yes, and how's the randy bachelor keeping?"

"Apparently his big Mega-Software floatation is giving him ulcers," said Alan, ignoring Diane's usual snub at John. "He said he could do with a crystal ball, to tell him what the markets will be doing on the big day. So I told him to read some of your books on OOBE's, then he could travel forward in time to get a handle on the situation."

Diane raised her eyebrows slightly and looked questioningly at Alan.

"How do you know about OOBE-time-travel, have you been reading my research books?"

Alan glanced at her innocently and then looked towards the TV in the corner of the room.

"I did pick one up the other day and flick through it," he said nonchalantly. "I read a few paragraphs on time and space travel and…"

"Darling," said Diane abruptly. "It's alright to show interest in the subject. We aren't living in the dark ages. The Witchfinder General isn't about to burst into the house, snatch all our books and have us burned at the stake."

"I know," he said irritably, it's just something that John brought up today when I mentioned the subject to him."

"Oh, you'll play the sceptic with me but you'll talk openly to John about it," said Diane teasingly. "Even recommend he reads-up on the subject!"

"Oh it's not that way love, honest. I just happened to mention it when he was going on about wanting a crystal ball; and he said to watch out, not to talk about OOBE's in the office. People might get the wrong idea about me, think I'm some sort of latent crackpot."

Diane fell silent for a moment and looked down at her hands, unconsciously playing with her rings.

"Is that what you think I am Alan," she said softly, "a latent crackpot?"

Alan slid along the sofa closer to Diane and with an affectionate gaze put his hand on hers.

"No of course not love. There's nothing latent about you!"

Diane grabbed a cushion and made to whack him and Alan instinctively ducked his head.

"Sorry, just a little joke. Seriously though, of course I don't think you're a crackpot, otherwise I'd be a hypocrite!"

"Hypocrite, why?"

Alan paused in thought for a second and then groaned loudly:

"Oh, okay, I'll come clean, but don't laugh," he appealed. "I have been reading your books and I find the whole thing really fascinating."

He took a sip of his coffee and looked at Diane like a schoolboy who's just about to confess to his parents that he's been caught smoking behind the school bike sheds.

"Look, I've never told you this before but I've had lots of dreams, since I was a snotty-nosed little urchin; dreams where I remember flying. Really flying like a bird; no, like Superman in the movies.

And when I started reading that book we bought at the kids' garage sale it said that everyone has OOBE's when they're sleeping but only a few people remember them. Most people just think they've had a dream about flying. Well maybe that's me. Maybe I'm having OOBE's and don't know it."

"Oh Alan why didn't you say so?" said Diane, putting her arm around his neck and stroking his cheek. "You know you can talk to me about anything.

Alan looked at her sheepishly.

I don't know," she said despairingly, "you men are so anally retentive."

"Now, now, there's nothing wrong with my lower bowel functions," joked Alan, trying to cover his discomfort.

Diane chuckled, snuggling up even closer, gently stroking his earlobe.

"Look, let's agree something right now. We'll both finish reading all the stuff we have on OOBE's and try a little experiment."

Alan frowned slightly but didn't interject.

"I've wanted to do this since I read that first book," continued Diane eagerly, "but I thought that you'd think I really was crazy."

Alan pulled away slightly and responded like a little schoolboy again.

"Ah, see, you were keeping that from me, I'm not the only one with little secrets."

Diane looked at him with a wry smile.

"Okay, that's a touché, but just listen to my idea about the experiment for a moment."

She sat back, pausing to collect her thoughts.

"I think that we can self-induce a state of conscious sleep it will give us a better shot at having an OOBE. According to some of the books I've read they do it all the time at that institute in America. All it takes is relaxation of ones body, a little patience and, apparently, a real belief in what you're doing and…"

"Hang on there," wailed Alan. "A state of self-induced conscious sleep! I'm not sure that I want to do this yet. I mean, what happens if one of us actually does have an OOBE? What if we can't get back into our bodies or something?"

Diane ignored his comments and continued her soothing manner.

"Darling, I've read lots more on the subject than you have and the consensus seems to be that it's not that hard if you really believe in what you're doing. Apparently some people have spontaneous OOBE's that they remember but they seem to be in the minority; or maybe those people just choose not to talk about it much."

Alan looked at her incredulously.

"Not that hard eh? Leaving our bodies at night, to travel the world; no, the universe; maybe popping back in time to see the birth of humanity, and all before breakfast, and you say there's nothing to it. Now that would raise questions as to our sanity if it got out."

Diane shelved his remarks again and continued her calming approach, but this time a little more steadfastly:

"Look, I'm way ahead of you in the research stakes, so you keep reading and I'll give it a try. Maybe even tonight, just to see if I can get to the conscious-sleep-state. And I promise that if I do manage an OOBE, which is highly unlikely at the first attempt, I won't leave the bedroom."

Alan decided he was on a hiding to nothing if he continued trying to discourage Diane and laughed in submission.

"Okay, have it your own way, but don't go spoiling my dreams if you can't get back in."

He paused momentarily, looking at Diane with a twinkle in his eye.

"There's one condition though," he said, moving closer and slipping his arm snugly around Diane's waist, giving her a teasing kiss on the nose. "I'd like to fool around with your physical body a little before you leave it. Just in case!"

Diane giggled and pouted as she ran her hand up the inside of Alan's thigh. They kissed passionately!

They were both deep in thought, lying in bed staring at the ceiling. Alan was the first to make a move, turning over to face Diane.

"Look love," he said in a slightly anxious tone; "I know that I agreed earlier, about you attempting this OOBE thing, but I really do believe that you should re-think trying it out, at least for a while. Who knows what might happen?"

Diane rolled over on her side, gazing at Alan sweetly.

"Thanks for the concern but don't worry, I'll be okay. I've researched this to death. No pun intended!"

She paused in thought for a second, plumping up her pillow with her fist.

"For instance, there's a tip in one of the books, on getting back into your physical body if you feel disoriented or lost. All you do is try to waggle your big toe on the real physical-you and that's supposed to have the desired effect."

Alan burst into uncontrollable laughter.

"Waggle your big toe?"

He raised himself onto his elbow as Diane looked on indignantly.

"Yes, waggle your big toe," she repeated firmly. "What you have to remember is that when you're having an OOBE it's not the physical-you that's out there, it's your ... well ... your consciousness; your spirit for want of a better word. And even though it's attached to our physical body, well at least for this particular life, it works differently when it's free of those physical constraints. Apparently it can pass through walls, steel, water, in fact anything physical, without any harmful effect to itself."

"It sounds more and more like my Superman-dream-scenario," remarked Alan.

"Maybe there is a connection," said Diane, looking at Alan with a thoughtful gaze. "Anyhow, according to people who've experienced OOBE's and recorded the results, all you have to do is think something and it happens. If you want to move, you think of moving. The same if you want to change direction. According to one book I read you don't even have to travel to get around. Well, travel as we understand it that is; you know, going from A to C via B? You just think of or visualise a person or place that you want to visit and hey-presto, you arrive there immediately. Apparently people are easier to find than places for some reason I've yet to fathom. Anyway, while all this out of body stuff is going on, ones physical body just sort of ticks over. You know, breathing, heart pumping away, etc.; but it says that if your sleep is disturbed, for whatever reason, your spirit automatically gets recalled, so the body can respond normally upon waking."

She looked at Alan who had an inquisitive expression on his face but he didn't interrupt her flow.

"Look darling," she purred, leaning across and kissing him tenderly on the cheek, "all I'm really saying is that if I do manage to have an OOBE, I'm sure I'll get back okay. So please don't worry."

Alan exhaled loudly but nodded his agreement.

"Okay, I'll stop hassling you but don't forget to wake me when you get back; if you get out in the first place that is. Goodnight love."

He turned over and assumed his usual sleeping position, on his side with his back to his wife, curled-up like a foetus "Goodnight darling," she said, as she snuggled down onto her back.

Diane lay there for quite a while, staring at the ceiling, trying to relax her body yet at the same time focus her mind; a technique that she had picked up from one of her research books. And as she lay there, quietly telling herself that she wanted to experience an OOBE, she eventually felt her body beginning to relax and her breathing became shallower. But try as she may she had a great deal of difficulty fighting her left brain – the analytical side of everyone's head – and it started to close down; and eventually she fell hard and fast asleep.

5

As the clock on the bedside table flickered over to two-thirty Diane slowly sat up in bed and surveyed the room. She looked over at Alan who was still curled up with his back to her and then casually glanced over her shoulder. With something akin to a double take she uttered a muffled scream and quickly clutched her hands to her chest in shock!

"Oh my God!" she wailed out loud. "How can this be possible?"

Diane could see herself, or at least her own head and bare shoulders, protruding above the quilt, lying back on the pillow seemingly fast asleep!

After a few seconds of near frozen terror Diane's fear slowly turned to bewilderment and then just seemed to ebb away as her senses sharpened.

"Oh my goodness, what a strange dream," she thought with relief, unfolding her arms from her chest and staring at her hands as if she'd never seen them before. "But if I'm really dreaming how is it I'm thinking I'm dreaming? Hang on, something's not quite right here."

She looked back again at her sleeping form and something stirred deep down inside her consciousness.

"Hang on a minute, maybe I've done it. Maybe I'm actually having an OOBE," she thought excitedly.

Very cautiously she tried to get out of bed, but instead of her hands pushing down on the mattress as they would normally, there didn't seem to be any real resistance and they seemed to sink, with a peculiar feeling, down into the bed. Then, quite slowly, and with a strange sensation deep inside her being, Diane started to rise upwards, towards the ceiling, and the panic briefly returned!

"What's happening?" she screamed.

But as soon as she'd thought the words, she stopped rising; and remarkably, a feeling of elation flooded through her and she laughed out loud, surprising herself that she could actually make a noise, or at least that was her current perception.

"This is incredible! Hang on though, this could still be a dream, one of those lucid dreams where you know you're dreaming and have some control over it. After all, I've been thinking about nothing but OOBE's since I got that article to edit. I've got to try and test this out somehow."

Very tentatively she reached forward with her arm and immediately seemed to glide effortlessly in the direction she was pointing, until she came up against a wall and gently bumped to a stop.

"This is unbelievable, it's like being Superwoman!"

And with that thought, she looked down at Alan and instantly floated towards him, stopping just a few inches from his sleeping form. She spoke softly at first:

"Alan, can you hear me?"

He didn't stir so she spoke louder this time:

"Hey Superman, its Superwoman. I'm here, floating above you; wake up will you?"

Still Alan didn't move, so this time she shouted loudly:

"Alan, look at me Alan, I've done it I'm having an OOBE!"

Nothing, Alan's nose didn't even twitch. Wondering what to do next she looked up and immediately began to float back towards the ceiling.

"This is staggering," she thought. "I've got to try some more manoeuvres."

Diane started a series of circuits of the bedroom, slowly at first but gaining speed with every lap and after a short time became quite adept at controlling her movements. Eventually she came to a halt by the window, looking out over the moonlit fields.

"I wonder if I should try to leave the bedroom?"

She looked around the room but there didn't seem to be any way out. The windows, apart from one that was slightly ajar for fresh air, and the door, were all closed.

"How can I get out though?" she thought, with a feeling of real frustration.

"I know I told Alan I wouldn't but … oh … I'd love to go outside."

As soon as that thought crossed her mind a bright blue-white flash blinded Diane's view and she felt a sensation of great acceleration, but only for the briefest of moments, and before she knew it she was outside above the front lawn; which suddenly seemed a very, very long way down! She began to claw the air and kick her feet, emulating a very bad doggy-paddle.

"Oh my God, what's happened?" she shrieked.

Looking around, Diane realised that she was actually floating about ten feet away from the house and a good fifteen feet off the ground; which was a totally different scenario from a minute ago. Floating three feet above a soft bed was one thing, but this! Yet slowly, as it dawned on her that she hadn't moved for the last little while and that she probably wasn't going to plummet down onto the lawn below, her panic subsided. She gradually stopped her doggy-paddle impression and lay there, floating still and silent. And then she remembered, and it was as if a light had just come on in her head.

"I know!" she exclaimed to herself, "It's like that book said. All I have to do is think of a destination or directions and that's where I'll end up."

Diane felt elated and with newfound confidence decided to try to move again.

"Let's check this out."

She thought of moving slowly towards the house and instantly had the sensation of gliding; as if in a swimming pool, when you're floating aimlessly and someone pushes you gently by the feet when you're not expecting it. She advanced nearer and nearer to the house and eventually ended up with her face just inches from the bedroom window. She looked inside but it was too dark to see anything, so she cautiously placed her index finger onto the windowpane and pushed gently. The finger went straight through the glass accompanied by a slight buzzing sound.

"Ooh, that tingles," she thought, pulling it back quickly and inspecting it closely for any damage.

To her amazement the glass didn't feel hard at all, in fact, the sensation was more like putting ones finger into a bag of those little polystyrene balls used for packing delicate objects. She tried again, this time placing the flat palm of her hand on the glass. Holding held her breath – or at least that was how it felt at the time – she pushed her hand through the window, but before she could withdraw it her whole body lurched forward and rapidly followed her hand; accompanied this time by a sound similar to that of the crackling-buzz of electricity that can be heard near high-voltage power cables on a damp day. She screamed again and when the sensation of movement had stopped Diane found herself back inside the bedroom, floating lazily over the bed.

"Wow, what a trip. That's amazing, and so incredibly easy too."

Easy or not, Diane still checked herself out for any damage but none was apparent, and for the first time she realised that her body felt to the touch much as it did in her normal state; and the sense of being touched, as she proceeded to prod herself, was also very similar. She looked down at Alan and her own physical body lying in the bed but neither had moved. So with her self-confidence gaining in strength by the minute, Diane had an urge to try out other feats, and she looked around the bedroom for inspiration, but nothing immediately sprang to mind. She scanned the room again and then had an idea.

"I know," she thought, "I'll do some exploring of the house. Let me see now, I wonder if I could pass through the wall into the next bedroom."

Diane cautiously touched the wall and felt a slight, almost imperceptible form of resistance but as soon as she pushed a little harder her hand started to disappear. And although she vaguely perceived the texture of the different materials that made up the wall, as she pushed her hand further in it still felt basically the same as the window had, like soft polystyrene balls. Holding her breath again she thrust her hand completely through the wall, and with the same sound of crackling electricity, was quickly in the next bedroom, floating over the chest of drawers.

"This is fabulous, I think I'll search the whole house and hone my skills a bit."

And with that Diane set out to get to know the house, probably more intimately than its original builders.

She passed through walls, floors, doors, ceilings, and even went up into the loft space where she found a family of bats popping in and out through a hole under the eaves.

"Bats, and I don't feel afraid of them. In fact I don't feel afraid of anything," she thought elatedly. "Wait a minute though what's that strange feeling, I'm coming over all woozy!"

A white flash filled the loft and instantly Diane was back in bed staring at the ceiling, totally confused. She looked at the clock, which showed two fifty-nine.

"Twenty-nine minutes since I woke up, well since I started my OOBE. Yes, my OOBE, it was an OOBE. I remember everything that happened"

She put the bedside lamp on and turned over to wake Alan, shaking him hard.

"Alan, wake up."

He moaned then slurred something incoherently.

"Alan, please wake up."

Alan turned over and put his hand to his face, to shade his eyes from the light.

"What is it?" he mumbled.

"Darling, I think I've just had an OOBE."

"You what?" he said, still half asleep. "An OOBE? What are you talking about?"

Diane leaned over him, close to his face.

"Alan, I've just had an OOBE."

Then she abruptly stopped and put her hand on her abdomen.

"Ooh, I need to pee; right now!"

6

Later that morning Diane was still in her dressing gown, sitting at the kitchen table with a mug of tea and a plate of hot toast and marmalade as Alan walked in, already dressed for work.

"Want some tea?" asked Diane, probably just a little abruptly.

Alan looked at his watch and checked it against the kitchen clock on the wall.

"No thanks, our little tête-à-tête upstairs has put me back a bit."

Diane sighed and got up from her chair.

"Look darling, I'm telling you it wasn't a dream. I really believe it was happening to me; or at least my spirit," she said firmly as she poured herself another cup of tea from the pot on the Aga.

"But you've been reading about and studying OOBE's for so long now, can't you at least concede that it's possible you just had a vivid dream?"

Diane was becoming just a little frustrated at Alan's obstinate stance and her voice reflected her feelings:

"Okay then, if you don't believe me go up into the loft and see if the bats I saw are there. That'll prove it."

Alan picked up Diane's mug and took a quick swig of her tea before assuming his all-knowing stance.

"Not necessarily," he said. "There are lots of bats in this part of the country and it would be safe to assume that an old house like this would have bats hanging around in the roof void."

"Alright then 'Mister Lawyer'," said Diane, raising a finger as an idea formed in her head. "You set me a test if you don't believe me."

Alan looked at her with raised eyebrows.

"What kind of test?"

"I don't know," she said quite casually, "you're the sceptic, you think of something."

He looked at his watch again and bent over, kissing Diane on the cheek. "Okay," he said, a little more light-heartedly, "I'll give it some thought at work today. Now I've got to go or I'll be late. See you tonight."

He walked out of the kitchen, collecting his briefcase by the door as he went. Diane shouted after him:

"Okay, but remember I'm going into the office today and while I'm there I'm going to talk to Susan about my OOBE!"

She paused briefly, then continued talking to herself in a low voice:

"She'll listen to me."

The front door closed with a thump as Alan left.

"Bye," said Diane gloomily.

It was a beautiful sunny morning as Diane stood on the platform of the pretty little village station, which like the majority of buildings in the area was built from locally quarried Yorkshire stone.

As the train pulled in she nimbly dodged a large puddle of water made by a member of the station staff who had inadvertently over-watered one of the colourful floral hanging baskets that adorned the whole station. Diane boarded the first carriage of the small commuter train, taking a backward-facing seat by the window; and as the train pulled out of the station Diane was lost in her thoughts of last evening's experience. Periodically she looked up at her fellow passengers, studying their faces, wondering if any of them could have ever experienced the same sort of thing that she had encountered last night?

"Surely not," she thought as she drifted off into reflections of OOBE's, pondering, trying to rationalise her dilemma.

And thirty minutes later, as the train ground noisily to a halt alongside the platform at Leeds Central station – which was still bustling with late rush-hour commuters, flexi-time workers and early shoppers – Diane was yanked back to reality and alighted, following the crowds heading for the exit.

Later that morning Diane was on the phone, sitting at her desk in the Magazine's slightly tired-looking but very busy office complex, when her friend and colleague Susan Turner dropped in for a chat.

Susan is a forty-something attractive red head with a slim but curvaceous figure, and was, as usual, dressed immaculately. Like Diane, she was originally from the South of England, but the similarity abruptly ends there. Susan, who was voted by her male peers as the best looking girl at her school, opted out of the education system at the age fifteen. Less than twelve months later she eloped and married a twenty-nine year old newly divorced car salesman.

At that time Susan thought she had the world in her hands, travelling up to get married in Gretna Green, Scotland, in an E-Type Jaguar, with a 'real man' by her side. She never could abide teenage boys; well, not until she was nearly forty! This, her first marriage, was over in less than a year, when her husband eventually went back to his ex-wife and their two children. So Susan moved up to London and lived alone for the next three years, working in various bars and clubs and going out with a variety of men.

One evening in a well-known up-market London nightspot, she met, in her words: 'A twenty five year old rich dish'. She played him like an expert angler plays a record-weight salmon and he was hers before the end of their first week together. She made absolutely sure of that! Within two months they were married, much to the displeasure of his family, who were something big in publishing.

But before long Susan had charmed her new father-in-law around to such an extent that he gave her a job on one of the family's magazines, as a researcher for the Agony Aunt column. The rest is history, as they say.

Susan very soon became the full-time Agony Aunt for that magazine and although her marriage failed after two years, the publication – which by then was the subject of a buyout by someone called Robert Maxwell – kept her on.

She met Diane when they worked together on the same trendy fashion magazine in London and Susan always maintained that she would never marry again. Last year she met this guy from Otley, near Leeds – a love at first sight job – and immediately wangled a position with a sister publication based in Leeds; which just happened to be Diane's current employer. Although the relationship only lasted six months Susan told Diane that she understood why she, Diane, was so happy with Alan. She said: 'Yorkshiremen are just so different from most others you meet. They have a certain ruggedness and a wonderfully loving nature, and they cry at soppy films.' And although

Diane couldn't ever remember Alan crying at a soppy film, for prudence sake she told Susan she was right.

Susan likes gossiping, designer clothes and big men, but not necessarily in that order! She is also a bit of a one-off, being the only extrovert woman that Diane knows, who is liked equally by both the men and women she makes friends with. Well, maybe the men do like her a little more!

Continuing her telephone conversation Diane waved Susan to a chair.

"Yes," she said into the phone, "I'll get that copy to you around the middle of next week if that's all right with you."

She paused momentarily while the other person spoke.

"Yes I will, bye."

Replacing the handset back on the receiver Diane smiled at Susan who returned her smile with an inquiring look.

"Under pressure my dear?"

Diane shook her head.

"No it's just an article they," she pointed up at the ceiling, "decided they want ahead of schedule."

Susan nodded knowingly.

"So, what did you summon me for, my Agony Aunt skills or a girlie chat?"

"A bit of both really," said Diane.

Susan settled further into her chair and smiled.

"Good, then I'm all ears. But it'd better be worthwhile, because you've just dragged me away from answering a letter from Wendy who lives in Wakefield. Wendy has a willy problem!"

Diane frowned.

"A what?"

"Not hers of course," corrected Susan with a smile. "Although I've had a couple of those in the post this week. You'd be amazed what people write in about nowadays; but of course the best ones don't get published. Well, not in our middle-class publication anyway. Now, where was I; oh yes, our Wendy says her husband's penis is much too big for her," she said, sighing sensually and rapidly fanning her face with her hand. "I don't know, one woman's plight is another's fantasy…! Still, Wendy says that big-uns are only really good for conventional sex and apparently Wendy likes a bit of variety," said Susan with a cheeky wink. "I suppose, put simply, Wendy's hubby is just as-big-a-pain-in-the-arse as the majority of men I know!"

"Oh my," said Diane, howling with laughter. "I didn't realise that you got that sort of mail, I thought that sort of stuff went to the 'top-shelf' type of magazine. Anyway, it's funny you should mention fantasies..."

Susan raised her eyebrows and squealed out loud:

"What do you mean? Have you been having fantasies like Wendy, because I'm sure that's what it is with her?"

"No you moron, not fantasies, more like vivid dreams; well more than that actually. You see," she said hesitantly, "I'm not sure if I had one or not last night."

"Which, fantasy, dream or the other?" enquired Susan suggestively.

Diane looked Susan straight in the eyes and tried to assume a serious demeanour.

"A dream, I think. Look, if I tell you this, you have to promise not to laugh and you mustn't tell anyone else."

Susan feigned an expression of hurt and put her right hand over her heart.

"It's okay, I've taken the Agony Aunt oath of silence. Imagine you're talking to your doctor or your solicitor, only with me it won't cost you!"

She leaned forward in her chair and looked furtively around the office, lowering her voice to a whisper:

"The only difference being that I may repeat what you tell me, but I promise that I'll change the names to protect the guilty. Like I'm going to do for Wendy from Wakefield, assuming I can get her letter past the editor that is!"

"Ha, ha, very funny," said Diane sarcastically before looking reflectively at Susan. "Joking aside Sue, I really do need to talk to someone about this,

Alan doesn't seem to be taking me too seriously. A bit like you in fact!"

Susan held up her hands and sat straight in her chair, shuffling in the seat to get comfortable.

"Okay, serious mode, fire away, I'm all ears."

Diane wavered slightly.

"I'm not sure where to start."

"How's about the beginning," suggested Susan, now sounding much more sympathetic.

"Okay, here goes. You remember that article I was sent on Johnny Bizarre? Well…"

Diane told Susan everything from the time that her and Alan had bought the first OOBE book and after about an hour of disclosure, periodically interrupted by Susan's questions, Diane concluded:

"…And Alan seemed a bit prickly this morning after I told him everything."

Susan looked visibly moved.

"Wow, so you really think that you had one of these OOBE things?"

Even though she'd now unloaded her thoughts Diane still sounded a little despairing.

"Yes I really do, and I need to be able to prove it, at least to Alan."

Susan got up from her chair and started to walk up and down in front of the desk.

"My dear, if you could prove it, and I mean scientifically prove it, you could make a fortune," she said, turning dramatically to look at Diane.

"Think of it," she said excitedly, "the book, the film, magazine interviews..."

"Sue, please," said Diane, cutting across her friend's verbal deluge. "I just want to prove it to Alan."

She stood up and walked around the desk to face Susan.

"And I suppose if I'm being truthful, I need to prove it to myself as well. You see," she said earnestly, "I really believe that what I experienced last night actually happened but at the back of my mind is always the question: if it's so easy to do then why isn't everyone at it?"

Susan smiled and adopted her Agony Aunt voice again.

"Look Di, throughout my career I've had letters from people all over the country describing similar events, asking what they can do to prove it. Some even think that they're going a little cuckoo, if you know what I mean. In fact that's probably the reason why most people don't confide in others about such phenomena, in case they're made a laughing stock, or get dragged off to the funny farm. However," she said, raising a finger and smiling warmly, "in your case, because I know you so well, I believe you. That is I believe that you believe what you've experienced. So I'd recommend you go along with Alan's suggestion for a test, whatever it turns out to be. It can't do any harm and hopefully it'll prove the case, or not, to both your satisfaction."

"You're right," said Diane with a smile. "Thanks a lot, that's all I needed to hear. You're a good friend for listening."

"No problem, that's what I'm here for."

Diane glanced at her watch.

"Hey it's gone twelve, come on, I'll buy you an early lunch."

You're on," said Susan. "Wendy's willy problem will have to wait."

The two girls waltzed out of the office arm-in-arm. Diane, especially, had a lighter step than when she came in.

Later that same day found Diane back at home at the farmhouse. She was sitting in the upstairs study going over the draft of an article when she heard the sound of a car approaching up the drive. After a moment or two the front door banged closed and Alan shouted from the hallway:

"Hi love, I'm home."

"Hi darling," she shouted in response, "I'm in the study, come on up."

She heard Alan's size-twelve's thumping up the stairs and he ambled into the room, kissing her on the back of the neck.

"Hi love, T.F.I.F! I'm whacked. You been back long?"

Diane swung around on her swivel chair and stood up.

"No, about twenty minutes. I just wanted to get this lot out of the way so we can sit down and discuss last night over an early dinner."

Alan put his hands around Diane's waist and looked softly into her eyes.

"That's fine by me. I've been giving some thought to what you said this morning, and on reflection I may have been a bit quick to condemn your experience. I'm really very sorry."

Diane snuggled up and embraced him affectionately.

"That's alright, I'm sure I must seem a little obsessed with this whole thing."

Alan held her at arms-length, shaking his head.

"No, not at all. I tell you what, you get some drinks sorted and I'll nip down to that Chinese Restaurant on the main Bradford road, for a take-out. That'll give us a good few hours to sit and chat."

"Oh you're such a wonderful husband," said Diane with a beaming smile, giving Alan another hug and kissing him tenderly. "I do love you."

"And I love you too," responded Alan, giving her a playful pat on her bottom.

"Now go on and get the drinks ready and I'll be back in about twenty-ish."

Having finished their dinner the couple curled up together on one of the couches in the lounge, in front of a roaring log-fire. Diane turned to Alan and kissed him on the cheek.

"Thank you darling, that was a fabulous meal. We must try an eat-in at that restaurant one night."

"Yes, we must, it's a big place and the staff are really efficient. Surprising really, for somewhere that's so far away from a large town. Anyway, let's get down to business and sort out last night's occurrence; or more to the point, how we can test your experience."

Diane got up from the couch and picked up a log from the copper bucket in the fireplace. Tossing it on the fire she reflected for a few seconds as the sparks flew up the chimney. Sitting down next to Alan again she took his hand in hers and smiled warmly.

"You know darling," she said sincerely, "I really do appreciate your support in all this and I just want to let you know that this test is as much for me as anyone. Last night seems more like a dream the more I think about it, and I just wanted to say thank you for being so tolerant."

"Hey, don't forget we're a partnership, the sum of the whole being greater than the sum of the parts that is, and you don't have to thank me for helping you. It's like helping myself."

"Okay pardner," said Diane with a pseudo American accent, "have any good ideas today?"

"Actually I did," said Alan, sitting up from his curled position. "I remembered a TV show that I saw years ago. It was about psychics or something. They wanted to find out if certain people really could tell what others were thinking; so they put someone in a different room from the psychic and asked them to write down a message or draw a picture, and the psychic tried to read their mind. Nobody got it exactly right although some were very near. I think that guy Uri Geller, you know, 'Mister spoon-bender', was one of those who came closest."

Diane frowned with uncertainty.

"But my OOBE couldn't be tested like that, could it?"

"Well, not exactly like that, but certainly a variation on that theme. You see I can write something on a piece of paper, in big print of course, in case you can't get up close. I then leave the paper on your desk in the study, just before we go to bed; and just to be on the safe side, in case you're sleepwalking or something and we don't know it, I'll lock the door and hide the key. Infallible, yes?"

Diane nodded in agreement.

"Seems okay to me. In fact I went into the study during my OOBE last night." She sat there in thought for a moment then jumped up off the couch.

"Yes, we'll do it. We'll try it tonight."

"Right," said Alan, pleased at being able to come up with an acceptable scenario for a test. "But do you think you'll be able to do it; have an OOBE that is, two nights on the trot?"

"I don't know," said Diane with a little shrug. "This is as new to me as it is to you. We'll just have to give it a go and see what happens, but please promise me something," she appealed.

Alan looked up and cocked his head to one side.

"What's that love?"

"If it doesn't work out tonight, that you'll persevere with me, until I decide I've had enough. I'm not sure I could explain why but this thing seems really important to me."

She smiled warmly and bent down, kissing Alan tenderly on the lips. Alan responded to the kiss and looked deep into her eyes.

"Of course I will," he said tenderly.

"Thank you darling, I do love you."

Later that evening while Diane was getting ready for bed, Alan went to the study and took a piece of paper from a drawer in her desk. He wrote on the paper and smiled inwardly.

"She'll never guess this, she'll have to see it to get it right."

He placed the message directly in the middle of the desk and left the room, locking the door behind him. He then proceeded downstairs to the kitchen and without putting the lights on walked over to the fridge and opened the door. The fridge light illuminated the contents and Alan secreted the key under a tub of cottage cheese! He closed the fridge door and left the kitchen smiling to himself again.

Back in the bedroom Diane was just coming out of the en-suite bathroom as Alan walked in.

"Left the message yet?" she asked.

Alan had a grin all over his face.

"Sure did, and you'll never guess it. You'll really have to see it to get it right."

"Good. Well, I'm just about ready for the sack now, I feel really tired."

Alan started to get undressed.

"Okay, I'm just going to have a quick shower," he said, disappearing into the bathroom as Diane got into bed.

7

The couple were hard and fast asleep with Diane on her back and Alan in his usual foetal position. The clock on the bedside table showed four-o'clock as Diane's spirit-form detached from her physical body and slowly floated up from the bed, eventually rolling over like a log in a river, leaving her looking face-downwards. She stared around with a smile of amazement on her face.

"Wow, I've done it again," she thought. "This is fantastic."

She looked down at the bed and gazed at Alan lovingly.

"Hi there sleepy-head. Oh yes, the test! Let me see if I can read your message."

She thought of the study and that white flash went off again; and once more, temporarily blinded Diane. When she next looked she was floating in the study, just inside the doorway.

"Wow," she cried, sounding like an excited child who'd just ridden it's bike without training wheels for the first time: "I did it, just like that."

She looked around the study, still amazed at her newly acquired ability, and then caught sight of the message on the desk. She slowly floated over and looked down.

"Now, what does it say?"

She wafted down closer to the desk and looked at the paper, which had the message clearly written on it.

'What was my Mother's maiden name? Love Alan XXX.'

Diane smiled to herself as she read the words.

"Not just a message but a question too. No wonder you became a lawyer Mister Smarty Pants! Well, that was easy enough."

Diane glanced around the room again.

"Now that's done with I think I'll go for a little exploration of the neighbourhood."

She visualised the garden and another white flash quickly ensued; and before she knew it she was floating in front of the mock-Victorian street lamp that lit the cobbled courtyard at the end of their drive.

"This is really great, I love it," she said to herself, taking in her surroundings.

Now feeling extremely elated and giggling like a young schoolgirl, Diane made for the village. When she eventually arrived there she flew up the centre of the main street, which seemed totally deserted, all but for a few cats that is. She followed one rather grubby-looking feline around the back of the pub – which was awash with empty beer barrels and crates of bottles, awaiting tomorrow's brewery delivery – and was surprised that it seemed to sense her presence, looking around hissing as she passed overhead. She banked right flying quite quickly around the corner of the pub towards the off-road car park and then! Diane screamed in horror as she saw a milk van just inches in front of her face. She covered her eyes, waiting for the inevitable impact, but none came. Stopping abruptly she looked back in disbelief at the vehicle.

"Where the hell did that come from?" she exclaimed.

But as she pondered her question was promptly answered. The milkman walked jauntily towards his truck from the pub doorway carrying a crate of empty milk bottles and whistling quietly to himself. Stacking the crate with all the others on the back of the vehicle he jumped into the drivers seat and drove off the car park onto the main-street.

As the van stopped again, opposite the village shop, Diane was still trying to work out if she'd somehow manoeuvred around the vehicle or gone through it without feeling anything. But with that question still unanswered, she gave a little shrug and set off again, this time much more slowly!

As she cruised past the church for the second time she saw a dim light coming from a bedroom window in a house around the corner and decided to investigate; and as she got closer she recognised the house.

"That's where Matt and Mark live, the kids we bought the OOBE book from."

She floated over to the bedroom window and came to a halt. Looking inside she saw Matt, the youngest boy, asleep in his bed. Then, to her utter amazement, she noticed a strange man, who seemed to be kneeling at the side of the bed, looking closely at the boy.

Diane was puzzled but strangely didn't feel perturbed.

"I wonder who on earth that is?" she thought.

The man immediately looked around and stared through the window, straight at her. Diane felt a peculiar sensation – if she'd been in her human body the hair on the back of her neck would have stood straight up – and she backed away slightly. As she came to a halt she heard a voice very close but couldn't quite pinpoint where it was coming from.

"I'm Arthur. I'm his father," echoed the voice. "Or rather I was the father."

Diane turned her head left and right looking for the source of the voice but couldn't see anyone, and although she felt a little anxious wasn't really frightened and decided to respond:

"Who said that?" she asked tentatively.

The voice answered but Diane still couldn't pinpoint its source; in fact, it seemed to be coming from inside her own head!

"Me, in the room here."

Diane looked back through the window into the bedroom, at the man knelt by the bed. He waved at Diane! Then the voice sounded again and this time she was sure that it was coming from inside her head:

"Have you just died my dear, you seem a little disoriented?"

Diane, although feeling a little apprehensive, responded somewhat indignantly:

"No, I haven't, I was just having a little exploration of the neighbourhood and saw the light from the bedroom window. I was just a little ... well ... curious."

The voice reverberated insider her head again.

"Well if you're not dead then how is it you're communicating with me and floating fifteen feet off the ground?"

Diane automatically looked down!

"Um, I'm having and OOBE," she answered, still sounding a little uncertain.

The man frowned.

"Excuse me?" questioned the voice in her head "A what?"

"An OOOBEEE," said Diane, stretching the sound of the word as if talking to someone who didn't understand English very well.

She saw the man frown again and shake his head.

"Sorry, that's our abbreviation word," she said apologetically. "I'm having an out-of-body experience."

The stranger's face lit up, literally, and he smiled warmly, and immediately Diane felt totally at ease as the voice echoed in her head again:

"Oh my goodness, of course," it said casually. "All those books I read when I was alive. I so much wanted to believe in that OOBE, as you call it, but I never was able to actually achieve anything. Well, well, how interesting. You know something; you're the first OOBE-person I've met since I left this life? Where are you from my dear?"

"My name's Diane Harris; I live just down the lane, in the farmhouse."

The man smiled again and his form seemed to glow.

"Well, let's start again shall we? Hi Diane Harris, my name is … sorry … was Arthur, Arthur Ayres; I was Mark and Matt's dad. People at work used to call me AA. You know, like the car breakdown company. They used to say: 'send for the AA, he'll fix the problem'."

Diane giggled.

"Hi Arthur. Now don't take this the wrong way but this seems a little bizarre to me; I mean, holding a conversation, if you can call it that, through a bedroom window. Would it be okay if I came inside?"

"Oh, I'm sorry," apologised Arthur profusely, "of course you can."

Diane reached out her fingertips and gingerly put them against the windowpane. As before, she screwed up her face and pushed, passing easily through the glass and straight into young Matt's bedroom.

"Wow, I've still got to get used to that," she remarked, looking down at herself, unconsciously checking out her spirit-form. "It doesn't half tingle."

She looked over at Arthur and as he smiled at her comments she saw that he had a very warm and kind face, his eyes as bright as two shiny blue opals.

"Please don't think me rude," said Diane, "but I wonder if you could explain something to me about…?"

Before she could finish the question Arthur spoke, and although the voice was still in her head, the experience didn't seem quite as strange as it first had.

"Sure," he said, "you want to know what I'm doing here; why I haven't passed-over, for want of better words. Also, what am I doing in my son's bedroom?"

Diane was totally gobsmacked.

"How on earth did you know all that?"

"Well," responded Arthur quite calmly, "I've been dead for over a year now, in earth-time terms that is, and you get used to communicating with other spirits in thought-packages, made up of images rather than words. I believe they called it NVC in the books I used to read. That's non-verbal communication."

Diane suddenly felt a really strong desire for knowledge.

"NVC, how does that work?" she eagerly enquired.

Arthur's appearance gently vibrated, or at least that was Diane's perception, and then his voice filled her head again:

"Well, when you're in your spirit-form as we are now, we don't talk per-sé; it's more like a telepathic communication, mainly using NVC."

He looked closely at Diane.

"You obviously haven't met many spirits, have you my dear?"

Diane shook her head.

"No I haven't, you're the only one so far. In fact, this is only my second OOBE; and my first was only last night."

Arthur smiled again and nodded slowly.

"Thought so. You see NVC tends to send a package of your thinking rather than individual words; like when you yourself recall something from your own mind. So when you thought earlier about what I was doing here, I picked up the whole concept in one. Hence, short question, long answer. Mind you, when lots of spirits are trying to communicate with you at once it can get a little hectic; especially when you're new to it," he said with a chuckle.

Diane looked at Arthur with wonderment written all over her face.

"That's truly amazing," she said, looking around the room, down at her spirit-form and then back at Arthur. "Even though I'm here experiencing this, it's hard to believe it's happening; it really does feel like a vivid dream or something."

"I know just what you mean," said Arthur with a fatherly voice. "That's exactly how I felt when I first died, but it won't be long before you don't even consciously think about being OOBE, as you call it. Even the act of passing through things that you'd normally avoid soon becomes second nature. After a while it just seems to happen. A bit like riding a bike I suppose."

Diane thought briefly of her encounter with the milk van and then looked down at Matt, who although sleeping soundly turned over and pulled his quilt up under his chin.

"Oh, he looks so peaceful," she said tenderly.

"Yes, but he's the reason that I'm still here," sighed Arthur. "I've been trying to find a way to let him know that I'm okay. He's the only one in the family who hasn't fully accepted my death yet. He's very sensitive you know."

Diane felt truly saddened by young Matt's quandary.

"Poor little soul. He did seem a bit melancholy when we met him at the garage sale the other week, especially when he was talking about you.

In fact it was buying that book on OOBE's, one of your old books actually, that influenced me to try to have an OOBE."

Diane paused in thought for a moment and Arthur looked at her and nodded.

"Yes, I do," he said. "I think I believed in it when I was alive, but now I'm dead I know for sure!"

Diane looked perplexed again.

"I'm sorry," she said. "Do what?"

"Sorry Diane, I was a little ahead of you again. You were thinking: 'Did I believe in fate'. The answer's most definitely yes."

Diane looked extremely impressed.

"Wow, I'll have to watch my thoughts," she said with a little giggle, "they could get me into trouble."

"I'm sorry," said Arthur, "in future I'll try to communicate in real-time, as if we were speaking normally, until you get the hang of NVC that is."

Diane looked down at Matt again and an idea sprang into her head.

"Maybe I can help you with young Matt. After all, as I'm not dead I could talk to him in the morning, when I wake up. I could pass on a message for you; discreetly of course."

Arthur's face beamed again!

"Oh would you Diane, that would be great if it worked."

He paused in thought for a moment and gently vibrated again.

"You will be careful how you broach the subject though won't you? I wouldn't want him spooked at the thought of this," he said, gesturing around the room with his arms. "I wouldn't want him frightened to go to bed because he thinks that I'm a ghost or something. I think he's a little frightened of the dark as it is, that's why he has this lamp on all night."

"You're right," concurred Diane.

They both went quiet for a moment and then Diane raised a hand in the air.

"I know!" she said excitedly. "I'll tell him I had a dream. A dream with you in it, and that you told me to tell him not to worry anymore, that you're safe in heaven."

It was Arthur's turn to look impressed.

"What a great idea Diane. It's probably a lot more believable than the reality," he said with a little laugh. "Especially to a young boy like Matt."

He vibrated in thought again.

"However, if you don't think he's taking the hook, about the dream that is, then tell him that his Dad said: 'His Mate Matt shouldn't worry'. That was a pet phrase I used when we were doing things on our own. It's something that you wouldn't really know unless you'd actually talked to me."

Diane looked concerned.

"Gosh, I hope I can remember all this when I wake up; along with my mother-in-law's maiden name."

"Yes, I picked up the NVC about your little test for your husband. Maybe you should write everything down as soon as you get back to your physical body, just in case you fall straight back off to sleep and only recall your OOBE's as dreams."

"Good idea Arthur, got any more tips?"

Diane listened enthralled as Arthur related some of his experiences in the spirit world and she got the feeling that he would have talked until dawn if she'd let him. But eventually she felt it was time for her to go; so when there was a lull in the conversation, or rather, the communication, Diane made her apologies for having to leave and said goodbye to Arthur. She passed through Matt's bedroom wall in one smooth action and flew off into the night, as silently as an owl on the wing.

As she approached the farmhouse Diane spotted one of their bats, which was just emerging from under the eaves, and to her utter amazement it flew straight through her, without her feeling a thing. She gave a little involuntary scream but then laughed inwardly at her misplaced fear.

Arriving at the farmhouse Diane passed straight through the thick stone wall without stopping; although she did close her eyes!

Back in the bedroom she floated over the bed and looked down at her physical body, with Alan sleeping soundly next to it.

"Well, I think I'm ready for re-entry as they say at NASA. I think I'll give the big-toe-wiggle a try."

But just as she was readying herself Diane noticed Alan start to move in bed, and as he rolled over he knocked her physical body with his elbow and all of a sudden a feeling of apprehension swept through her whole being.

"Oh my goodness there's that strange feeling again?"

That white flash appeared and Diane's spirit streaked back into her body and she immediately awoke with a jolt, opening her eyes to find herself in bed, staring at the ceiling. She turned to look at the clock, which showed five-forty and her OOBE recollections started to flood her mind.

"Wow, the OOBE, Arthur; I must write down what just happened."

She reached for the pad and pen on her bedside table and smiled to herself as she remembered Alan's message. She looked over at him sleeping soundly. "Cheeky Tyke," she said affectionately.

8

The birds had been singing outside for quite some time but the couple was still in bed. Alan roused first and turned over to look at Diane who was just stirring.

"Morning love," he said kissing her on the cheek. "Sleep well?"

Diane yawned and stretched.

"Oh yes, thanks," she groaned, opening her eyes and smiling as she remembered what day it was.

"Oh great, Saturday."

Diane ran her tongue around her mouth and made a yukky face, then stroked Alan's stubble-coated cheek and smiled sweetly.

"I could murder a cup of tea darling."

"Okay, I'll make one," he said, smiling inwardly at the ease with which Diane could twist him around her little finger when she really wanted to.

He swung his legs out of bed and searched with his feet for his old deck-shoes. Although far too tattered to wear outside the house – at least according to Diane who was extremely conscious about how she looked – these old shoes were much too comfortable to part with. So he compromised and wore them inside, instead of slippers.

"Oh, by the way, how did your OOBE attempt go last night" he asked, stifling a yawn and wrestling with the sleeve of his bathrobe.

Diane sat bolt upright in bed and checked her bedside table.

"Oh thank God, my notes, they're here. It did happen. Alan, I did it again. It was incredible. Go make the tea while I go for a pee and I'll tell you all about it. Oh this is so exiting, and a little spooky too!"

"Well, come on then, don't keep me in suspenders," joked Alan, spreading copious amounts of Marmite on a slice of heavily buttered hot toast. "Did you manage to read my message or what?"

The couple were in the kitchen having their usual tea and toast for breakfast. Diane looked at Alan across the kitchen table and smiled from ear-to-ear. She pouted her lips and made three kissing sounds towards Alan; matching the three crosses he'd put at the end of his message.

"All I have to say to you is Pilling!"

Alan stopped in mid-bite and his chin dropped as he stared open-mouthed at Diane.

"Oh my God, you did see the message! My mum's maiden name, Pilling".

He dropped his toast in shock, jumped up from the table and rushed over to the refrigerator, nearly pulling the door off its hinges. Diane looked on baffled.

"What's the matter darling?" she enquired with a frown.

Alan rummaged in the fridge.

"I'm looking for the key to the study, I put it in the fridge last night, under the cottage cheese."

He found the key and held it up, looking at it in disbelief. Diane laughed with incredulity.

"In the fridge, under the cottage cheese. Gosh, you're a trusting soul aren't you? No wonder you took up a career in law."

Alan looked a little sheepish.

"But I told you I was going to hide the key," he moaned defensively.

Diane didn't comment.

"Well it seemed like a good hiding-place last night. I got the idea from a film I saw, years back; only they put the key inside the tub of cheese! Anyway, It's not that I don't trust you, I just wanted to make sure that there could be no doubt; for both of us."

Diane feigned a frown.

"Okay, I'll believe you but I know some that wouldn't."

Alan looked at her expectantly.

"Well?"

"Well what?"

"The OOBE last night, tell me all about it, I mean, you got the message in the study. God, I can't wait to try it for myself."

Diane interjected firmly, shaking her head.

"Let me tell you Mister Lawyer, you don't know the half of it! After I found your message I went outside and…"

Alan sat dumbfounded as Diane related every detail of last night's OOBE, referring to her copious notes when necessary.

"…And then you turned over and whacked me with your elbow and before I knew it I was back in bed staring at the ceiling. Apparently what I read about the OOBE instantly ceasing when ones normal sleep pattern is disturbed was correct."

Alan gawked at Diane with his mouth half-open.

"That's the most incredible thing I've ever heard. And these notes you wrote down," he prodded Diane's pad, "they're amazing. It's a good job Mister Ayres, or should I say: 'the late Mister Ayres', gave you that idea."

He shook his head in disbelief, stood up and started pacing the kitchen floor.

"Diane, this thing is awesome. Do you realise what you have here? This could bust open all sorts of things. I mean religion to name but one, and..."

Diane waved her hands in front of Alan to stop him pacing and then put them together in a 'T' sign.

"Time-out, hang on there a moment. You're as bad as Sue."

Alan stopped and gave Diane a miffed look.

"Susan?"

"Yes she reacted just like you when I told her about my first OOBE."

"Oh, you didn't mention that you'd told her."

"Look never mind that now, let's just take a look at the facts. Now I know I'm not the first person to have an OOBE," she continued, "and I'm damned sure I'm not the first to understand what it can mean from a personal perspective. If you remember, I got the idea from a book, which was just one of many on the subject. And that Institute in America has conducted hundreds, if not thousands of experiments on the OOBE phenomenon."

She paused for a second to collect her thoughts, taking a sip of tea before continuing:

"Just consider my position logically for a moment. Why do you think that most people who've had OOBE's don't go around telling others about their experiences, unless they're amongst like-minded people that is. Just remember what John said to you, about not letting your senior partners hear you talking about it. Most people would listen politely and then call the shrink before you were halfway out the door."

Alan nodded his head slowly.

"You're right, they'd think we were a couple of Loony Tunes. Oh this is so bloody frustrating!".

"Why?" asked Diane, her voice raising an octave. "We don't have to tell anyone. Anyway, to be honest," she continued, quickly regaining her composure, "I think it's a gift, that it was meant to be; some sort of fate. In fact I've already decided that I don't want to tell anyone else, not even Sue; at least not yet. Let's live with this for a little while and see where it takes us."

Alan exhaled loudly through pursed lips.

"You're right," he said, sitting back down at the table and retrieving the toast he'd lost earlier; which had, as usual, landed face down. "And I'm not just saying that because of the Loony Tunes tag. Anyway, I'd like to try it for myself. It sounds like it could be fun as well as educational."

He grinned at Diane who smiled back as she watched him scoop up the globs of butter and Marmite from the table, licking his fingers like a two-year-old.

"It is fun," she confirmed, "but do you know what the strangest thing is?"

"What's that?" he mumbled through a mouthful of toast.

"The fact that if something half as weird as last night had happened to me in my normal awake-state, I'd have been scared to death. But for some reason, everything that happened during my OOBE seemed so normal, well at least at the time it did; even talking to someone who is physically dead didn't faze me one iota. And talking of AA," she said, getting up from the table, "I have to try and wangle an accidental meeting with young Matt Ayres."

The screeching sound of tyres fighting tarmac was quickly supplanted by the staccato noise of spinning wheels throwing up gravel. Alan's head snapped up, breaking the daydream that was carrying him through the chore of raking leaves from the lawn.

"Who the bloody hell's that idiot?" he cried irately.

A few seconds later his question was answered as a very sleek and low sports car quickly appeared round the bend of the drive, eventually coming to an abrupt halt in the courtyard.

John jumped out of his new silver Mercedes and waved at the couple. Alan had an uncomfortable expression on his face as he looked down at Diane, who was knelt on a pad, weeding the lawn's border.

"Oh shit, sorry love; I forgot that John was coming around. I arranged to go to the game with him this aft'. It completely slipped my mind what with all this OOBE stuff. Honest!"

John carefully flicked a foreign body off the bonnet of his new pride-and-joy before greeting the couple:

"Hi there you guys," he shouted.

Diane arose from her kneeling position and straightened her back with a slight groan, glad for an excuse for a break. She looked at John's new car and responded glibly:

"I see you bought that penis-extension then?"

Alan winced visibly. John ignored the remark and glanced back once more to admire his silver chariot before walking across the cobbled courtyard towards the couple.

"What a wonderful picture of matrimonial bliss," he remarked sarcastically.

"Relish the scene," retorted Diane with a slight edge, "It's probably the nearest you'll ever get to settling down."

John smiled and gave Diane a rakish wink.

"You always were such a perceptive woman Diane; which makes me wonder why you dumped me after only two months."

Alan quickly jumped in to defuse the banter.

"As I keep telling you John, she dumped you for a better man, and because she's intelligent."

Diane held her hands up in an attempt assuage any further verbal conflict.

"Okay lads," she said with a grin, "let's turn down the testosterone taps and make peace. Come on inside and I'll make us some coffee before you both leave me for your real truelove."

She walked off towards the house shaking her head as John gave Alan the once-over.

"Well old buddy, unless you're intending to make a new fashion statement, by the way you're dressed I assume you forgot all about the game this aft'?"

Alan nodded, forcing a smile.

"Sorry mate but it won't take me long to change. We had a rather long breakfast this morning, talking about ... erm ... things. You know!"

"Yes Al, I know. So you old married couples call shagging, talk; eh?"

He winked at Alan and laughed. Alan slapped him on the back shaking his head slowly.

"Bloody one-track-mind you; dirt track! Come on, let's go inside and you can have that coffee while I get changed."

John sat at the kitchen table and looked longingly at Diane's firm bottom, accentuated by her tight jeans. And as she turned his eyes roamed upwards, gazing at the protrusion of her nipples showing through her clinging tee shirt; and he salaciously remembered their times together at university.

Diane couldn't help but notice John 's stare, and knowing him extremely well correctly assumed that he was mentally undressing her. So she slowly turned to lean against the Aga, crossing her arms tightly over her breasts.

"Rugby eh?" she remarked, making a little tutting sound.

John snapped out of his semi-pornographic daydream.

"What? Oh yes the game. And you're a rugby widow for the afternoon; yet again!"

Diane pulled a sour face.

"Yes, me and a few million other wives," she derided. "It never ceases to amaze me that when the weekend comes around, half the men in the world feel the need to congregate with others of their species and watch a few of their perceived peers beat the hell out of each other while chasing a funny shaped ball around a muddy field."

She took a quick breath and continued before Alan could comment:

"Of course it's essential that this senseless pastime be followed by a period, at least equal to that of the duration of the game they've just watched, drinking beer and going over the highlights of said game."

John pursed his lips.

"Ooh Diane, you always did understand men so well," he joked. "I really shouldn't have let you go all those years back."

Diane leaned further back against the warm Aga and surveyed her ex-lover.

"You didn't have any say in the matter my dear boy. I knew from the outset that you were a confirmed bachelor, I just gave myself a couple of months to try to change you."

She sighed and shook her head.

"I liken the experience to that of trying to push water uphill with my bare hands. Impossible! So let's drop the subject, eh?"

John grinned, and as was his wont, ignored her request.

"But you must admit that you had fun trying didn't you?"

Diane turned around and shifted the coffeepot onto the hot plate, mainly to hide the hint of a blush on her cheeks.

"That's for me to know," she said, just as Alan walked into the kitchen.

"What's for you to know?" enquired Alan, looking from Diane to John and back.

Still a little flushed, Diane turned around and fiddled with the Aga as she racked her brain for an adequate response.

"What this man's laundry service has to put up with," she lied, pointing a finger at John. "His socks had to be the worst in the whole university that particular year. They had a sniff'o'meter reading of ten. And his under-shorts, well! I didn't know if it was the beer or the curries but they sometimes had skid-marks longer than those Michael Schumacher lays down on his approach to a tight corner!"

John looked at Diane in disbelief and even Alan was too mortified at her comments to laugh. Diane looked up at the clock on the kitchen wall and quickly tried to change the subject:

"Anyway, you guy's are going to be late if you don't watch out."

Alan looked inquisitively at Diane.

"Are you okay love?" he asked with a concerned voice. "You look a bit flushed."

She brushed the hair back from her forehead.

"No I'm fine. It must be the heat from the Aga."

Alan shrugged and turned to John.

"Okay, you ready Schumy?"

"Oh piss off Al, she's pulling your plonker; there's nothing wrong with my Jockeys, never has been. Anyway, now I've got a brand new car with ABS brakes I don't have any skid marks whatsoever, so there," he quipped, giving Alan the finger as he swigged down the last of his coffee.

Alan laughed and turned to Diane.

"Okay then, we'll be back…"

Diane cut across his words before he could finish.

"I know. Around seven-ish if your lot wins. A little earlier if they don't."

Alan smiled and kissed her on the cheek.

"You're so understanding. See you later."

John approached Diane with a lecherous grin on his face and tried to kiss her on the lips but she turned her head slightly at the last second and all he managed was a glancing peck on the cheek.

"Goodbye Di," he said with a little wink, "see you around."

As the two men left the kitchen, Diane leaned back on the Aga again and sipped her coffee, smiling inwardly!

9

After her little mental tussle with John, Diane suddenly felt the need to expend some more energy, so after finishing up in the garden she set off for a walk around the village; virtually retracing her OOBE jaunt of the previous night. As she passed the Ayres house she noticed that Matt and Mark were playing rugby with some of their friends on the large lawn at the side of the house. Mark kicked the oval ball hard and, fortuitously for Diane, it bounced sideways, straight towards the gate. Young Matt chased the ball and caught up with it as it came to rest near Diane's feet and she grasped the opportunity.

"Hi there Matt, not going to the big game today?"

The young lad wiped a blob of dirt from his face with his shirtsleeve and looked up at Diane.

"Oh 'iya Missis Arris, wot game's that then?"

Diane smiled inwardly at the young boy's old-fashioned narrative.

"You know, Bradford and Wigan, at Odsal Stadium this afternoon."

Matt whistled out loud.

"Oh reight, no. A wish wi could but our mum wo't lerrus go on us own and shi's not thar interested in rugby anyroad."

His eyes looked past Diane with a distant gaze.

"Wi used t' go a lot tho', wi' our dad."

"Oh dear, if I'd known that earlier I'd have asked your mum if Alan could take you and Mark. He loves going to the home games."

At that moment Mark shouted to Matt from the rear garden:

"Matt, bring t' ball back."

Matt ignored his brother's shout and turned back to address Diane:

"Thanks fer't offer Missis Arris but am not sure me mum'd lerus go wi' a stranger."

Again, Diane smiled inwardly at the maturity of Matt's words.

"Well let's see if we can change that shall we? Is your mum in now?"

"Yeah, shi's just tidyin' t' house."

"Then may I come in, just for quick chat, so I can introduce myself properly? I should have done it long before now, being a new neighbour and all. Maybe I can ask her about Alan taking you and Mark to a game sometime?"

Matt clenched his fist with approval.

"Yeah, that'd bi great. Come in an' A'll call 'er."

He opened the gate for Diane as Mark shouted again, this time more impatiently:

"Matt! a' yer playin' o' what?"

"Ang on a minit," retorted Matt, "am just showin' Missis Arris in' t' house t' talk wi' our mum."

He kicked the ball to his brother and their friends.

"Ere, an' mek sure yer wait fer us!"

Matt took Diane into the house and showed her through to the lounge before running off upstairs to find his mum.

Diane casually browsed the room, catching sight of the family photographs on the shelf above the fireplace. Wandering over for a closer look she gasped gently at what she saw. There, in pride of place in the centre of the shelf, was a picture of Arthur Ayres, with a big smile on his face and his arm around a very attractive woman. She picked up the picture and was taking a closer look when a rather dishevelled, but none-the-less attractive Mrs. Ayres, the woman in the picture she was holding, entered the room. Diane was a little embarrassed at being caught prying and muffed her greeting somewhat.

"Oh, hi Mrs. Ayres," she said, putting down the picture and extending her hand to the other woman. "I'm Diane Harris, from down the lane, the farmhouse. I've only moved in recently and I'm sorry to disturb you but me and my husband, Alan, met Matt and Mark when they had their garage sale the other week and I felt I ought to introduce myself."

The woman seemed a little flustered herself and pushed a lock of loose hair away from her face before wiping her hand on her apron and shaking Diane's.

Becky Ayres is a forty-something widow with two young sons – Matt aged twelve and Mark aged fourteen – from her seventeen-year marriage to Arthur, her deceased husband.

Born one of three children in Gloucestershire, in the South West Midlands of England, Becky was an average child who had an average upbringing. Always a home girl it was expected that she would settle down and get married locally, as her elder sister had. However, in the June of the year that she was twenty-five she went on a two-week holiday to North Yorkshire, with a friend from work who had family in Skipton; a market-town that was colloquially known as the gateway to the Yorkshire Dales.

On her second day in Skipton – a wonderfully sunny Sunday – Becky was out for a lunchtime drink in a local pub with her friend's family when she, literally, bumped into a young man who was standing at the bar, spilling his pint of beer all down his front. After much nervous apologising on Becky's part, the young man brushed the beer off his jacket and began to, in her words, 'chat her up'. Which made her feel, for some unknown reason, very comfortable with one Arthur Ayres, a junior newspaper reporter from Bradford.

Becky and Arthur saw each other several times during those two glorious summer weeks; including one memorable day when Arthur hired a tandem bicycle and they went off for a ten-hour tour of the extremely picturesque Yorkshire Dales.

For the next six months Becky and Arthur wrote to each other weekly, and that Christmas Arthur went down to Gloucestershire to be with her. They announced their engagement in the January and by August they were married, moving into a two-bedroom terraced house in Thornbury, on the outskirts of Bradford. Becky got a job in a large bakery, just up the road from their new abode, and very soon felt quite at home with her lot.

Within a year Arthur got promotion to the sports-desk of the Telegraph & Argus newspaper where he worked, and with their joint incomes now quite sizeable, at least for those times, they began to save like mad, planning for a family. The next fifteen years went as planned. They had two children two years apart and moved house twice; and Arthur managed to progress up the management ladder at work, eventually becoming assistant editor.

Life for those years was great for Becky, who gave up work to become a full-time mother and housewife just weeks prior to the birth of Mark; and things stayed that way until that fateful day last year, when Arthur dropped dead of a heart attack at work.

Totally devastated by this unexpected and tragic event, and still missing her husband dreadfully at times, Becky has struggled since his demise to keep their two boys on the straight and narrow. However, deep down inside, she sometimes wonders, and worries, what the future might hold for a middle-aged widow such as she.

"Hi Diane, I'm Becky. I'm sorry about these old clothes, I must look a sight, I was just cleaning the house when…"

"It's okay, interjected Diane, "I know the feeling, and again, I'm sorry for calling unannounced but I was just passing when I bumped into Matt at the gate and we got talking."

Becky smiled warmly at the mention of her youngest.

"Yes, Matt talks to everyone. He's such an inquisitive and trusting child. Takes after his father."

She paused and looked at the picture that Diane had just replaced.

"I'm sorry Diane, my husband died last summer and … well … things have been a little difficult, what with the children and everything."

She unconsciously wiped her hands on her apron again.

"Look, would you like a coffee? I put some on about ten minutes ago."

Diane, still feeling a little guilty about picking up the picture gave a small nod of her head.

"Only if it's not putting you to too much trouble."

Becky, suddenly realising that she still had her apron on, started to nervously fiddle with the knot behind her back.

"No, not at all Diane, I think that I've earned one by now."

She won the struggle with the apron ties and whipped it off, screwing it up in her hands as if to make it disappear.

"Anyway, I don't get many visitors, apart from other peoples' kids, so I'd be glad of some adult company for a while."

Diane smiled, feeling a little more comfortable.

"In that case, I'd love a coffee, thank you."

Becky headed towards the lounge door.

"Come on in the kitchen then," she said glancing back, "it's much cosier through here."

Diane followed Becky's lead, looking round admiringly as they walked through the large but very warm and friendly Victorian house.

"You have a lovely place here Becky."

"Thanks. When we found it, about seven years ago, it was in a real bad state. But we love this village and we made this place into a home over the years. The kids got to the local school and have all their friends nearby, and the family aren't too far away; well my mother-in-law and her sister that is. My own elder sister lives in the Forest of Dean, near Gloucester, where we were born."

She laughed as she filled the percolator from a packet of coffee grounds.

"That's why I haven't got a Yorkshire accent like the boys, in case you were wondering."

She pulled a chair out from the table and gestured for Diane to sit down as she continued her potted-history:

"My brother, the youngest, lives in America and only comes back for holidays once a year. So I suppose, all things being equal, I'll be here for some time yet."

She stared out of the window with a faraway look in her eyes and Diane felt a little uneasy.

"It must be difficult for you, I can't ever imagine what I'd do if I lost Alan, and we don't have any children yet."

Becky still looked distant.

"Yes, it would probably have been a little easier with no children but we were married for seventeen years and it's like a part of you just went away one day and you keep waiting for it to return. But you know, deep down, that it won't."

She momentarily turned away from Diane, and pulling a piece of kitchen-towel from a roll hanging from the wall, dabbed her eyes. Diane took a deep breath.

"Look Becky, maybe it would be better if I come back at some other time?"

Becky turned to Diane and smiled, seeming to snap out of her contemplative mood.

"No, I won't hear of it," she said resolutely. "I'm sorry I was going on a bit. As I mentioned, I don't get too many adult visitors and now you're here your not escaping that easily. Anyway, I'm usually too busy thinking of the boys to feel sorry for myself."

She looked over at the coffee percolator.

"Ah, I think the coffee's ready. How do you take it?"

"Oh, white please, no sugar."

Becky poured the coffee and handed a steaming mug to Diane.

"So what do you and your husband do for a living?" she enquired.

Diane took a sip of the hot coffee.

"Well, I work for a women's magazine..."

"Really!" exclaimed Becky loudly, looking truly surprised. "Arthur used to work for the Telegraph and Argus, that's the local newspaper for Bradford and the surrounding area."

She paused for a second and her eyes went glazed again.

"He loved his job, died there in fact. Heart attack."

She paused again then put her hand to her mouth as she realised that she'd interrupted Diane mid-sentence.

"Oh I'm sorry Diane, that was terribly rude of me, you were saying?"

Diane smiled sympathetically.

"It's okay Becky," she said, continuing her story: "I used to work in London, for the same company I'm working for now, in Leeds. I say in Leeds but I work from home most of the time, thanks to the wonders of modern communications. And Alan, he's originally from round here, near Bradford. We met when he was at University in London and I was at college, studying journalism. He's a fully-fledged corporate lawyer now and his firm recently promoted him to junior partner; and then within a couple of weeks of his promotion the opportunity arose to move to the Leeds office. Well you know what Yorkshiremen are like?" she quipped. "Give them a chance to drink real Tetley's Bitter, anywhere within fifty miles of the brewery, and that's it! So we ended up here, in the village. Anyway, Alan went off about an hour ago, with his friend John, to watch Bradford play Wigan at Odsal Stadium; so I decided to have a wander round on my own."

Becky nodded her head and smiled knowingly.

"A few pints of good beer and a game of rugby and men are as happy as pigs in … you know what!"

They both giggled.

"How true," agreed Diane.

Suddenly there was a loud bang from the back door and Diane jumped.

"Oh my, what's that?"

Becky looked round.

"Good grief, those boys, they're like a couple of miniature tornadoes."

Mark and Matt burst into the kitchen looking as grimy as a couple of young hippos straight from a mud bath.

"Hi you guys, beaten the opposition?" asked Diane with a benevolent smile.

Matt looked up as he kicked off his boots.

"It were only a friendly, so wi weren't too 'ard on em."

Mark chimed in:

"Yer mean y' di'n't play too good, so wi nearly lost."

Becky stared sternly at her two sons.

"Now then you two, we have a guest in the house, so save the post-game analysis until later."

Diane came quickly to the boys defence:

"It's okay Becky, I'm used to it. Alan and John try to get to all the Bradford Bulls' games and they go through this nearly every week, and they don't even play the game. Oh, that reminds me; If the boys would like to go to a game sometime, let me know. I'm sure that Alan would love to take them."

Mark and Matt leapt in the air.

"Oh yeah, great! Bull Power, Bull Power," they chanted loudly.

"Quiet down you two," shouted Becky, trying to make herself heard above the din.

She looked at Diane with a pained expression.

"I'm not sure that Alan would want these two fanatics hanging on, especially if he goes with a friend."

"It's alright Becky, John's a bachelor and there's many a game-day when he's not fit to go with Alan, if you know what I mean?"

Becky nodded in silent agreement.

"Especially," Diane continued, "after a heavy night on the town. So Alan goes to quite a few games on his own and I'm sure that he'd be glad of the company."

Becky glanced at the two boys who were hanging on the two women's every word.

"Okay then," she agreed.

Matt and Mark punched the air with their fists and did a little dance, whooping like American-Indians dancing around a campfire.

"But only," postulated Becky loudly, "if Alan meets these two before he makes up his mind. He should know what he's letting himself in for before committing."

"That's a deal then," said Diane, laughing at the boys' antics.

She looked at Becky and an idea began to form in her head.

"In fact," she said, "if your not doing anything this evening, why don't you guys come around for dinner, then Alan can properly meet these two little tykes? Nothing home cooked I'm afraid; I was going to call Alan and ask him to bring a Chinese meal back after the game. We had one last night, from that restaurant down the Bradford road, and it was really good."

Matt and Mark looked at their mother pleadingly.

"Oh can wi mum," appealed Mark, "please se yes."

Matt chipped in:

"Wi luv a chinky tek-away do't wi?"

Becky sighed resignedly.

"That's very kind of you Diane, and if I'm being totally honest with myself I can't think of one good reason to turn down your offer."

Then she raised a cautionary finger.

"However, I insist that I pay for our meals."

"Absolutely not," responded Diane, giving Becky a firm look. "This treat's on me, and I insist that Alan pays."

They all laughed as Diane glanced at her watch and stood up.

"Well I must go now but thanks for the coffee and the chat Becky and we'll see you around seven-thirty if that's alright."

"That's fine Diane and thanks again. Next time we'll eat here and I'll cook."

Matt touched Diane's sleeve.

"It's alreight Missis Arris," he said reassuringly to Diane, "Mum's a fabby cuk."

The girls looked at each other and burst into laughter.

10

"...And don't forget, enough food for five adults. I know they're only boys but I've got a sneaking suspicion that they eat like elephants."

Diane was back home, talking to Alan on his mobile phone as he watched the rugby game.

"Yes darling I just heard on the radio, six-all after fifteen minutes. Now get back to the game and I'll see you later."

She paused as Alan spoke.

"And I love you too, bye."

Diane hung up the phone and looked over at the kitchen clock, which showed three-thirty, and she smiled inwardly.

"I think I'll pamper myself."

Diane went upstairs into the en-suite bathroom and turned on the taps of the large, Jacuzzi-type bath, pouring copious amounts of sweet-smelling bubble bath into the steaming water. Once it started to froth she went through into the bedroom and turned on the CD player. Slowly, Diane undressed in time to the soft music, swaying deliberately to the rhythm of the soulful tune; and when she was completely undressed walked back into the bathroom and turned off the taps, swishing the foaming water with her hand.

"Ooh lovely," she said to herself.

Tentatively, Diane stepped into the steaming tub and knelt down, basting herself with the hot fragrant water; then, very slowly, she slid under the thick bubbles and lay back with only her head showing above the water.

"Oh that feels so good," she thought with a sigh and yawned loudly. "Gosh, I feel tired, it must have been that walk and tidying the garden this morning."

And with that Diane closed her eyes and before long, soothed by the warm perfumed water and lulled by the soft music, she fell asleep.

Diane's spirit-form started to slowly detach from her body and rise from the bath, taking her totally by surprise.

"Oh my, I don't believe it. Another OOBE, but it's the middle of the afternoon!"

She looked down at her physical body, lying in the bubbles of the steaming bathtub.

"My God! I'm naked. Does that mean I'm naked as a spirit?" she thought, looking down at her spirit-form. "It's difficult to see myself like this."

She looked around the bathroom and floated over to the mirror and was amazed and somewhat shocked when she couldn't see her reflection.

"Oh my, this is weird," she thought as she waved her arms around in front of her. But to no avail, she couldn't see even the slightest movement in the mirror.

The reality was that Diane looked just the same as her physical naked body; only the outline of her spirit-form appeared slightly softened, as if it had no real definition.

She looked in the mirror one last time and shrugged her shoulders.

"Oh well, what does it matter, I mean, who am I going to meet?"

She floated slowly into the bedroom where the CD player was still running.

"Well I can hear properly, the music doesn't sound any different."

Floating over to the window she looked outside at the sprawling green fields of the valley.

"I think I'll go for a little daylight exploration."

She started to visualise the outside of the house but as she did she got a picture of Alan superimposed over it. A white flash filled the room and Diane felt a rush of speed.

Within what seemed like no more than a couple of seconds to Diane, she found herself in a large and very crowded room and panicked, automatically trying to cover her nakedness. The room was packed with people, all standing facing the same direction, looking out of a big window at a game of rugby being played on a lush grass pitch below.

All of a sudden a loud groan emitted from the crowd as one of the players on the pitch, a tall blonde young man in a red and white shirt, dived over the touchline at the far end of the field, scoring a try. When the conversion was successfully kicked the referee blew his whistle for half time; but Diane was still somewhat perplexed.

"Where am I? Why did I arrive here," she pondered?

With her hands still modestly covering her chest and her legs firmly crossed she looked around, taking in the scene in more detail. Then it suddenly struck her!

"Of course, I'm in a hospitality box at the rugby stadium at Odsal."

She looked around again, this time searching the faces of the throng, which had now formed into small chattering groups for the half-time break; and as she surveyed the extremities of the room she saw him, in the corner by the bar. Alan was standing chatting with John, and two young women!

"Of course, I thought of Alan at the same time I thought of going outside and people take precedence over places."

Having now become accustomed to her surroundings and in the firm knowledge that her nakedness was invisible to the crowd – she wasn't yet used to mingling without being seen – Diane, intrigued at the seemingly cosy foursome over at the corner of the bar, moved a little closer.

"I wonder if I can hear what they're saying above all this din," she thought, and slowly floated towards the group.

As she got nearer, she picked up the conversation. John, who had a big grin on his face, was talking to the chest of a tall, quite attractive, and extremely well endowed blonde girl.

"...Yes that's right," said John grandly to the blonde. "In fact both Alan and myself are very senior partners in the firm, although I do tend to get the more interesting jobs, such as large..." he leaned over and whispered loudly in the girl's ear, "…and I'm talking hundreds of millions of pounds here, what we call IPO's. That's initial public offerings to the uninitiated; when a privately owned company comes to the market for the first time and…"

"John!" said Alan firmly, cutting across his friend's verbal diarrhoea. "I'm sure that these young ladies aren't interested in IPO's. In fact I'll bet they aren't interested in listening to any old, boring, legal shop-talk."

"You're right, as usual old buddy," agreed John, finishing the last of his drink in one gulp. Ladies," he said, turning to address the two girls, "would you allow me to re-fill your glasses?"

The blonde girl nodded at her friend with a 'told-you-so' smile.

"Oh, that's very kind of you John," she quietly exclaimed in mock surprise. "I'll have another glass of the chilled Australian Chardonnay if that's okay."

John nodded, smiling a salacious acknowledgement to the blonde before turning his attention to the elegantly slim, Italian-looking girl.

"And what about you my dear?"

"I'm okay for the moment thanks," responded the girl, politely but curtly.

"No, I insist," persisted John. "Have another. We'll be here for ages yet. What is it? No, let me guess?"

He gently took hold of the girl's hand that was clutching her glass and lifted it to the light, scrutinising the drink and then looked straight into her big brown camel-eyes.

"It must be a Chianti Classico, right?"

The girl raised her expertly fashioned eyebrows.

"And why's that?" she enquired, giving John a piercing look.

"Because it has to be like you," he replied with just a hint too much lechery in his voice. "Italian, great body and smooth on the tongue."

She smiled cordially and put her head on one side.

"Is that so? Well I'm afraid you're wrong on that count. It's actually Lambrusco, which is much more like me."

"How's that then?" asked John with a puzzled expression.

The girl licked her full, pouting red lips with the tip of her moist pink tongue and responded, quick-as-a-flash.

"Because it's full of fizz and goes down incredibly easily!"

John's chin dropped with astonishment and for once in his life he was lost for words. Alan stared in amazement at the girl, who had now turned her back on John and was facing him, giving him an 'I'm more interested in you' look.

"I must apologise for my friend's manner," said Alan, glaring at John.

But John, having the thickest of skins, had quickly recovered and was already back to chatting with the blonde girl. Alan turned back to the dark-haired girl.

"He's actually quite harmless," he said with a laugh. "It's just that he's been working long hours during the week and he grabs any opportunity he can find to push the boat out of a weekend."

The girl looked at Alan with the sexiest of smiles and fluttered her long eyelashes.

"Don't apologise for him. Anyway, I was only having a bit of fun."

While all this was unfolding Diane was still hovering unseen above the small group and was astonished at what she was hearing.

"I don't believe this," she thought angrily. "These two have the temerity to tell me that they go out to watch a game of rugby ... it looks to me like they've got a game plan of their own!"

Annoyed, but at the same time intrigued, Diane couldn't resist continuing her surveillance of the cosy quartet. However, at that particular juncture Alan had already decided that the dark-haired girl was taking far too much interest in him and he looked conspicuously at his watch.

"They'll be kicking off the second half in a minute," he remarked, to no one in particular, "so I'm off back to my seat."

He turned to address John who was now casually stroking the back of the blonde girl's hand and staring lovingly into her eyes:

"As soon as the game's over I'll have to find a cab. I've got to get a Chinese meal for Diane and our new neighbours."

John grabbed Alan's arm and pulled him near so he could whisper; although in his current imbibed state and surrounded by the hubbub of the crowd, his whisper was more like that of a town crier making an announcement.

"Wait a minute Al old buddy, you can't go off and leave me with these two lovely ladies," he insisted, looking lecherously at the two girls.

"John, my old mate," said Alan scathingly, "Diane's arranged this dinner for tonight and I promised I wouldn't be late."

He glanced over at the girls who were now huddled deep in conversation.

"Anyway, as much as this little gathering is very pleasant, I came here to watch the Bulls play the Warriors."

He started to move off and turned to the girls.

"It was a pleasure to meet you ladies."

They both looked at him disappointedly, especially the dark-haired girl.

Alan looked back at John.

"And as for you, I'm sure that you can manage on your own. And don't drive when you leave here. Pissed in charge of these two in your car wouldn't look too good on your résumé."

So as the two rival teams came back out onto the pitch, Alan walked towards the door, waving his arm without turning around.

"Bye now," he shouted.

Diane stared at the scene in disbelief and shook her head; although inwardly she was smiling at the way Alan had handled himself.

"John should know better than to pit girls against rugby where Alan's concerned. No competition!"

And as the referee blew his whistle and the game kicked off for the second half, Diane, now feeling good again, swooped down over the pitch, through the high hanging rugby ball, and disappeared in a white flash directly between the goal posts!

Diane immediately found herself back in the bathroom, floating over the bathtub, looking down at her physical body asleep in the soapy water.

"Wow, back again. Let me get back in that lovely bathtub"

Suddenly she felt extremely uncomfortable.

"Oh my, what's that strange feeling?" she thought, looking down at her spirit-form, which had suddenly started to go hazy. Another blue-white flash blanked out the scene and Diane disappeared!

11

Diane reappeared instantly in a dark warm place, floating quite still and calm. It wasn't totally dark as she could see a slight glow, but she somehow sensed that the light emanated from her own form. And even though she couldn't see anything Diane had a perception of immense space around her; as if she were floating in the vast night sky, looking out towards the stars. Only on this occasion there weren't any stars, or a moon; in fact there wasn't anything but a mass of blue-black openness.

She wasn't sure why but somehow she felt quite tranquil and totally at one with herself. No panic, no claustrophobia, no agoraphobia, no fear whatsoever; just total peace and tranquillity. She floated there quite happily for what seemed like an age but then slowly became aware of another presence, and before her very eyes a figure materialised, surrounded by a glowing aura. And although not exactly as she remembered him – he looked a little fuzzier around the edges of his shape – Diane knew that this was Arthur Ayres.

"Hi Diane," echoed the familiar voice in her head. "I'm sorry to drag you out here but I wanted to thank you for what you've done for Becky and the boys."

Diane was still a little perplexed as to where she was and how she'd come to be there.

"It's … um … it's okay Arthur. It was great talking with Becky; I really like her. In fact I think that we could eventually become really good friends. But can you just tell me where…"

Arthur jumped in before she could finish.

"Oh, yes, I'm so sorry," he apologised profoundly. "I should have explained straight away. We're in, what they call in your earth-time, the Ether. It's a place that's still within the earth's boundaries so to speak, but it's sort of on another plane; not in earth-time-space as you know it. In fact you could stay here for what seemed like days to you, but in your earth-time it might only be a few minutes. I suppose that you could call this place the life/death way station," he said with a childlike chuckle. "Or maybe a better way of putting it, to fit your particular circumstances, is physical/spirit way station. That's to say it's a place that every spirit visits to make its decision as to whether it needs to go back to earth as another person, to learn more about human life, or whether it feels it's learned enough and should go on to the next level."

Diane's face portrayed her utter bewilderment.

"Next level? It sounds a bit like a computer game."

"Well, I suppose they do have a lot of similar attributes but I think the Ether was here long before the Sony Play Station," said Arthur with a playful smile.

As in past conversations with Arthur, Diane felt a powerful impulse to learn more.

"I don't mean to be rude, she said cautiously, but if this place is, as you put it, the only life/death way station, then how come it's so empty and such a quiet, dark place. I mean, we seem to be the only ones here but people are dying all the time back on earth. Where are they all?"

"Good question Diane, and a hard one to give a plausible answer to; but I'll try. After a spirit leaves its physical body it eventually ends up here," he said, gesturing around the open blackness. "Once in the Ether a spirit can create its own surroundings. At the moment all you can see is a vast, dark open space; but I can see a wonderful view of Malham Tarn, in the Yorkshire Dales. In fact, from my perspective you are standing on a grassy patch of ground just in front of the little waterfall at Malham. It's a place I like to recreate and visit quite regularly; it's where I took Becky on one of our first outings, before we became an item as they say."

"Oh, how wonderful," said Diane. "Is there any way that I can see what you are seeing?"

"Yes, eventually, but you have to tune-in to my particular spirit-vibration and I'm not sure that you could achieve that at this moment. As a new OOBE practitioner you still have a lot of skills to learn, skills that you will automatically acquire when you permanently leave your current physical body."

"You mean when I die?" asked Diane.

"Putting it bluntly, yes. But I'm sure that with enough practice you'll be able to achieve this, even though you're only temporarily in your spirit-form."

"Oh, I do hope so Arthur, that would be fantastic."

"As for the other spirits," he continued, "they are here, all around us; coming and going all the time. But, believe it or not, there's a very strict privacy policy out here and you have to be invited into another spirit's personal space; you can't just gatecrash."

Diane looked totally perplexed at Arthur's words, so he endeavoured to explain further:

"As you spend more and more time out here in the Ether you'll learn all the communication skills, and eventually you'll be able to contact other spirits, but it will take practice. All spirits can communicate with each other but they have to agree to so do. Believe me my dear, you will learn over time.

Diane was having trouble absorbing all this information but she still felt a need to know more:

"You just mentioned that you called me here," she said, "how does that work?"

Arthur paused for a moment as if he were thinking and his form vibrated gently before speaking:

"Everyone, be they alive or dead, on earth or in the Ether, has an individuality. This identity, or ID as I prefer to call it, is unique to that spirit no matter what physical characteristics they have taken on as a human being. So once you know a spirit's ID, and it's more an intuitive feeling for that spirit rather than the name of a person, you can sort of home in on it. If you were back in your physical body and I tuned in to your ID I would actually go to where you were on earth at that particular earth-time; although you wouldn't know I was there because I'd be in my spirit form and you in your physical."

"You mean you'd be like a ghost or something?" asked Diane incredulously.

"In non-technical vernacular yes," replied Arthur with a warm smile. "Man originally created the concept of ghosts to explain occurrences that he didn't fully understand at that time. As you know, most famous ghost stories emanate from past-times, past to your particular earth-time that is, and these stories tended to be a little gruesome. Nowadays, in your current earth-time, people seem to be far more open minded about such phenomenon, and ghosts are portrayed much more realistically, as kind helpful entities, which is what most spirits really are."

"This is fascinating," said Diane. "So if I understand correctly, we are, right now, in a sort of spirit limbo-land, where time is irrelevant?"

"Yes, sort of," laughed Arthur. "In fact it's possible, with a little experience, to go from here to any point in earth-time."

Diane looked askance.

"What, past and future?"

"Yes," he said in a quite matter-of-fact tone. "As there's no time out here there's no past and no future. Earth-time-space is unique to your physical earth, and as such, can be accessed from here like … well … like driving a car off the motorway. You just have to pick the correct time-and-place-exit-lane for your particular destination and voila, you're there."

"That sounds just a little bit too easy," laughed Diane. "Mind you, if it's anything like getting off the M1 motorway in the rush-hour, maybe it's not that easy."

Arthur, who was now sounding more like a friendly schoolteacher than the spirit of a recently deceased newspaperman, was most definitely on a roll.

"It's probably about the same degree of difficulty," he continued, "once you know how. One thing to remember though, you can't affect anything in the time you're visiting, you can only observe. But it's still pretty good because you can see and hear as though you were actually there. Like being a visitor on a film set."

"I don't suppose that I could do that, could I?" asked Diane hopefully. "Even though I'm not really ... well ... dead."

Arthur chortled.

"Au contraire my dear, you're one of the lucky ones; well as far as I'm concerned you are. You've got the same attributes as any spirit but you can go back to your own current physical body whenever you want; and actually remember the experience."

He paused and vibrated – something Diane had noticed happened whenever Arthur seemed to be thinking – then looked at her inquisitively.

"Tell me Diane, do you remember everything when you get back from an OOBE?"

She thought for a moment.

"Well, I think I have, at least up to this particular OOBE. Why do you ask?"

"Oh, nothing really. It's just that after telling you that you were the first OOBE-person I'd met, I met another."

He laughed and glowed.

"It must be that time of year in your current earth-time. Anyway, he could only remember his OOBE's on earth, not the ones in the Ether."

"Well I hope I remember this," said Diane, "but as this is my first visit to the Ether I'll only be able to tell you that the next time we meet. I tell you what, let's arrange to meet back at our original meeting place, tonight, after I've given Matt your message. Assuming, that is, I get the opportunity to pass it on."

"You mean my old house?"

"Yes."

Arthur nodded in agreement.

"Alright, we'll give it a try; and if you want, I'll work on a time-trip for us, together. You may find it a little easier the first time around with someone more experienced tagging along."

Diane's voice gave away her excitement at the prospect.

"Oh yes, that'd be great. Okay, If I have an OOBE I'll see you tonight, or whenever that is for you."

After Arthur had given Diane a few more tips on travel techniques they said their goodbyes and she visualised home.

In a flash she was back in her bathroom, floating over the bath. She looked down at her sleeping form and marvelled at her new abilities.

"Well, I have to get back in there. I think I'll give the big-toe wiggle a try."

She screwed up her face and with a small rush she was back in her body, immediately waking with a jump, sitting up in the bath with a splash.

"I remember, Arthur, the Ether. I must make a note while it's fresh in my mind."

She leapt out of the bathtub and ran naked into the bedroom, dripping water and bubbles everywhere. She picked up her notepad and pen from her bedside table and took them back into the bathroom. Getting back in the bath she lay there thinking:

"Wait till I tell Alan about this one!"

Then she paused in reflection for a moment.

"And what about Alan; should I tell him about seeing him in that bar? I'd better not. He'll never stop looking over his shoulder and it doesn't really seem fair to be able to spy on people. Still, I could ask him a few searching questions when the time's right. Just to verify the accuracy of my OOBE of course!"

Diane smiled to herself and carried on writing her notes.

12

Diane was preparing the dinner table for the imminent arrival of Becky and the boys; and Alan, with the Chinese food. She was just making her way from the dining room to the kitchen to get a few condiments when the doorbell chimed. She walked through the hallway and pulled open the heavy oak door to find Becky and her two sons standing there smiling.

"Hi there Becky, come on in, and you too boys."

Becky ushered the boys through the door.

"Thanks Diane," she said, looking around the hallway admiringly. "Oh I do love this house; oh and way you've decorated this reception hall! It's just fabulous, this wallpaper's lovely."

"Of course," said Diane; "you knew the house when the Ryan's had it?"

"Yes I did," concurred Becky. "They had it nice here but you've gone one better than nice. In fact maybe two better," she concluded with a laugh.

"Well, thank you very much," said Diane, swelling visibly at the compliments. "We decided to have it decorated before we moved in, to save all the upheaval."

Becky looked round at the boys who were stood quietly with their coats still on.

"Come on then you two, take your coats off and make sure that you wipe your feet properly; we don't want any dirty marks on Mrs. Harris's new carpet."

"It's okay Becky," said Diane smiling at the boys. "You make yourselves at home lads."

"Thank you Missis Arris," replied the boys in unison.

"You're welcome," retorted Diane. "Here, give me all the coats and I'll put them in the closet. You guys go into the lounge over there and grab a seat and I'll be back in a moment."

"I'll come with you and help," said Becky, trying to take some of the coats from Diane.

"No, absolutely not," retorted Diane, seizing the coats back and frowning at Becky with mock intent. "You just go into the lounge there and make yourself comfy and I'll fix everyone a drink."

"Okay, if you insist," yielded Becky, holding up her hands in submission.

"I do," replied Diane resolutely. "Tonight's your treat."

Diane showed the trio into the lounge and put their coats away in the cloakroom and was on her way back to the dining room to fix the drinks when Alan came through the front door, loaded down with copious bags of food.

"Hi love," he said genially, kissing her on the cheek. "I hope everyone's hungry? There's enough here for an army."

They went through into the kitchen and Alan put the food on the table, giving Diane another kiss, this time a more lingering one on the lips. He took off his coat and put it on the back of one of the chairs.

"Have they arrived yet?" he asked.

"Yes, they're in the lounge. I was just about to get them a drink."

"Okay then, why don't I do that while you sort the food out? It's Becky isn't it?"

"Yes, and you remember the boy's, Mark, he's the biggest, and little Matt."

"Right, I'll go introduce myself and see what they want."

He set off for the lounge and was nearly through the kitchen door when Diane called out:

"Oh, Alan."

He stopped in his tracks and spun around.

"Yes love?"

"Don't forget," she said, grabbing a prawn cracker from a big bag on top of the pile of food containers, "I have to engineer a chat, with Matt. Hey that rhymes, a chat, with Matt," she chanted. "Anyway, If I manage to get him on his own, will you keep the others occupied for a while to give me a chance to talk to him?"

Alan winked.

"No problem," he said, continuing out the door.

As Alan entered the lounge Becky got up from her chair smiling sincerely and offered her hand in greeting.

"Hi there, you must be Alan; I've heard lots about you."

Alan smiled back grasping her hand firmly.

"Good to meet you too Becky. I hope what you heard wasn't all bad?"

"Quite the contrary," she said, raising an eyebrow cheekily.

She looked over at the boys who were sitting uncommonly quietly on the couch.

"I believe you briefly met my two sons, Mark and Matt."

Mark forced a smile.

"Hiya Mister Arris," said Matt cheerfully as he turned to address his mother: "Mister Arris bought a book from our garage sale t'other week."

Becky looked at Alan enquiringly.

"Oh really, which one did you buy Alan?"

Not wanting to bring any attention to his and Diane's newfound interest in OOBE's, Alan feigned reflective-thought for a few seconds.

"Um … I think it was about the paranormal or out-of-body experiences; well something like that."

Becky nodded mindfully.

"Right, Arthur was into all sorts of things like that. Though I'm not sure if he took it seriously or not."

Matt quickly interjected in his father's defence:

"E did, fo' sure. 'E used t' talk ter us about it."

"It's a load o' old rubbish if yer ask me," said Mark, looking scornfully at his younger brother.

"Mark, don't be so rude," scolded Becky. "Mr. Harris may find the subject interesting."

Alan cut in, hastily trying to smooth the situation:

"It's okay Becky, everyone's allowed their own opinion in this house, no matter what their age."

Becky looked at her two boys and then back to Alan.

"It's easy to see that you and Diane don't have kids," she said with a little laugh. "You know, if these two were allowed free rein they wouldn't get to sleep until three in the morning, especially that one," she said, nodding at Mark. "They'd be watching satellite TV all the time; especially that music channel. What is it that you watch incessantly Mark?" she asked, glancing at her eldest through narrowed eyes. "Music Television or something like that?"

Mark's face brightened at the mention of his favourite TV channel.

"Yeah, MTV, it's cool."

"And loud," exclaimed Becky.

"Oh, cum on mum," groaned Mark, "get wi' it, it's rad!"

Alan jumped in on the exchange again:

"Hey, I'll have you know young man that there was some great, and loud music in our time too," he said, looking across at Becky and winking cheekily. "In fact a lot of the stuff they put out today originated in our youth; they're nearly all remixes nowadays."

Mark looked dryly at Alan and, unsure of which side this adult was on, made a non-committal comment:

"Yeah, right."

"This is true." chipped in Becky, "But we weren't allowed to play it loud; not at home anyway. We had to go down to the local coffee shop or to the youth club; or at least wait until our parents were out."

"Ah yes," said Alan, with a reminiscing sigh. "The good old days. And everyone has them at some stage in their life, don't they?"

Matt, who had been listening intently to the conversation thus far, looked somewhat bewildered at Alan's last statement.

"As what?" questioned the young lad.

His mother laughed.

"Good old days," she answered. "When you're our age you'll have them too."

Oh, right," said Matt, still unsure of the real gist of the adult's conversation.

"Well, enough of this merry banter for now," asserted Alan. "Diane will be after me in a minute if I don't get you a drink. So, Becky, what would you like?"

Alan went back into the dining room just as Diane had finished laying the table. The food was sizzling away on several food-warmers, and plates and bowls aplenty covered the table.

"You took you're time taking the drinks order," said Diane.

"I know, I was just saying hello; and of course we had to have a quick discussion about pop-music!"

Diane looked at Alan with puzzlement.

"Of course, who wouldn't?" she said, quickly changing the subject. "Hey, do you think that everyone will be able to handle chopsticks?"

"I hope so," laughed Alan, "I wouldn't like to see them use their feet."

Diane threw a napkin at him.

"Uncouth moron," she exclaimed with a chortle, "I was only wondering if I should put out some forks, just in case."

"Come on love, it's only an informal dinner with the neighbours; If they can't manage chopstick I'm sure they'll say so. Anyway, it'll probably be obvious if they can't. Don't you think?"

"Alan!" said Diane with a warning note in her voice. "I don't want to embarrass them at out first dinner together."

"Okay," said Alan, raising his hands submissively, "I'll ask when I take the drinks in, but I bet they'll think I'm a jerk. Everyone knows how to use chopsticks nowadays."

"Thank you Mister Never-Wong," replied Diane sarcastically.

She slinked over to Alan and stroked his cheek, pouting sexily.

"Oh, by the way waiter, as you're getting the drinks, mine's a morning-glory!"

"I know madam," he said with a wink. "In fact, yours is a glory anytime!"

He smiled wickedly and grabbed his wife around the waist, pulling her body to his and firmly stroking her bottom. Then, hooking a finger under her skirt he pulled the hem up and caressed the inside of her warm silky thigh. Diane succumbed for a moment, enjoying Alan's amorous attentions and then pulled away, straightening her skirt and wagging a stern finger at him.

"Now then, no sex in the dining room, especially with juveniles in the house."

Alan adopted a hurt expression.

"Sorry madam, I'll get madam's drink then shall I? One long, cool, morning-glory, coming up," he said slowly, rudely parodying the last two words. This and similar comments being a remnant of Alan's days at his old rugby club, where he was known as the 'dude with the double-entendre'.

Alan returned to the lounge with the drinks loaded on a tray, closely followed by Diane.

"So, who's the Coke and who's the Pepsi?" he asked setting the tray down on the coffee table.

Matt jumped up from his seat.

"Mines t' Coke please Mister Arris."

Alan handed him a large glass of fizzing brown liquid.

"So Mark, yours must be the Pepsi; 'For The New Generation', eh!" he said, remembering the words of a TV advert he'd seen, and passed him an identical-looking drink to the one Matt had.

"Thanks Mister Arris," said Mark, slurping half the drink before he'd even sat down.

Alan handed a glass of wine to Becky who was busy frowning at Mark's lack of manners.

"And for you madam, une vin blanc de maison."

Becky switched her attention from Mark to Alan and turned on a beaming smile.

"Merci monsieur," she laughed. "You'd make a great French waiter Alan."

"Why sank you Madame," replied Alan in his best Franglais, bowing his head to Becky. "Actually I did a bit of bar work when I was a struggling young student, but unfortunately it was restricted to a large pub in Highgate, North London."

"Yes, I think you missed your way darling," concurred Diane. That must have been where he picked up most of his diabolical chat-up lines. I couldn't repeat the one he used on me when we first met."

"Oh, please do," appealed Becky, raising her eyebrows.

"Maybe later," said Diane, "when the kids aren't around. Anyway, it's nearly time for dinner now, so if you'd like to finish your drinks..."

She quickly held up a halting hand as the boy's glasses went straight to their lips.

"No rush though, Alan will bring you through in a few minutes, won't you darling?"

He bowed his head as if addressing royalty.

"Yes ma'am."

Diane left the room shaking her head.

"Men," she remarked sarcastically, as she closed the door behind her.

As soon as Diane had exited the room Alan looked over at Becky.

"Are the boys okay with chopsticks?" he quietly enquired.

"Oh sure," she said, nodding vigorously. "After all they're just an extension of ones fingers, aren't they?"

They both laughed as the boys looked on in bewilderment.

13

The dinner with Becky and the boys was just about over and everyone seemed to have thoroughly enjoyed the meal. Alan gestured toward the boys' empty plates and the empty bowls scattered around them.

"I see what you meant about these two and chopsticks Becky. And I thought that I could eat quickly!"

Becky smiled, nodding her head in agreement.

"Yes, it's amazing how quickly kids can adapt their eating habits when food's at stake; or should that be a lack of it? I remember the first time that Mark used chopsticks he..."

"Mum! D'yer 'ave t'?" said Mark indignantly.

"Oops, very sorry," apologised Becky. "If you two ever have kids," she said, addressing Diane and Alan, "you'll find that once they become teenagers they very quickly want to become adults and forget their childhood. It's absolutely forbidden to talk about the things they did when they were little, especially around other people..."

Becky's words trailed off as her attention was suddenly drawn to Matt who was staring around the room as if following the passage of an invisible fly. Everyone else followed her gaze.

"Matt," queried Becky, "what are you looking at?"

Matt immediately snapped out of his daydream.

"What? Oh, nowt," he said, looking down at the table and muttering quietly to himself. "A just gorra feeling that dad were around," he mumbled hesitantly.

Diane glanced at Alan who raised his eyebrows and shrugged.

"Oh, not tharagen," said Mark, making a face and prodding his brother firmly in the ribs.

"Please, don't start Mark," snapped Becky.

Matt looked at his mother with a sullen expression.

"It's alreight mum, 'e thinks thar a'm weird," he said, looking at his elder brother with no perceivable expression. "Do't yer?"

"Well y'are," replied Mark, giving Matt another prod and increasing his voice a few decibels. "Yer alas sayin' y' think our dad's still around. Well 'e i'nt. 'e's dead and 'e's niver comin' back, an' that's that."

"Look you two," interjected Becky sternly. "We're guests of Mr. and Mrs. Harris, so let's not spoil it with the usual mealtime arguments, alright?"

"It's okay Becky," said Diane calmly. "We understand," she said, looking at Alan with pleading eyes.

"Yes," said Alan, "don't worry about it Becky, things must be tough for all of you at the moment. Look, why don't the boys go into the TV room if they want?"

Mark's face beamed.

"Grand, 'ave yer got Sky Mister Arris?"

Becky shot a mean look at her son.

"Mark don't be so rude," she snapped again.

Alan quietly cut in, trying to defuse the situation:

"Sure we do Mark; we've got all the digital channels, mainly for the sport. The remote's on top of the TV," he said, getting up from his seat. "In fact, I'll show you."

"Great," yelled Mark, leaping up spiritedly from his seat.

Becky gave Matt an inquiring look but her youngest looked a little glum.

"A'll stay ere if it's okay mum."

"Are you sure?"

"Aye, A'm not that keen on MTV."

"Come on then Mark, this way," said Alan opening the dining room door.

Everyone apart from Mark was in the kitchen. They'd just about finished stacking the dishes in the dishwasher when Diane saw an opportunity to get Matt on his own. She looked at Alan with a little nod of her head and winked.

"Alan, why don't you take Becky into the lounge while Matt gives me a hand with the coffee. That's if you don't mind Matt?"

"Aye, oky doky Missis Arris."

Alan grabbed Becky by the hand and started to gently drag her across the kitchen.

"Okay Becky, we're excused. Let's make a run for it before they change their minds."

"I'm right with you Alan," she laughed, "I really think I could get used to being spoiled."

Alan and Becky went off into the lounge, leaving Matt alone in the kitchen with Diane, who was just finishing spooning coffee-grounds into the cafetière. Standing with her back to Matt she decided to go straight into her planned piece:

"What did you mean just now in the dining room Matt?" she said without turning to face the young lad. "You said you thought you had a feeling that your dad was around."

Matt didn't speak straight away but when he did his voice was shaky:

"Oh it were nowt Missis Arris."

He paused again for a few seconds shuffling uncomfortably.

"A'm sorry fo' startin' an argument wi' our Mark."

"It's okay Matt," said Diane forgivingly as she turned to face the boy. "No harm done."

As Matt wasn't readily taking the bait Diane decided that a little white lie was in order, just to get her point across.

"You know, I get the same feeling sometimes, about my mother. She passed away a few years ago and I still feel, on the odd occasion, that she's still around."

"Do yer Missis Arris?" said Matt, warming visibly to Diane's words.

"Yes, I do," said Diane, sounding quite sincere. "Tell me, what do you feel?"

Matt sounded quite emotional as he spoke:

"Am not shuwer. It's just a feelin' thar e's nearby. It meks mi feel reight strange. Not scared or owt, just a funny feelin'. Like A use't t' get when wi' did stuff together. 'e were great at that, 'e alas did things wi' our Mark an' me. But A suppose thar our Mark grew out on it, bein' older an all, an' 'e started t' go off wiy 'is friends, so it wa' just our dad and me over t' last year. Before 'e died like."

Diane responded soothingly to the young lad.

"If I tell you something, do you promise that you won't tell anyone else; not even your mum or your brother?"

"Aye, A promise," replied Matt, looking at Diane with obvious interest.

Diane paused for a second, and with a warm smile looked softly at Matt.

"Well, last night I dreamed that I was flying around the village like Superwoman, and all of a sudden I saw this man. He was a kind looking man and he said his name was Arthur."

"That's our dad's name," exclaimed Matt excitedly, before looking down at his feet and shuffling uneasily. "Well it were 'is name."

"It's okay Matt," said Diane sympathetically.

Matt looked up at her but didn't speak.

"Anyway, in this dream Arthur said to tell 'His Mate Matt' that he's okay, and not to worry about him."

Matt's eyes widened as Diane spoke those words so familiar to him.

"He knows you're worried," she continued, "but really he's fine. He said he wants you to try and cheer up a bit. It makes him sad to see you unhappy and he doesn't feel he can move on until you're your old self again. He knows that it's difficult for you but he said that he knows you can do it, especially for him."

Matt's eyes glistened.

"Did 'e really say "is Mate Matt', Missis Arris?"

"Yes Matt, he really did," said Diane, this time with real conviction.

Matt looked down at his feet again and a little tear rolled off his cheek onto the terracotta tiles of kitchen floor, leaving a little dark patch where it burst on impact.

"That's whar 'e all'as called mi."

After a short silence Matt wiped his eyes and with a little sniff seemed to visibly warm, looking up at Diane with a tearful smile that would have made his dad melt, spirit or no spirit!

"D'yer really think it were mi dad in yer dream Missis Arris?"

"Yes Matt, I really do, and I think that one of the things he was trying to say to you is that when people pass on they sometimes find it difficult to let go, especially if their loved ones are still grieving for them. And when those of us left behind say that life must go on, we don't mean that we should totally forget the one that's left us, just that we should try to continue as best we can in their absence."

"That's whar our mum sez," said Matt, seeming a lot perkier now.

"And she's right. We should remember them for all the good times that we had with them, and try, as difficult as it seems sometimes, not to be too sad at our loss. After all, I'm sure that your dad didn't want to leave you and your mum and Mark.

But these things are decided by a greater power than us, and obviously that greater power thought that your dad was needed somewhere else, and it just couldn't wait until he got old."

Matt went quiet in thought for a moment.

"Y' know Missis Arris, yer probably right. 'e wa' real smart, in lots o' ways were our dad. 'e understood all them books 'e use' t' read an' 'e'd tell mi that wi shunt bi frightened o' dying. Thar it wa' just another part o' t' journey t' ower final restin'-

place. An' that when wi eventually get there wi'll bi together forever."

"Well, for what it's worth," said Diane, "I think he was right on the button, and one day we'll all be reunited with those we love."

Matt looked thoughtful again and then seemed to visibly brighten.

"Missis Arris, If yer 'ave another dream wi' our dad in it, will yer tell 'im thanks fo' t' message? But tell 'im thar 'e should go where 'e's supposed t'. A mean, it's no good 'angin round here if 'e's got important thin's t' do fo' God. An tell 'im not t' worry about our mum or our Mark. A'll see their okay."

He suddenly stopped and looked over Diane's shoulder.

"Eyup Missis Arris, A think coffees' boilin'!"

Diane looked at Matt in total bewilderment and wondered how one so young could be so mature in his reasoning and she smiled lovingly at him, ruffling his hair.

"Come on then," she said with a little laugh, "let's finish making the coffee and take it through to the others."

The group had been sat in the lounge drinking coffee for about an hour, chatting about all sorts of things, when Becky suddenly glanced at her watch.

"Well, as much as I hate to say this, I think it's time that we made a move. Matt, would you get Mark please?"

"Aye, alreight mum," said the young lad, springing up from his seat and leaving the room.

Becky smiled at Diane.

"All I can say is thank you Diane, and you Alan; and I really mean that. I don't think I've had such an enjoyable evening since ... well, you know."

"Yes we do," said Diane, "and you're more than welcome, you and the boys. You've made our first dinner-party in our new home a real success. Isn't that right Alan?"

"Absolutely, and don't forget, if the boys want to go to any of the rugby games, I'm your man!"

Becky smiled again but with a somewhat wistful tinge.

"That's very kind of you Alan, they miss that sort of thing more than they let on but I just can't stand the crowds. I never could; I must be claustrophobic or something. Even when Arthur used to take them he'd always invite me but I only went the once and I'm afraid the huge crowd put me off for life."

"Don't worry about it" said Alan, getting up from his seat and feigning a whisper towards Becky. "It gives me an excuse to go to more games."

"Ha, that's a laugh," shrieked Diane. "You don't need an excuse to go to any rugby game, especially the Bulls. You're what's classed as a fanatic."

"Hey, don't make me feel guilty," laughed Becky, "It's okay, I'm only joking assured Diane."

They all looked round as Mark and Matt entered the room. Mark had a typical teenage pout on his face.

"Oh mum, ca't wi' stay fer another arf-hour?" he winged. "Theza great concert on MTV."

"No!" said Becky firmly. "You can watch the end when we get home; if you behave!"

Mark's arms seemed to grow six inches as his shoulders slumped and he adopted a defiant yet vanquished face. Becky ignored this familiar adolescent gesture and turned to face Alan and Diane.

"Thanks again you two, it's been really great."

Becky gave her two boys a quick glance and they sounded off in unison as if they'd been rehearsing for weeks.

"Thanks fer 'avin' us."

Diane walked over to the boys and ruffled Matt's hair. Mark ducked!

"You're welcome boys, and don't forget, if you're ever at a loose end or want to go to a rugby game, then give us a call or pop round."

Matt gave Diane a little wink.

"Thanks Missis Arris."

Mark looked at Alan.

"Yer an' thanks fo' lerrin us watch MTV."

"Okay tribe," said Becky, making a move towards the door, "let's go."

Alan got their coats from the closet and the couple saw the Ayres' clan to the door and waved them goodbye as they walked across the courtyard and down the drive.

An hour later and Diane and Alan were in bed. Alan was reading the programme from the rugby game earlier in the day and Diane was thumbing through the latest edition of her company's magazine. She looked up having just finished reading Sue's agony page; which, unsurprisingly, didn't have a letter from anyone called Wendy from Wakefield!

"I think this evening went well from all perspectives. What did you think of Becky?"

"I think she's a great gal," said Alan, putting down his programme. "She seems to be coping quite well with the loss of Arthur. Well, what I mean is, as well as anyone can cope with such a loss; especially for a couple so obviously as close as they were."

"Yes," said Diane, pausing in thought for a moment. "But I think she's covering up a lot of hurt for the sake of the boys."

"I'm sure you're right, all I meant was she comes across as coping well."

"I don't suppose she has any choice in the matter. Mothers tend to automatically do what they have to, especially where their children are concerned. I really hope that I got it right with Matt tonight. Do you think it was okay to take the 'little-secret' tack?"

"Sure, he's only young. Young boys actually like to have secrets with adults, especially non-relatives, it makes them feel more grown-up."

"How do you know that?" asked Diane.

Alan laughed out loud.

"I was that boy," he said, picking up his rugby programme.

Diane paused in thought for a few moments before pursuing something that had been niggling at her since she got back from her OOBE that afternoon:

"Alan?"

He looked up from his reading.

"Yes love."

"Do you think we have a strong bond, like Becky and Arthur had?"

Alan seemed puzzled by the question.

"Of course we do. Why do you ask?"

"Oh, nothing really. Well ... actually it is something," she admitted, sitting up straight. "Do you ever find yourself attracted to other women?"

"What do you mean by attracted?" he asked rhetorically, searching for some hidden meaning behind the question.

Diane responded in a matter-of-fact manner.

"Well, let's say you were out on your own; or with male friends and an attractive young girl came-on to you. How would you react?"

"You mean apart from being flattered?" he said with a nervous laugh.

"Obviously apart from being flattered," said Diane, slightly peeved at his flippancy.

"Well, I suppose I'd enjoy the moment, but that's about all."

He looked straight into Diane's eyes.

"Is this questioning leading to something love?"

"No darling, I'm sorry," she said, averting her eyes momentarily. "It's just that since I first chatted with Becky I've been thinking about us a lot and I can't imagine life without you. So I suppose I transposed death for a younger woman," she lied.

Alan slowly shook his head.

"Firstly, if I have anything to do with it I don't intend to die until I'm well past eighty; and secondly, no woman could tempt me to do anything that would hurt our relationship."

He put his arm around Diane and looked deep into her eyes.

"I love you. I have from the moment I first saw you with John all those years ago. And I don't intend to let…" He paused in thought momentarily, searching for the right words. "…As you might put it, 'a lack of testosterone control', spoil what we have. Okay?"

"And I love you too," sighed Diane. "I suppose that I'm letting all this OOBE stuff, and Becky's situation, get the better of me. Anyway," she said, snuggling down with her face in Alan's chest, "I think it's time that you got the better of me. Right now!" she said sexily, letting her hand wander down Alan's torso and around his genital area.

Alan involuntarily responded to her advances!

"Oh, you little vixen, you've got eight hours to stop that."

"Is that all?" asked Diane in a low husky voice, as she slid her head under the covers!

14

Later that night Diane's spirit detached itself from her physical body and as she rose slowly towards the ceiling there was a white flash and that sudden rush of travelling at great speed; and before she knew it she was back in the warm, friendly darkness of the Ether. But before she had time to wonder why she was there, Arthur appeared, as if from nowhere.

"I was just about to come down to meet you," he said.

Diane looked down at her OOBE form admiringly, as if viewing an outfit of new clothes.

"I still can't get used to this incredible transformation."

Arthur smiled his all-knowing smile.

"Oh, by the way, before I forget, you did a great job with Matt. Thank you, most sincerely; I really think that your little chat may just have done the trick there."

"You're more than welcome, It wasn't a difficult task, I mean he's such a warm friendly boy and he has a very strong feminine side to him. Not that I mean he's..."

"It's okay Diane," said Arthur sympathetically, "I know what you mean. All people on earth have both male and female sides to them. In fact the men who let their feminine side show through seem to relate better to everyone, regardless of sex. Matt's fortunate as his feminine side comes through so naturally; I just hope that it stays that way as he matures."

Arthur sighed slowly and seemed to reflect for a moment before continuing:

"Mark, however, is the total opposite. He tries to suppress his feminine side so much that he comes across as such a young macho thing. But I don't suppose that he's much different to the majority of teenage boys. He probably thinks that being the eldest male it's expected of him. In fact, it's his overt masculinity that's helped him handle my absence. He's literally blocked it out of his mind and put on this rough, tough exterior; that's why he gets so annoyed when someone brings up the subject."

"I'm sure you're right," agreed Diane, "but I can't help thinking that his grief at your loss, because he's totally blocked it out for now, may come back at a later stage in his life."

"Oh it will," said Arthur, nodding his head in agreement, "but there's nothing that we can do about it at this moment in earth-time. But then that's one of the unknowns of taking potluck when acquiring a physical body at birth. You have to accept the physical genetic profile that comes with that particular life in the queue."

"Potluck?" said Diane incredulously.

"Yes, good old potluck. When we're in our spirit form after we've died, we, our spirit that is, must decide whether or not it needs to go back to earth to further its enrichment. And as a free spirit we normally take the first earth-life that's offered to us; unless there's a very specific experience that we wish to live through. So mainly it's a potluck scenario. Simply put, we go through our lives on earth to obtain the experience of each particular life, no matter how good or bad it is. At some stage, after one or more lives on earth, we instinctively know that it's time to move on to the next stage. However, once we've moved on to that next stage, we never need, or would want for that matter, to come back to what you and the rest of mankind know as life on earth."

Diane was visibly stunned at this revelation.

"Wow, that must be the decision of all time; should I stay or should I go?"

"Not really my dear. As I mentioned before, one's spirit instinctively knows when that time comes, when other earth-life experiences are, how shall we say, surplus to requirements. Mind you," he continued, "there's always the exception that proves the rule, even for spirits, and earth-life can become addictive to a few errant souls; and those poor jerks just keep going back for more, even though they know they don't really need to."

Arthur moved nearer to Diane and visibly brightened.

"Okay Diane, that's enough of the educational talk for now, you ready for that journey of a lifetime I promised you? I only call it that because not many living people make this kind of trip and remember it. Most who do, and strange as it may seem that's actually the majority of earth-population, only remember it as a dream. But of course you can do anything in your dreams, can't you?"

"I have to admit," she nodded in agreement, "when you put it that way it starts to make sense. Nobody really questions the content of their dreams, we just seem to accept them at face value; and blame their occurrence on something we ate before we went to bed," she concluded with a laugh.

"Well there's always a basis for those old wife's tales Diane, even that one! Anyway enough dream chat for now, hold on to your hat, metaphorically speaking," he said with a little chuckle, "and let me lead the way."

Diane and Arthur were streaking through the darkness and Diane felt a real sensation of moving at phenomenal speed; like being on the downward slope of a big dipper, but strangely, without a wind blowing in her face. Suddenly it became light and they seemed to decelerate, eventually coming to a complete halt.

"Well how's that for you Diane?" asked Arthur, gesturing majestically at the incredible sight before them.

Diane was momentarily speechless. What she saw was better than any picture or film she'd ever seen, even those sent back from outer space. The curvature of the earth was laid out below them in bright, clear and vivid colours. Diane could see both Lands End in Cornwall and John o' Groats in Scotland, and in the distance to their left the rough coastline of Ireland; and directly beneath them the coastline of northern France.

"Oh Arthur, It's absolutely spectacular," she gasped in wonderment. "The colours are so intense, the blues and greens, and the white of the clouds. Wow, is that really earth?"

"Most definitely," he replied. "In fact, to be precise, earth 55BC; earth at the time of the Roman invasion of England. That's why the air is so clear. No real industry or pollution yet."

"Roman invasion?" blurted out Diane with total astonishment.

"Yes," said Arthur, quite casually. "At this particular earth-time the Romans have only been in England about six months. I believe that Julius Caesar is currently in charge but not actually down there yet; he's still back there in Rome," he said, gesturing over his right shoulder. "You know of course that the Romans civilised the English and many other peoples, in many and varied ways."

"But how do you know the year?" asked Diane. "How did you get us here at this time? Did you use that motorway-slip-road technique you mentioned last time?"

Arthur smiled inwardly at Diane's appetite for knowledge.

"Not quite. I used a method that's virtually the same as the way that you get from your bedroom to wherever you want go when you're having an OOBE; except I added the time element. If you think back, to when you first moved around in your spirit form, there were two options for getting from A to B. One is to move in conjunction with your surroundings, like flying. A slow method but to newcomers it can be quite fun. The other is to think of, or visualise, a person or place and you immediately find yourself there. Yes?"

"Yes," agreed Diane, "although I'm still working on mastering it!"

"Well it's just about the same with time-shifting, but you think of, or visualise the time-slot before the person or place. And that's really all there is to it. I tell you what, when we move on you can set the time and place if you want."

"Oh can I?" asked Diane with obvious excitement. "That'd be great. I think I'd be much happier trying it while you're around."

They both stopped communicating for a few moments to take in the fabulous scenery. Diane looked across at Arthur who was just floating there peacefully; face down wearing a big smile.

"Can we go down and take a closer look please?" she asked.

"Sure," he replied. "In fact we'll go down the conventional way. Well, what most people would call conventional anyway; as if we were a couple of eagles soaring on a thermal."

And with those words hardly spoken, they began to float down towards the earth below, eventually breaking through the lower clouds, revealing a verdant coastal landscape. Diane broke the silence first:

"This is great. Where exactly are we, geographically speaking that is?"

"Oh, let me get my bearings," said Arthur, vibrating momentarily. "We're travelling north-west, over what will eventually be known as Dover; the Roman's called it Dubris."

"It all looks so strange," said Diane. "No roads, no big towns or cities, just mile after mile of forest from the coast inland."

"Yes, it's a shame man had to spoil it, don't you think?"

"I suppose so. It does look rather beautiful down there."

"It is aesthetically beautiful but don't forget that man's struggle to expand his territories at this particular earth-time is a bloody affair. As we may well observe!"

They floated down lower towards the land.

"Arthur, I assume that we can't be seen by anyone?"

"No my dear, nor heard. But we can see and hear everything. Come on, let's go down for a closer look."

They were now skimming the tops of the trees and Diane moved closer to Arthur, just in case!

"I know that I'm guiding myself," she said, "but I don't know how."

"And they thought that in your current earth-time an aeroplane's GPS-autopilot was a clever piece of electronics," said Arthur with a laugh. "If they only knew what they were really capable of, and without any form of electronics! Anyway, I digress. You are guiding yourself, sort of sub-consciously. In your spirit form you guide by thought and an inbuilt knowledge gained through the vast shared-experience of billions of spirits. Something that's inherent in all spirits but that you, as a relatively new OOBE exponent, may find takes a little time to come to the fore. And as you already know, you can go through things too. Come on."

Arthur swooped down and disappeared into the treetops. Diane followed nervously and tentatively penetrated the top of a few of the higher trees at what she guessed was around sixty miles an hour. Arthur appeared again, right in front of her.

"See, easier than flying through tissue paper. And those are pretty big oak trees, extremely dense."

Diane was now laughing like a child on a roller coaster.

"Wow it tingles. This is fun."

Diane banked to her left and then to her right.

"Wee, I feel like a bird."

Arthur swooped in front of her and gestured with his hand.

"Come on, this way."

And as the pair glided silently over the trees a clearing appeared and Arthur pointed down.

"Look, over there."

Diane looked down and saw what appeared to be a small village or settlement.

"Oh my, I can see people. Look," she exclaimed excitedly, "children."

They slowed down to a near stop and Arthur came alongside Diane.

"Come on then, let's mingle with the natives for a while."

The pair floated down into the middle of the group of huts, which were about twenty in all, arranged in a circle and constructed from twigs and mud with a thatch-type roof.

"This is phenomenal," said Diane. "Look at those women around the fire, they're cooking something. It doesn't look too appetising though."

"No, it's probably a piece of that deer carcass that's hanging from that large hut over there," he said, pointing towards the largest of the dwellings.

"It's funny," said Diane, "but I don't seem to be able to smell anything."

Arthur pulled a face and laughed.

"Then think yourself lucky, because it's not that pleasant I can assure you. It'll probably take you quite a while to get your smell-senses; they're the last to develop. In fact, as an OOBE practitioner you may never get them. Still the sights and sounds aren't bad, are they?"

Diane moved around inspired, trying to take everything in, and then suddenly realised that she didn't recognise the language the villagers were using.

"Arthur, I don't understand what they're saying, do you? It doesn't sound like English. In fact it doesn't sound like any language I've heard before."

"It's probably some old Celtic tongue, a forerunner to modern-day Gaelic, but it'll slowly change over the next few decades. By AD 47, In a hundred years or so, the Romans will control all the land from the south coast of England up to York and everywhere east of the river Severn, and most town people will be talking a mixture of this language and Latin, courtesy of their Roman invaders. In fact, you probably wouldn't recognise the language here as what you now know as basic English for many hundreds of years."

Diane was truly fascinated by everything she saw and continued her exploring, watching the women in particular. Clad in what looked like a mixture of rough cloth and animal skins, they went about their daily chores, oblivious to the two airborne spectators. Little children were playing in small groups, throwing sticks at each other and cheering when one hit the target. Most of the women were sat around in groups, some cooking, some preparing food and one group scraping a large animal skin which was stretched out on the ground and pegged at all four corners.

"You know Arthur, there's something strange about this village."

She stopped and looked around more intently.

"I know!" she exclaimed. "There aren't any adult men here."

"Your right my dear but it's not unusual in these times. The men are probably out hunting somewhere."

Diane was suddenly drawn to the entrance of one of the smaller huts on the edge of the village and slowly floated over, cautiously looking inside.

"Oh my goodness, look at this," she cried. "That young girl's having a baby."

Arthur joined her and peered into the hut at a young pregnant girl squatting on a reed mat on the floor.

"Yes, it's fascinating isn't it? No matter that we understand how a baby is created and no matter how many newborn babies we may see, it's still a marvellous thing to behold."

"But the mother-to-be only looks about thirteen or fourteen," said Diane. "It's hard to believe that we used to live like this. I mean, I've seen this sort of thing on the BBC and National Geographic TV, but to actually be here and experience it is something else…"

Diane's words were suddenly obliterated by a loud crackling sound as a streak of bright blue-white light shot through the roof of the hut and seemed to enter the young girl's heavily pregnant stomach. Diane immediately backed away startled.

"Oh my goodness," she cried out, "did you see that Arthur?"

"Yes, I did," he said, looking at Diane inquisitively. "Can you guess what it was?"

Diane turned slowly and looked at Arthur with a frown and then the realisation hit her.

"It was a spirit wasn't it?" she answered quietly.

"Well done," effused Arthur, "your senses are improving in leaps and bounds."

"The beginning of life," she murmured, turning back to view the scene.

"Yes my dear," concurred Arthur, to whom a murmur sounded like a shout. "The true beginning of a human life."

"Goodness," said Diane abruptly. "You know, I always thought that the soul, or spirit of a person, was created at the time of conception. Well, that's what they taught us at school anyway."

"There are many belief systems on earth, whether it's this earth-time," he said, gesturing at their surroundings; "your own current earth-time, or hundreds of years into your future; and they all have their own way of explaining how and when people come by their spirit. But I suppose their misunderstanding is understandable, if you'll forgive the oxymoron? After all, even though all of mankind really knows the truth subconsciously, they can't normally access that information and they don't have the benefit of your OOBE recollections."

Diane was still staring at the pregnant young girl, who was now well into the birth process, red in the face with pushing.

"All this makes me wonder," she said thoughtfully; "why, of all the billions of people on earth, have I been given the opportunity to experience all this?"

Arthur smiled knowingly.

"I'm sure that eventually it'll be made clear to you Diane but don't go thinking that you're all alone in your abilities in your own earth-time. There are thousands of people who have OOBE's and actually remember them. It's just that most of them don't talk about it much. I mean," he said with a wry smile, "just think, if someone had told you before you'd had your first OOBE that you'd experience a fraction of what you have recently; would you have unreservedly believed them?"

Diane looked thoughtfully at Arthur.

"You're right, of course," she agreed with a slow nod of her head.

The young woman cried out loudly again and Diane turned to watch in awe as a little, pink, baby boy was born onto the reed mat of the hut and immediately started wailing. The girl picked up her baby son and laid him on her chest, stroking his head lovingly; and after a few minutes of mother and baby bonding, the young girl instinctively bit through the umbilical chord. Then, cradling him gently in her arms, she placed her baby onto her distended breast, where it snuffled for a second before latching firmly onto the swollen, dripping nipple. Diane was completely overwhelmed.

15

The invisible time travellers watched the young mother and her new baby for quite some time before continuing their exploration of the village and its surroundings; observing the women and children of some long-past time go about their daily lives. Eventually, they slowly rose up above the huts and Arthur floated over closer to Diane.

"May I make a suggestion," he requested politely.

"Of course," said Diane.

"Well, if you've seen enough here we could do a few increasing circles from the village; we might just find the men-folk."

"Let's go then," she said enthusiastically, still a little overawed by the countless revelations that this fantastic journey was providing.

They streaked off together over the lush treetops and after only a few minutes of searching Diane pointed away into the distance.

"Arthur," she shouted, "look, by the foot of that small hill."

Arthur followed her gaze and saw the group of people that Diane had noticed.

"Let's go in for a closer look," he said.

And as they approached the hillside the image unfolded like a scene from a Cecil B. DeMille movie. Hoards of men were engaged in a ferocious battle, and as the pair got closer the noise increased accordingly, almost deafening them as they arrived overhead. Diane shrieked above the din:

"Oh my God, they're fighting, they're killing each other; this is awful."

"They sure are," said Arthur, "and I don't think the locals are going to win this one. It looks like they're up against a crack unit of Roman soldiers."

The pair were now virtually in amongst the fight and Diane was appalled by the sight and sounds of this gory battle. The Romans, who really looked like soldiers, with their pleated skirts and leather tunics, had short fat swords and small shields and were ferociously hacking at the Celtic men. The Celt's, who although armed with little more than wooden spears and seeming grossly outclassed in the battle-technique department, were doggedly standing their ground; causing some casualties from the Roman ranks.

Diane and Arthur watched the scene develop, although Diane periodically averted her gaze when she noticed a particularly gruesome occurrence. But eventually the Romans started to make inroads into the slowly decreasing ranks of Celts, and the dusty brown earth became dark and sticky with drying blood. Diane still believed she had to shout to make herself heard above the clamour of the battling men and the clash of steel on wood:

"Arthur," she yelled in a concerned voice, "look at that man, the one over there."

She pointed towards one of the Celts standing in the middle of the melee, looking decidedly lost. Arthur nodded.

"Let's go over to him."

Diane silently complied and they drifted over to the man. As they floated overhead, the young Celt warrior looked straight up at Diane and with a shocked expression on his face, held his arms defensively to his face, apparently overwhelmed with fear.

"Arthur," said Diane bewilderedly, "I'm sure that young man just looked straight at me."

"Yes," he replied cautiously, "it seemed so didn't it?"

"But he can't see us, can he? You said that we couldn't be seen or heard."

Arthur floated up alongside Diane to explain the occurrence.

"In the village back there you saw the birth of a baby; not just the physical birth but also the spirit entering the physical body just prior to birth. What you are now observing is the inevitable conclusion of that process. The reason why the young man looked at you with some recognition is that he can see us. He's just been fatally wounded by one of the Roman soldiers. In fact if you look carefully, you can see his physical body lying on the ground about six feet in front of him."

Diane floated in more closely, much to the consternation of the recently deceased Celt, who seemed more afraid of Arthur and Diane than he ever had of the Romans.

"Oh my goodness, you're right," she exclaimed.

"If you look around you'll see lots more," said Arthur. "Look over there."

Arthur gestured towards another older Celt who was lashing out at the Romans but to no avail, as his blows were seemingly going straight through every soldier he attempted to attack. Diane, not for the first time on this trip, looked on in total bewilderment.

"What's he doing?"

"It hasn't yet dawned on him that he's no longer physical and he's still trying to fight the…"

Diane interrupted Arthur, pointing across the battlefield.

"Look," she shouted, "they're going."

One-by-one the spirits of the Celtic warriors started to streak up into the cloudy sky, all that is except the older man, who still seemed a little disoriented and just stood in the middle of the melee looking totally confused.

"He'll be fine," said Arthur sympathetically. "Someone will be along to help him if it looks like he's going to be really stuck." Anyway, I think that we should get on with our little exploration. Let's take another quick look around the area and then you can take us somewhere else."

They left the remnants of the fighting behind and took off over the English countryside. As they went, they saw lots more small villages and farming-type communities, and a great many of those industrious Romans, building roads and settlements; with the help of a few reluctant locals, of course!

Eventually Diane and Arthur came to a halt over what would, in the due course of time, become the sprawling Metropolis of London, but was currently just a small settlement on a large bend in a winding river, surrounded by thick lush forest.

"Well my dear, what did you think of all that?" asked Arthur.

"I can honestly say that it's the most incredible thing I've ever experienced," said Diane looking around at the tremendous view. "You were right again, as usual. Mind you, if I ever told anyone about this they'd think I was ready for the psychiatrist's couch. Still, I'll at least attempt to explain it all to Alan."

Arthur interrupted Diane with a cautious tone:

"Of course that's your prerogative my dear."

"It's okay Arthur, Alan knows all about my OOBE's. In fact he helped me set up the little talk I had with Matt."

"I know he did, and I'm very grateful for his assistance; but I think that his acceptance of what you tell him still has more to do with the fact that he loves you, rather than his belief in OOBE's. Anyway, you can deliberate that in your own good time; let's continue our little adventure. It's your turn to choose our time and destination. Have you given it any thought?"

"Yes I have. I'd like to go to…"

That familiar white flash blanked out the scene.

16

With that usual feeling of rapid acceleration Diane streaked back into the warm darkness of the Ether and again experienced the perception of phenomenal speed. Within a few seconds the light returned and she found herself motionless about five hundred feet up in the air, staring down on the city of Leeds. And although it was a lovely sunny day she immediately noticed the difference in visibility. Compared with ancient Britain, the air here was positively gungy.

For a few moments Diane was totally engrossed in the view, trying to pick out familiar landmarks, but eventually, as she looked around, and for the first time since she'd had her first OOBE, she truly panicked. There was no sign of Arthur, anywhere!

"Oh my God I'm lost in time," she thought anxiously.

She looked around wildly again.

"Arthur," she shouted, "Arthur, where are you?"

Arthur materialised by her side.

"It's okay, I'm here. I was just getting my bearings on you."

To say Diane was extremely relieved was an understatement but when she communicated with Arthur her thoughts had a slight edge to them.

"I thought you'd know exactly where we were going, and when."

"No, not at all. I didn't have an inkling as to your intended destination before we set off. I didn't actually think that you'd get your co-ordinates so right so quickly. But I'm a bit surprised at your choice," he said with a touch of bewilderment. "I mean, when you could pick any venue in the world at any time in its history, and you choose Yorkshire, just one month ahead of you own earth-time … well, thirty days to be exact."

Diane grimaced, feeling a little silly.

"Oh dear," she said disappointedly. "If we're only a month ahead of my own earth-time then I don't think I did get my co-ordinates right, at all."

"Ah, I see, right place wrong time?"

"Yes. It was supposed to be thirty years ahead, not thirty days. I wanted to see what things would be like around here when I'm at retirement age. For some reason I got my years and my days mixed up."

Arthur picked up on her sense of failure.

"Not to worry," he said in a sympathetic, fatherly voice, looking at the city of Leeds sprawling beneath them. "Practice makes perfect as they say down there. Try again, and this time when you formulate the co-ordinates, put the time first, as an actual date. Like: earth-time September 29th 2030, and try to visualise the verbal description."

"Seeing that we're already here," said Diane hesitantly, "do you mind if we take a quick look around? I've got a strange urge to go down there."

"Of course, no problem. Anyway, I've got something to see to, so I'm just going to pop off, but I'll be back when you need me."

Diane felt a little apprehensive at being left alone, especially after her last mistake.

"Please don't go Arthur," she said tensely. "I don't want to screw-up again. Anyway, aren't there things I should know about before I go wandering around in the future on my own?"

"Such as?"

"Well, you know ... what if I see myself or something?"

Arthur laughed out loudly.

"Oh Diane, you've been watching too many science-fiction movies. Remember what I said earlier? The only thing you can do during your OOBE is observe. You can't touch anything, or be seen; well by anyone alive that is, so you can't really change anything on earth in this form."

He paused in thought for a second and vibrated, then looked straight at Diane.

"However," he continued, "you could see something now that you may be able to use when you get back to your physical body."

"How do you mean?"

"Well, let me give you a couple of brief historical examples," he suggested, assuming his tutorial voice. "Remember the great artist Leonardo da Vinci, earth-time 1452-1519; and Michel de Nostradame, 1503-1566, better known as Nostradamus."

"Yes, of course," said Diane. "In fact I did da Vinci as part of my A-level art exam at school.

"Alright then," said Arthur with a little grin, "instead of me telling you about this I'll give you an NVC thought-package; it's sort of like a full-length feature film that will play in your mind. Although it only takes a few seconds to run the result is the same as if you had sat through a two hour film."

"Okay then, I'm up for that. I haven't seen a good movie for ages," she said with a smile; that is until a strange vibration consumed her whole being. "Ooh, wow, this is incredible and I love the sensation that comes with it. Wow, It feels like an extra-strong orgasm."

Diane's form vibrated and gyrated as the NVC package unfurled in her consciousness and she moaned lustily. Then, just as she thought she'd explode with ecstasy, it ended. She lay back and opened her arms, feeling spent.

"Oh, wow! That's such a wonderful feeling. Who needs sex in this realm?"

Arthur looked away demurely.

"Well, did you get the message my dear?"

"You bet I did, and more! What a rush."

Diane had received the full low-down on Leonardo da Vinci; who 'anticipated' many of the developments of modern science and technology, including a design for a helicopter; and Nostradamus, who, in 1550, started writing 'prophecies' of future world events that are still being studied to this day. But this NVC package also included information on their little-known ability to effect the OOBE!

"I understand!" she cried ecstatically.

"So those two both had the ability to effect OOBE's but they couldn't apply what they learned in their spirit travels due to a lack of critical materials and technology in their particular earth-times. All they could really do was try to remember and record their experiences. And they never told anyone about their OOBE's in case they were looked upon as male witches, or something equally as unacceptable in those heavily religious times. That's incredible," she said shaking her head. "Well, I suppose that told me in no uncertain terms?"

"Yes," replied Arthur, " if things aren't meant to be, they just don't happen. Anyway I'm off, so you pop down and have a look around and I'll see you later, or earlier!"

And with a final chuckle Arthur disappeared in that familiar blue-white flash. Diane looked around apprehensively at his departure, but with a small shrug of her shoulders commenced a slow descent towards the hustle and bustle of Leeds city.

As soon as she got down near to street level – about ten to fifteen feet off the ground – Diane started to waft around the roads, pedestrian precincts and parks that make up the centre of Leeds; enjoying the real sense of freedom that she had in her spirit form. Everything looked the same as when she was there the other day. Busses plied the busy thoroughfares, jockeying with cars for the limited road space, while suicidal cyclist nipped in and out, taking their lives in their hands. She followed one particular cyclist as he used the city's underpass as a shortcut from the west to the east, and Diane felt quite exhilarated as she sped through one tunnel the wrong way.

"Well, at least there aren't any spirit-cops to pull me in," she thought, smiling inwardly.

As she mingled unseen with shoppers near The Headrow – which used to be the main road through Leeds before the by-pass was built – she seemed to be drawn, for no apparent reason, to the window display of a Sony TV and Hi-Fi store.

"That's strange," she thought, "I feel as though I'm being pulled."

She tried to move on by pointing in one direction and then another, but to no avail. She seemed to be firmly stuck there.

It was just on the hour as Diane looked at the sea of television screens that made up the majority of the store's window display, and while she was wondering what to do next the news came on. The televisions were all tuned to the Sky News channel and the first item up seemed to be some kind of financial news, and as Diane watched, the name Mega-Software flashed up on the screen.

"Mega-Software," she thought, "that rings a bell. Oh yes, Alan said that John was working with that company."

She could see that the newscaster was talking but Diane couldn't hear from outside, so without a seconds thought she poked her head straight through the plate-glass window! It was as if someone had just released the mute-button on the remote control.

"Today's top stories," announced the newsreader. "One of this years biggest U.K. financial deals has totally collapsed. Very few Institutions have bought shares in the multi-billion pound Mega-Software floatation today and one of the syndicate of brokerage houses that helped underwrite the deal may be at risk of collapse. This was only one of many deals world-wide that have failed today due to a massive fall-off in world stock markets; the worst daily drop since October 1987..."

"Well, well," thought Diane, as she pulled her head back out into the street, "John won't be too happy at that news."

She tried to move again but couldn't seem to free herself from that particular area outside the store. The news-headlines continued with a few more short items and then the sports headlines came on; and with that Diane started to drift on as if nothing untoward had happened.

"About time," she said to herself indignantly, "mobile at last."

Not understanding why she had been temporarily immobilised and not wanting to repeat the anomaly, Diane floated upwards, until she could see the whole city beneath her. As she rose through the haze she could see planes passing below; on their way to land at Leeds-Bradford airport, over to the North-West.

"I wonder if I can get high enough to see across the sea?" she thought.

Diane floated up and up until she could see for miles in every direction. However, she was so absorbed with the fabulous view – she could now just about make out both the east and west coastlines of northern England – she didn't realise that she was close to leaving the earth's atmosphere. It was only when she actually passed outside the upper atmosphere and it started to get dark that she realised what had happened. But as it didn't seem to affect her progress or well-being one iota and with a real feeling of euphoria, Diane decided to become an unseen satellite and make an orbit or two of the earth.

As she was crossing over the Atlantic Ocean for the second time she noticed a glint in the distance and out of the sun appeared the outline of an aircraft, approaching her at great speed.

"Oh my goodness, what's that doing out here," she thought.

Instinctively she changed course to avoid a collision but as the craft got closer she realised, with a chuckle of glee, that it wasn't a plane. The craft bearing down on her was one of the NASA Space Shuttles.

Now infinitely more skilled in her flying techniques, Diane, like a little girl who had found a new toy, began to follow the shuttle on its course for earth.

"I wonder if I can actually get inside for a look," she thought.

That white flash went off again and Diane instantly found herself inside the shuttle, looking over the shoulders of the astronauts; who were busy flicking switches and talking to their ground controllers. Diane chortled with delight.

"Well I never. Who'd have believed it? Diane Harris, astronaut. I can't wait to tell Alan. He'll freak out over this one."

Momentarily the shuttle started to enter the earth's atmosphere and flames erupted all around the craft.

"Oh wow, phenomenal," cried Diane.

After a bumpy but nonetheless exciting couple of minutes the spacecraft eventually emerged into earth's atmosphere and the cabin became eerily quiet until the silence was broken by a jubilant voice from the radio speaker:

"Welcome home boys," said the voice as the astronauts cheered loudly.

Shortly, Diane was treated to a perfect landing at Edwards Airforce Base in California; and as the crew unbuckled their harnesses and started to congratulate each other, Diane mistakenly wondered what to do next. That white flash appeared, removing all options.

Diane awoke with a jolt and opened her eyes, quickly realising that she was back home in bed.

"Damn, how did that happen?" she said angrily to herself. "I must have thought it. Shit, I must learn to control my thoughts."

She turned over and looked at the clock. Not believing what she saw she rubbed her eyes and looked again.

"Good lord, all that in just five minutes. Arthur was right about the irrelevance of time out there in the Ether. Wow, I must write everything down, before I forget."

Diane got out of bed softly, so as not to disturb Alan, and took her pen and pad into the bathroom; and sitting down on the loo seat started to document her night's incredible adventure!

17

It was ten-thirty on Sunday morning and Diane was still asleep when Alan awoke. He got up quietly and went downstairs to make a pot of tea. Diane woke-up about ten minutes later roused by Alan's activities below but lay quietly in thought for a few moments before rising. She walked into the kitchen just as Alan was pouring the tea. He turned at the sound of the door.

"Morning love, sleep well?"

"Yes thanks. Especially when I got back from my OOBE," she said, a big grin spreading over her face.

Alan looked at her sideways.

"Another OOBE so soon after the last?"

"Yes, another OOBE," she repeated, still grinning. "But this one was totally out of this world, literally! Arthur took me…"

Alan immediately interjected.

"Arthur again eh. How is the … erm … old spirit?"

Diane laughed at Alan's choice of words.

"He's fine and he said thank you for helping me to side-track Matt last night."

Alan looked inquisitively at Diane, pausing in thought for a couple of seconds.

"Did you tell him that I assisted or does he see everything we do?"

"What do you mean?"

"Well, if he does see everything that goes on here," he persisted, "I can tell you, I could have a problem with this."

"What are you talking about?" asked Diane, somewhat perplexed at Alan's train of questioning.

"Well, if he knew that I'd helped you, without you telling him, then that means that he was here," he said, gesturing around the kitchen. "And if he was here, then who knows where else he might go in the house; what else he might see. In the bedroom for instance," he protested, his voice decreasing to a whisper, as if someone might be listening in.

Diane couldn't help but laugh at this ludicrously misplaced concern.

"Oh Alan, don't be silly. Fancy thinking Arthur's a voyeur."

Alan put his finger to his lips.

"Shush, he might be here now."

He looked furtively around the kitchen and Diane suddenly realised that Alan was really serious.

"For goodness sake," she said tersely. "Arthur's not interested in our sex life, or any other part of our life for that matter … well, unless it's to do with Matt that is."

"Yes, of course young Matt," said Alan. "I'll bet Arthur was here last night, when Matt said he thought he was; remember, in the dining room when Mark had a go at him."

"Look darling, pour me a cup of tea and I'll tell you what happened last night. It might put things a little more into perspective for you."

Diane sat down at the table with her back to the warm Aga, taking a sip of her tea before recounting her story:

"I met Arthur in…"

For the next hour or so Diane related her memories of last night's OOBE to Alan, covering virtually all points bar one!

"…And there I was on the ground in California," she concluded excitedly. "And then, before I knew it, I was back here in bed. I never did get to say goodbye to Arthur. Still, I know how to get him now, if I want to."

Alan stared wide-eyed at Diane, looking as stunned now as he had since she started her tale.

"If I didn't know you better and hadn't been a part of what you've been through these last few weeks, I'd have you certified first thing tomorrow morning. What an incredible revelation," he said shaking his head in wonderment.

"Isn't it just," agreed Diane excitedly, "but I must admit that re-living it like this does help me. I feel much better now. It's strange but every time I wake up after an OOBE everything that's happened seems so dreamlike. But I just know deep down that it's for real. After all, I passed your little test didn't I?"

"Sure," he agreed hesitantly, giving a quick glance out of the window as he mentally prepared his words. "But this really is something else love, this is awesome; I mean, time travel, wow! From Ancient Britain to the Space Shuttle, and all in one night ... sorry ... all in five minutes! It is rather a lot to get one's mind around. Still, It's a shame that you screwed-up ... oops ... sorry, I mean got your co-ordinates wrong when you went forward in time. It would have been fascinating to hear what's happening around here thirty years from now."

However, as he spoke, Diane was in deep thought, only half-listening to Alan's words.

"Darling?" she said cautiously, pausing slightly to gain his attention.

"Yes love."

"Do you really believe me; I mean about the OOBE's and everything?"

"Of course I do. I mean, you just said it yourself. You passed my little test with flying colours, if you'll excuse the pun."

"No, I mean really believe?" said Diane earnestly. "Not believe me just because we're married, and you love me. I mean really deep down believe, everything?"

She took his hand in hers and squeezed it softly.

"It's very important to me," she explained tenderly. "I don't think that I could've got this far without your support. But I really do believe in my OOBE's, absolutely believe, and so I suppose I want you to have the same sort of understanding."

"Look love," said Alan with a sigh, pausing in thought, wanting desperately to get his words right. "You're certainly correct about one thing, I do love you, and I wouldn't do anything to hurt you. And I really believe that you believe in your OOBE's. I mean, if anyone else had told me ten-percent of what you have, I'd certainly have been sceptical, to say the least. But you've definitely been through what you just told me. I can tell by the way that you just re-lived last night to me..."

"But?" said Diane, letting the question hang.

"No buts," said Alan firmly. "I just think that this is the sort of thing that you have to experience personally, to truly deep down believe as you put it. After all, it totally flies in the face of convention and everything that we've been taught since we ... I don't know ... since we first went to Sunday school as little kids. And all those years of learning take a lot of hard evidence to counter. Look love, this is very difficult to verbalise without sounding negative but you have to believe me, I'm not being negative. I'm just trying to be objective. Do you understand what I'm trying to say?"

"Yes, I do," said Diane with a loving smile. "And I'm so glad that you're being totally frank with me; I feel much better knowing exactly how you feel," she concluded, kissing him on the lips.

Alan's face wore a puzzled frown, somewhat taken aback by his wife's response.

"You're welcome," he said. "Any time."

Diane was about to get another mug of tea when she put a finger in the air, remembering something she'd forgotten to mention about last night's OOBE.

"Oh, by the way, I nearly forgot this with everything else that happened last night. You remember I told you that I got stuck outside the Sony shop?"

"Yes."

"Well at the time the news was on the television's in the window display and there was mention of that big deal that John's working on, the one for Mega something."

Alan's ears pricked up at the mention of his firm's largest client.

"Mega-Software," he enquired eagerly, "what about them."

"Yes, that's it, Mega-Software. Well the news that I watched said their deal totally collapsed."

Alan responded with a half-choked yell.

"Collapsed! What do you mean collapsed?"

Diane looked at him with a frown.

"I don't know," she said guardedly, "that's what the newsreader said. Something to do with the current ... well ... current in twenty-nine days that is, fall-off in world stock markets. That most of the underwriters had been left with their allocation of stock or something. Do you understand that?"

"Is that what was said, I mean are those the exact words they used?" asked Alan pointedly.

"Well, near enough, I wasn't really taking that much notice, I was too busy trying to get free."

Alan got up from his chair and sat on the table by Diane.

"Think carefully love, can you remember, did he say that it was a temporary fall-off in the markets or had it been going for some time?"

Diane screwed up her face in thought.

"Well, I got the impression, from the fact it was the first item in the news programme, that it was big-news; if you see what I mean. And he did say something about worst world-market-fall since October 1987."

"Oh my God," cried Alan. "If that's right, it could be big trouble for the firm and a bunch of our clients, especially the Mega deal."

He rubbed his unshaven face, thinking for a moment.

"Shit!" he exclaimed, with a worried expression.

"What?" demanded Diane.

"This is crazy. Even if you're right on the button with this, I can hardly tell anyone now can I? They'll put me in the post-room forever; or worse!"

"But it's the future, I mean, how can we do anything to change it. Remember what I told you Arthur said. If things aren't meant to be they don't happen."

"Yes I know love."

Alan paused in thought again for a few seconds then his face lit up.

"Ah, but he also told you about Leonardo da Vinci, and Nostradamus. They're supposed to have had OOBE's and done something about what they learned, only the technology of their time wasn't advanced enough for them to capitalise on it, just record it in the best way they knew how. Otherwise they might have changed history!"

"But I don't think that you can change history. What they did was all that they were supposed to do."

Alan looked exasperated.

"I know that love, but this isn't history yet; and who's to say that you weren't meant to have this information, and us do something with it. After all, if Arthur was right, then we can't possibly do anything that's not supposed to be. Can we?"

"Well, if you put it that way, I don't suppose so. But can we do anything to help John."

"Never mind that randy bachelor," wailed Alan, using one of Diane's favourite sayings. "What about the firm? If they go bust or get a lousy name because of all this, it could seriously neutralise my career prospects."

Diane sat back in her chair.

"Okay, let's just calm down and think rationally about this for a while. Look, let's go for a walk and get the papers, then we'll come back and have some lunch. Alright?"

She got up from the chair and hugged Alan.

"Okay," he said reluctantly. But I'm sure there's a way to use this information to our benefit!"

That evening Alan was in bed reading the newspaper when Diane wandered into the bedroom from the en-suite bathroom, rubbing hand-cream vigorously into her hands. Alan looked up and put his paper down as she approached the bed.

"Diane, how difficult would it be for me to have an OOBE?" he asked nonchalantly.

Diane was momentarily taken aback by the question.

"You?" she said in a surprised voice.

"Well we did plan to do this thing together one day, didn't we?" he questioned with a hurt expression.

Diane sat down on the bed, taking his hand in hers.

"Oh I'm sorry darling, I didn't mean it to sound like that. It's just that you surprised me a bit with that one."

Alan put his paper on the floor to make room on the bed for Diane.

"It's okay love, it's just that I've been thinking about all your OOBE's and I really would like to try it out for myself."

Diane raised her eyebrows and cocked her head on one side.

"Has this got anything to do with this Mega-Software thing?"

Alan looked sheepish, adopting his little-boy-lost expression.

"Well, sort of I suppose. I mean it does add a whole new dimension to this OOBE thing. And it's got me thoroughly intrigued."

Diane got under the covers and kissed Alan on the cheek.

"You're right," she agreed, "let's give it a try."

Alan's face beamed.

"Really?"

"Yes, really, but you have to promise me that you won't be too let down if it doesn't work the first time."

"I promise," he said eagerly. "But I should tell you that I have tried before but nothing happened, well nothing I can remember that is."

Diane looked surprised.

"When was that?"

"Oh several times actually. Whenever I've woken up in the night, I've tried to do that relaxing thing, when you try to send your body to sleep but keep your mind awake."

"I know what you mean but I'm a bit surprised you didn't tell me."

"Oh, come on love, you know me. I don't like admitting that I can't do something."

"I don't know. Men!"

She prodded him in the ribs and he fended her off, laughing loudly.

"Okay," said Diane, "lets go over everything you should do, including the big-toe-wiggle."

"The big-toe-wiggle?"

Alan screwed up his face in thought and then remembered.

"Ah yes, to get back in. Still, I've got to get out first. Now how do you..."

18

The clock showed three-fifteen as Diane's spirit detached from her body and floated up to the ceiling, and with the usual log-type rollover she looked down at the two forms sleeping soundly in bed.

"Now what do I do?" she thought. "If Alan manages to get out and I'm not here, he'll panic, I'm sure of it."

As she was pondering Diane got a strange but somehow familiar feeling and instinctively looked round. There, outside the window, was Arthur Ayres with a big smile on his face, waving as if he'd just seen her get off a train.

"Hi there Diane," echoed the familiar voice in her head. "I got a vibration that you needed me."

Diane was briefly taken aback.

"Hi Arthur. I didn't call for you, well not consciously anyway. Come on in."

Arthur floated effortlessly through the glass.

"Not to worry," he said, "now I'm here is there anything I can assist you with."

"It's silly really," laughed Diane, "it's just that Alan said he wanted to try to have an OOBE and I said that I'd wait for him here, in case he did."

Arthur raised an ethereal eyebrow.

"Oh, I see."

Diane felt a little embarrassed.

"I know it probably seems silly to you, but he so wants to have the experience, and it really would make my life a lot easier if he could do it, at least once."

"I know," conceded Arthur, "and I do feel a little responsible. I shouldn't have put that doubt in your mind about him really believing you."

"Oh no," said Diane quickly, "It's okay. It's not your fault. If I'm being honest I think I knew that before you mentioned it."

"Nevertheless, there is a way I might be able to help you."

"How's that then?"

"Apparently it's possible, under certain circumstances, for a spirit to assist another spirit that's trying to separate from its physical body but is having a little trouble fully detaching."

He looked down at Alan and then back at Diane.

"When do you think Alan's going to try?"

"I'm not sure," he said that he'd try when he'd had a sleep. Sometime around now I guess."

Arthur looked more closely at Alan.

"It looks to me like he's trying to get out right now, look at the luminescence around his body. How's about we give him a little helping hand?"

He floated down to Alan and took hold of his arm.

"Come on Diane, you get his other arm and on my word we'll pull him out. But don't let go when he's out," he chuckled, "otherwise he might go straight back in with the shock."

"You mean we're going to actually pull his spirit out of his physical body! Is that allowed?"

Arthur looked up at Diane and smiled.

"I don't think anyone's written a rule book on this but I have it on good authority that it works and it won't damage him, so hurry along there, he's starting to fade."

Diane looked closely at Alan and could see that the glow was beginning to fade, so she floated down and grabbed his arm.

"Okay, I've got him."

"Right, pull."

Diane and Arthur pulled on Alan's arms and then his legs and torso but for a while it seemed their efforts were in vain. Then, all of a sudden, Alan's arms and chest started to emerge from his physical body; and slowly but surely, inch-by-inch, his spirit form started to ease out from under the duvet. Diane was amazed at how Alan seemed to have two identical bodies. The physical one, that didn't seem to be affected in the slightest by their pulling and twisting on it; and his spirit-form that was identical to his physical body but was being affected by their efforts.

Then, with a sound like lightly tearing Velcro, the last thing to exit Alan's physical body was the back of his head, which released suddenly. Once free, Alan's spirit floated upwards, stopping a few inches from the ceiling, leaving him temporarily oblivious to Arthur and Diane's presence. He stared at the ceiling and yelled out in panic:

"Oh my God! ... What's happening?"

He looked around and immediately saw Arthur, still holding on to his arm.

"Who the bloody hell are you," he demanded aggressively, "get your sodding hands off me."

Arthur smiled and spoke calmly but didn't release his grip on Alan.

"I'm Arthur Ayres; I believe that your wife Diane may have mentioned me?"

Alan, not yet having caught sight of Diane, looked down and saw his and Diane's physical bodies lying in the bed, apparently fast asleep. He instinctively adopted a 'panic-bordering-on-fear' demeanour.

"Oh dear God, somebody help me. I'm having a nightmare."

Diane spoke soothingly to her husband's spirit:

"Alan, Alan, over here."

Alan looked around and saw Diane.

"It's okay my love, it's only Arthur and me. You remember I told you about Arthur, Becky's husband."

Alan seemed to calm slightly.

"But what's happening, why are you all in this dream? How come we're all talking in my head?"

Diane smiled reassuringly at him.

"It's not a dream darling. Don't you remember you were trying to have an OOBE tonight?"

Alan looked perplexed.

"OOBE?"

"Yes. You were trying to detach from your body but you seemed to be a bit stuck, so we gave you a helping hand, so to speak."

Diane floated slowly to Alan's side and took his hand.

"Oh my goodness, it feels just the same as normal."

Alan was now coming round a little more.

"What do you mean, normal?"

"Well, ever since I had my first OOBE I've wanted to touch another spirit but never had the opportunity."

"You only had to ask Diane," said Arthur, with a cheeky grin.

"Hey that's my wife you're talking about mister," yelled Alan.

He looked at Diane, who was shaking her head but had a warm smile on her face.

"I see you're back to normal now Sir Gallahad," she joked.

Alan looked a little embarrassed.

"Oh, I'm sorry you two, I'm just starting to remember everything."

"That's alright Alan," said Arthur, "It must be a bit of a shock being dragged unceremoniously out of yourself on your first OOBE, as Diane calls it. You know, I think I'm getting to like the sound of that word. OOOBEEE. It sounds like something out of a Star Wars movie, don't you think?"

Diane chimed in to correct Arthur's recollection:

"That was Obi-Wan-Kanobi Arthur."

"Oh that's right, I..."

Alan made an attempt at a throat-clearing sound but as he didn't really have a throat in his spirit-form, it came out more like a stifled grunt.

"I'm sorry to break up this little conversation," he said, trying to regain his composure, "but could someone please tell me what I'm supposed to do, now I'm OOMB!"

Diane repeated the word with a little laugh.

"OOMB?"

Alan replied sarcastically:

"Yes, Out Of My Body."

Arthur and Diane looked at each other and burst into laughter. Alan looked at both of them in turn and now, just about fully cognisant, joined in. After a few moments of highly contagious laughter Arthur tried to get the couple's attention.

"Enough, enough," he wailed, holding up his hand. "Look you two," he said in a more serious tone. "I think I'd better get off now. After all, we've achieved our main objective for the evening; you're out now Alan, and I'm sure that Diane has a lot to show you."

"Oh, don't go Arthur," she said with a tinge of melancholy.

"You know I always feel more comfortable having you around."

"Don't worry my dear," said Arthur with a little wink.

He looked across at Alan who was just floating there above the bed.

"You're a lucky man Alan. This wife of yours is a wonderful person, only she doesn't always have the same faith in herself that others quite rightly have in her. So take it from me, she's quite capable of looking after you out here. She's been a great student and there's not much left that I can teach her."

He floated over and took Alan's hand.

"It was good to meet you young man and I'm sure we'll meet again, somewhere."

He turned to Diane who had floated over next to him and he hugged her warmly.

"Pass that on to Becky and the boys for me will you my dear?"

"I certainly will Arthur. But we'll see you again, won't we?"

"Of course you will," he said softly, "somewhere, sometime."

Diane smiled sombrely but before she could say another word there was a bright flash and Arthur was gone. She looked around the room and gave the spirit equivalent of a sigh. Alan, who had sensed during this meeting a certain closeness between Diane and Arthur, felt a little uncomfortable and broke the silence:

"Wow, some guy."

"Yes he is ... was ... oh I don't know. I'm getting confused with all this time and space stuff."

There was a pregnant pause, then Diane snapped out of her malaise as quickly as she'd taken it on board.

"Okay," she said brightly, "let's not waste time now that you're eventually out. Where shall we go?"

"What are the options?"

"Limitless but let's stay in this earth-time eh, we can try some time travel on another occasion."

"Okay," but you'd better show me how to go through stuff, or I'll be staying in this room all night. The door's closed."

Diane laughed.

"Right, of course. I'm so used to being the student I'll have to change and put on my teacher's hat. Okay, just think that you want to float slowly towards the wall here. Visualise yourself actually moving towards me."

Alan screwed up his face in fierce concentration and, much to his amazement, moved slowly towards Diane, who was stationary by the window.

"Wow, that's cool," he said. "It's like being on a flying carpet, without the carpet."

Diane seemed to be thoroughly enjoying the role of her husband's teacher.

"If you think that was cool, just wait until you go through the wall."

Alan looked pensive but awaited further instruction.

"Okay, now put the palm of your right hand on the wall here and think the same moving-forward thought." And don't be alarmed if you feel a slight tingling sensation, or feel the roughness of the wall as you pass through," advised Diane. "It's quite normal."

"Bad choice of words love," he said pensively, "there's nothing normal about any of this."

He put his hand on the wall and screwed up his face again and slowly but surely started to pass through. Outside, Diane emerged from the stone wall of the farmhouse first, slowly followed by Alan; whose face was a picture of concentration.

"Oh my, what a strange feeling. It reminds me of something, though God knows why."

"Like sticking your head in a bag of polystyrene balls?" asked Diane.

"Not that I've ever done that," he said dryly, "but yes, a good analogy."

He looked around at the scenery in awe, and then, just as Diane was going to tell him not to look down yet, he looked down!

"Big mistake," thought Diane.

Alan immediately started thrashing around like a drowning man and squealing like a young piglet. She went to his side and caught hold of one of his flailing arms.

"It's okay darling, stop thrashing and just lie still."

Alan complied obligingly, grabbing Diane tightly around the waist.

"Sorry love, I just panicked there for a minute. It looks a long way down."

"I know, I did exactly the same thing on my first foray outside."

Alan calmed as he held on to Diane and looked around again, this time taking in the view more thoroughly. The moon was shining on the fields and a few sheep wandered around silently nibbling the grass.

"Oh my, what a wonderful evening," he said, tentatively letting go of Diane and looking down at their cobbled courtyard some fifteen feet below.

"Yes it is, wonderful," uttered Diane dreamily.

She looked at Alan and felt good about the whole experience. Somehow it was as if all this was meant to be! She floated into an upright position.

"Right, let's do something," she said enthusiastically.

"About time too," joked Alan.

"Wise guy. Now you must remember not to think of anyone or anywhere other than me, or where we are, otherwise I'll spend all evening trying to find you. It's highly unlikely though, because I'll be right with you all the time but if you do happen to find yourself on your own just think of, or visualise me, and you should automatically find me. And I'll do the same."

"I'm not at all keen on that word 'should', 'will' has a much better ring to it," declared Alan.

"Look darling, if you think that you're lost or you need to get back here, just use the big-toe-method, that'll get you straight back to bed. Alright?"

"Alright teach," he said impatiently. "Now can we go somewhere?"

"Yes, of course, I'm sorry for being a bore but I really want you to enjoy this experience. Okay, take my hand."

Alan complied and the couple moved slowly off over the Yorkshire countryside.

They started off around fifty feet above the ground but Diane quickly took them higher, to avoid tall trees and power pylons. She looked over at Alan whose expression was one of total disbelief.

"We could go straight through all this stuff," she said, "but I don't think you're quite ready for that experience yet. It can be quite unsettling first time around, especially at speed."

Alan was awe-struck.

"Whatever you say love, you're in charge."

They flew higher and higher until they were about ten thousand feet off the ground. Alan hadn't said a word for a few minutes and Diane looked around to check on him.

"Are you alright darling?"

"Alright?" he cried. "I'm fantastic! This is the most incredible thing ever. Look at all the lights down there. I don't think that flying by aeroplane will ever be quite the same after this. This view's better than the pilot gets."

"How would you like to head towards the daylight?" asked Diane. "It's probably morning in Russia."

"Russia, cried Alan incredulously."

"Sure. Let's do some real international travel. Hold tight."

Diane thought of accelerating and before they knew it the couple were travelling faster than Concorde, heading towards the brighter sky in the East.

They passed over southeast England, crossing the Channel in seconds; then streaking over northeast France they continued on to perform a high-speed aerial tour of Germany. They crossed Poland in a heartbeat and entered Russia, where the sun was in the early morning sky, at a speed that seemed to Alan like Mach five or more. They turned south and headed for Turkey and then west over Greece. They flew over Italy and the Côte d'Azur towards Spain, then headed north, over the

Pyrenees and eventually arrived in Paris. Diane picked out the Eiffel Tower.

"Look Alan, let's go down and do a circuit of the Tower."

Alan felt totally invigorated.

"Great, let's go."

They swooped down hand-in-hand, like a couple of swallows in early spring, flying under and around the majestic tower; which was still lit by a thousand bulbs in the early dawn. As they were just about to leave Paris and head towards home, Alan squeezed Diane's hand tightly. She stopped and turned to look at him, his face full of bewilderment.

"Di, I feel strange," he said in a concerned voice.

And as he spoke, the glow of his outline started to fade in and out.

"Oh my, I think you're on your way back home," said Diane with some apprehension. "Keep thinking of me darling!"

But before Alan could acknowledge her request he vanished in a flash of white light.

"ID Alan, quickly," thought Diane in a bit of a panic.

And with that she too disappeared in a flash, leaving the Eiffel Tower alone in the early morning light.

The couple arrived back in their bedroom at the farmhouse at exactly the same time, Diane seemingly having caught Alan up on the way back. As they appeared over their bed in the usual flash of white light, they dropped down simultaneously, into the two sleeping bodies.

Diane stirred and then threw back the quilt. Still half-asleep she groped her way to the bathroom but after only a few moments in there uttered a choking yell:

"Oh my God Alan, come here, quickly!"

Alan roused and sat up in bed, puzzled at the strange-sounding voice coming from the bathroom.

"What is it love?" he shouted, immediately crying out in anguish at the sound of the strange voice issuing from his own mouth!

Jumping out of bed he rushed into the bathroom but wasn't at all prepared for the sight that confronted him! His own body was sitting on the toilet, staring down at itself with astonishment! He yelled again, even more loudly.

"Oh fuck, it's me," he shrieked. "I mean you're me."

He rushed to the mirror to look at his reflection, only it wasn't his reflection; Diane's face was staring back at him with a contorted look of complete and utter disbelief!

"Oh Christ," he howled, "I'm you!"

They looked at each other with absolute horror.

"We've gone into the wrong bodies," said Diane, just sitting there quietly on the toilet, appearing completely confused. "When we came back from the OOBE, we ... we went into the wrong bodies!"

The couple stared at each other open mouthed, totally dumbfounded.

19

AUTHOR'S NOTE: *For clarification and ease of reading from hereon, please remember that Alan's physical body is now occupied by Diane's spirit/consciousness, and Diane's physical body is occupied by Alan's spirit/consciousness. So when reference is made to Alan, it is his physical body but Diane's spirit/mind that is being referenced, and vice versa.*

It was early morning and the couple were in the bedroom sat on the bed. Alan was rummaging through the drawers of the bedside cabinet on his side of the bed, while Diane was doing the same on her side.

"I thought I always put your socks in the bottom drawer?" queried Alan.

"You do," said Diane, "but I always move them back to the top. Where are your knickers?"

"Second down," he said.

They both stopped and looked at each other across the bed and burst into laughter at the absurdity of their situation. Then, somewhat clumsily, they finished dressing and went downstairs.

Alan and Diane eyed each other with keen interest across the kitchen table as they ate breakfast. It was Monday morning and Alan, dressed in a smart suit and tie, was clad for a day the office.

"So you think it was me … correction … my body," said Diane," pointing at Alan, "that wanted to pee, that brought me back like that?"

"Yes," agreed Alan, "well probably, but it wasn't your fault. I should have told you to make sure you took an extra pre-bedtime pee! Anyway, I really think we should be trying to get back into our own bodies not planning this 'trading places' charade. I mean, look at me in this suit."

He stood up to get across the full effect of his words but Diane was indignant.

"What's wrong with the suit? It's a Hugo Boss and if I remember rightly, you were there when I bought it. You said it looked great, then."

Alan capitulated.

"I'm sorry darling," he apologised, "you're right, it is a nice suit. It's just that I'm not used to looking down at myself and seeing … well … seeing this," he said, gesturing at himself with both hands. "I'm used to seeing that," he said, pointing at Diane who was dressed in jeans and sweatshirt.

"Well how do you think I feel with these?" said Diane indignantly, fondling her breasts under her sweatshirt.

"That's nothing," riposted Alan, "at least they're passive! This thing," he said," grabbing the bulge in his trousers, "has a mind of its own. I nearly soaked the bathroom floor taking a pee this morning, it just wouldn't … well … you know, relax."

"Well I did tell you to sit down instead of standing," said Diane tersely. "At least until you got used to it."

"But I don't want to get used to it," he wailed abruptly. "Anyway it's better to get the practice in now and pee all over our bathroom floor, rather than someone else's later."

Diane laughed loudly.

"I suppose you're right, you did get the 'more-difficult-to-handle' equipment, didn't you? But don't worry about it, I still miss now and again and I've had it all my life."

"I know," said Alan firmly, "I clean the bathrooms! Anyhow, were digressing. I just don't see how I can go to your office and pull this off. Someone's bound to notice."

"No they won't love," stressed Diane reassuringly, "not if you do as we planned. Like I said earlier, all you have to do is go into my office and tell Julie, I'm sure you'll recognise her from the last time that you were…"

"Who could miss her," Alan cut in sarcastically, "She's got a chest that a 'Playboy Playmate' would be envious of."

"As I was saying before you interrupted me," Diane continued coolly, "just tell Julie that you're not to be disturbed, by anyone, and then get the files out of my credenza; I gave you the keys didn't I?"

Alan fished the keys out of his pocket and jangled them in the air.

"Yes," he said sullenly.

"Good. So when you've sorted out the right files call me here and I'll tell you how to mark them up. After that you can come home, but don't forget to tell Julie that you're going out to see a client for the rest of the day and if she wants to get you she should call you on the mobile. So don't forget to take it with you."

"It's on the hall table with the car keys," sighed Alan.

"Oh, I'm glad you mentioned the car. I always park in the office underground car park when I don't get the train. Parking in the centre of Leeds can be a bloody nightmare. Leave the car in space 42, on level B2. That's two floors down from the side street entrance…"

Alan, who was unconsciously arranging his manly parts, interjected:

"Okay, okay," he said, tiring of Diane's briefing. "I'm sure that I'll find it. Now can you remember what to say if anyone from the magazine calls here?"

"Ah ha," cried Diane, "trick question. I don't answer the phone. I leave the answer machine on and only answer if it's you calling. And will you stop playing with my ... sorry ... your privates!"

Alan looked down at his hand.

"Sorry, it just seems to wander down there for some reason."

"See, it's a genetic thing that all men do," she said in a told-you-so voice.

Alan adopted a serious air:

"I think you could be right," he agreed. "When our spirit leaves our physical body that body has to keep working, you know, breathing, heartbeat, etc., and I suppose that goes for all its other involuntary functions too. So when we came back into the wrong body, we kept all the physical attributes of that body."

He paused for a second screwing up his face with effort.

"Like your farting!" he said, letting rip with a rasping fart. "Oh, pardon me, that feels much better."

Diane laughed hysterically.

"You see. If I'd done that, you'd have told me off. Some things are just meant to be," she crowed.

"Whatever," said Alan, looking slightly embarrassed. "Anyway, I've got to go or you," he pointed at Diane, "will be late for work."

Diane got up from the table and the couple approached for a hug and kiss but Alan started to kiss with a little more passion than seemed necessary for saying goodbye. Diane pulled away and frowned at him.

"Hey you, your supposed to be saying goodbye, not come to bed."

"I'm sorry darling," he said apologetically, "it just came over me all of a sudden, when I hugged you. I felt strangely sexy, no, not sexy, horny! My … sorry … your todger started to rear up."

He grabbed the offending appendage and squeezed.

"That'll show him," he said with a grimace.

"Hey, be careful love," warned Diane, "I want that back in good working order."

"I'm sorry darling, just playing," he said with a wink.

They kissed briefly and Alan walked out of the kitchen towards the front door, closely followed by Diane.

Outside, they walked across the courtyard to Alan's car.

"This is the first time that I've been able to get into this car without having to adjust the seat," he said, sliding into the driver's seat. It's weird."

"Yes and don't forget, you've got my body there. It's bound to take a little time to get used to the extra size and strength. I know! I felt a right bloody wimp when I couldn't get the top off the new coffee-jar this morning; well, not without using that weird kitchen-tool thing."

"Stop worrying," chided Alan, "I'll be okay."

He started the car and lowered the window, smiling cheekily.

"Oh, by the way, I managed quite well with your razor this morning," he said rubbing his smooth chin. "So why don't you wash your hair and put a little makeup on? You'll feel a lot better. Bye."

The car engine revved and Alan pulled away, waving out of the open window. Diane turned and with an indignant look flicked her head, running her fingers through her hair as she walked back towards the house.

"Cheeky bitch," she fondly cursed under her breath.

20

Alan stepped out of the elevator into the reception area of Alan's offices and smiled at the girl behind the desk, who immediately smiled back with a twinkle in her eye. He walked through the open-plan area towards Alan's private office, where he saw Alan's secretary, Julie, sat outside at her workstation. Julie looked up, gave Alan a big smile and rose from her chair. Alan stared at her long, perfectly shaped legs, hardly covered by the short red dress she was nearly wearing, which had a scooped neckline, revealing a goodly measure of her ample cleavage. Julie noticed this unusual once-over from her boss and smiled again, this time a little more coyly.

"Hi Alan, how are you this lovely morning?"

"Oh fine thanks … um … Julie," he replied nervously. "How are you?"

"Oh, feeling just wonderful," she said blissfully. "I had a great weekend. Lots of shopping, eating and drinking; you know, the usual stuff, but still great."

"Good," said Alan hesitantly.

He paused momentarily in thought and then, taking a big breath, went straight into his planned lines:

"Look Julie, I have lots of papers to go through this morning, so I don't want to be disturbed, by anyone. And when I've done I have to go to a meeting with a new client and I won't be back for the rest of the day."

Julie picked up her diary and looking at that day's corresponding date gave a little frown.

"Oh, I don't seem to have a note of any meetings today," she said with genuine surprise. "Who's it with?"

Alan was momentarily flummoxed, she wasn't supposed to ask that.

"Oh, that's right, you wouldn't. Um … it's someone that I met on the weekend. They want me to take a look at their operation and see if the firm can help them. So you see, it's sort of a potential-new-client."

Julie was standing with diary in hand and pen poised.

"Do you want me to put them in the diary then?" she enquired.

"Um … no … I don't think so," stuttered Alan. "Well, not just yet that is, until I've seen them. Until I know that they're really going to appoint me … um … us … the firm that is. Anyway, I must get on."

He smiled and headed toward his office door. Julie shouted after him.

"Usual coffee Alan?"

"Oh, yes, thanks Julie, that'd be nice."

He went into the office and closed the door behind him, leaning his back against it for support and exhaling loudly.

"This is not going to be easy!"

Back at the farmhouse Diane was in the bathroom. Having taken Alan's advice she had just showered and washed her hair and was standing naked in front of the mirror towelling herself dry.

She stopped and looked admiringly at her reflection. Dropping the towel she started to run her hands over her body, slowly fondling her naked breasts, quivering slightly as she brushed her erect nipples.

"Ooh Diane," she said out loud to her reflection, "you should have told me it felt this good. I'll have to spend a lot more time on this when we make love in future."

Slowly she slid her hand down over her flat stomach, across her pubic mound, and slipped it between her legs, fondling the softness of her labia and gently parting the lips of her vagina.

"Wow, that's a different feeling, it sort of glows and tingles."

She slowly caressed her clitoris with the index finger of her right hand, simultaneously rolling alternate nipples gently between the fingers of her left.

"Oh, this is nice; I wish I had three hands!"

As she continued to explore her body her vagina became extremely moist.

"Ooh, that's wonderfully slippery," she said out loud.

She slid two fingers carefully up into the lubricated passage and then back onto her swelling clitoris.

"Oh that's much better," she thought as she fervently viewed her every action in the mirror.

Her slow gentle caressing became more rapid and less gentle as the glow inside her abdomen began to spread over her whole body, subconsciously urging her fingers on. Suddenly she began to tremble uncontrollably.

"Oh my God I'm..."

She quickly removed her left hand from her breasts and grabbed hold of the towel rail for support. After a few moments the trembling subsided, at least enough to allow her to release the towel rail and she looked at her reflection in the mirror again. Her face was flushed and her upper chest pink between her throat and breasts.

"Bloody hell!" she said out loud to her reflection, "and I thought my male orgasm was good."

Then, very slowly, Diane became aware of a sound in the background. The telephone was ringing!

She rushed into the bedroom and staggered towards the phone on the bedside table and was just about to pick it up when she remembered the answering machine, and quickly pulled her hand away.

"Oh bollocks," she muttered.

She ran naked across the landing to the study just as the machine was giving out Diane's recorded message.

"Thank you for calling," said the machine, "you can send a fax or leave a message after the tone."

The machine beeped and Diane heard Alan's voice through the answer machine speaker.

"Alan, are you there?"

Diane pushed a button that turned on the hands-free function of the phone and spoke in a sexy low voice; which in reality was how she still felt.

"This is the lady of the house speaking, how can I help you?"

Alan sounded irate:

"Will you stop messing around," he said tersely. "Julie will be back in a minute."

"Ooh, testy, what's up?" said Diane quite calmly.

"I'll tell you what's up. You didn't tell me that Julie would give me the third degree about my … sorry … your so-called appointment today."

Diane sighed.

"Cool down love. I told you to tell her about the meeting when you were on your way out, not on your way in. That way you could make like you were running late and she wouldn't ask too many questions."

"Well I'm sorry," said Alan somewhat defensively, "I forgot; or rather, I was distracted. I mean, how long has she been coming to the office dressed for a night out on the town. She looks like a slightly taller version of Pamela Anderson and just about as covered up as Pammy is in those re-runs of Baywatch that you fastidiously watch."

Diane answered in a matter of fact tone:

"Really love, I can't say I've noticed her clothes," she lied.

"Is that so?" replied Alan sarcastically. "Well, then I'll just have to get her to book you … me that is … an appointment at the opticians! On the other hand I can understand why you haven't noticed her clothes," he bellowed loudly down the phone. "She hardly bloody-well wears any."

"Calm down love," appealed Diane softly. "Julie's just a young gal who lives for today. And she does sometimes go out on the town straight from the office. You do remember being twenty don't you?"

"Of course I do but…"

Diane lost her cool and jumped in with both feet.

"Look, stuff the way she dresses," she said sharply, "she's a damn good secretary and as long as she is I don't care what she wears to work. I mean, let's face it, it took you women long enough to gain your equality and I'm sure that included giving women the right to wear what they want, when they want. Just because you've temporarily got a man's body don't start getting sexist, for Gods sake."

A long sigh emanated from the speakerphone and then, after a couple of seconds Alan spoke, a little more calmly:

"Okay, you're right, let's get off this subject. What do I say to her then? She'll be back with a coffee in a minute and I don't want to say anything that might get you in trouble."

"Don't say anything, unless she brings it up again. And if she does, just say it's a new potential-client and you'll give her the details tomorrow."

"I've already said as much."

"There you go then, just leave it at that. After all, she's only trying to be super-efficient. She's paid to look after my administration and she does it well, so give her a break, eh?"

"Okay, I'll call you back in about half an hour," said Alan dejectedly, "when I've got the files out."

"Okay love, bye then."

"Bye darling," said Alan, a little more affectionately. "And I'm sorry for that outburst. "It's just that I'm a bit nervous and I don't want to screw-up for you."

"Don't worry love, you'll be fine. I'll talk to you soon, bye."

Diane pressed the button to disconnect the phone and padded back into the bedroom. And with another quick admiring glance at her reflection in the mirror picked up a pair of knickers from the bed and held them up in front of her with outstretched arms.

"Now which way around are these chuffing things meant to go on?" she said with a puzzled expression!

21

Alan was going through the file drawer of the credenza when Julie knocked on the office door and immediately entered carrying a large mug of steaming coffee. Alan looked up startled.

"Here's your coffee boss," said Julie.

"Oh, thanks Julie, could you just pop it on the desk please?"

"Sure. Can I help with anything?" she asked cheerily, noticing all the files that Alan had piled on the top of his credenza.

Alan glanced over at the pile.

"Oh, no, it's okay Julie, I'm just getting out some files for review. Thanks all the same."

Julie smiled and turned to leave but hesitated at the door.

"So that's no one at all to disturb you?" she enquired again.

"Yes, that's right Julie, thanks."

Julie left the office, giving Alan a quick puzzled glance as she closed the door behind her. Alan looked at a file he had just extracted.

"Okay, I think that's the last one," he said to himself.

He went over to the desk with the reclaimed files and took a welcome drink of the hot coffee.

He was just about to call Diane when he put his hand on his stomach.

"Oh heck, I think I need a pee."

Getting up from his desk, he left his office. Smiling at Julie as he passed, he mouthed to her 'loo', and pointed in the general direction of the reception area, and as he walked away he could feel her eyes following him.

Not having ever been to the gents before Alan scanned all the doors in the vicinity of the ladies toilet to ensure he got the right one.

"That's all I need," he thought to himself, "getting caught walking into the ladies loo!"

Once found, he tentatively entered the opulent marble and mahogany-clad gent's washroom and decided, for prudence sake, to use a cubicle rather than the stalls. When he'd finished his pee he went over to the washbowls to wash his hands and as he turned on the gold-plated tap, John walked in!

"Hi Al old buddy," said John, with a beaming smile. How'd your dinner go on Saturday night?"

Alan looked away as John stood at the urinals and got his todger out to pee.

"Oh, fine thanks, it was lovely."

John looked across at Alan with raised eyebrows.

"Lovely?"

Alan mentally kicked himself and immediately adopted a more macho approach:

"Yeah, you know, okay; great in fact. That Becky's quite a gal."

John looked more interested as his favourite subject was mentioned.

"Who's Becky then?" he nonchalantly enquired.

"You know, our new neighbour, the widow with the two teenage boys."

"Oh, right. So, she a good looker or what?"

"She's very attractive."

"As good looking as those two at the rugby on Saturday?"

"Undoubtedly," responded Alan, with a sarcastic edge to his voice, "but in a totally different way; more mature and definitely not tarty!"

John shook his todger and replaced it in his trousers and struggling with his zipper, walked over to join Alan at the washbowls.

"You thought they were tarty?" queried John, frowning again. "I thought they were great, especially the blonde. That Italian-looking one was more interested in you, though God knows why," he said with a laugh. "You know, you're becoming a real old stick-in-the-mud. We could've had a great time with those two."

John started to wash his hands as Alan had a devious thought.

"I'm sure we could have," said Alan in as matter-of-fact a voice as he could conjure up. "It would have been like that time at … oh … where was it?"

He looked at John as if trying to remember a specific venue. John returned the look with a furrowed brow.

"What time? I don't remember us having a night out with a couple of gals since we were at Uni. You always run off nowadays saying you're happily married. You must be day-dreaming old buddy, or having wishful thoughts."

Alan looked visibly pleased.

"Yes, you're probably right. Anyway, how did you get on with the two tarts?"

"Well," said John, ignoring Alan's comment and eagerly returning to the subject; "after the game finished all the players came up into the player's bar. That Italian-looking gal, the one that fancied you, was all over one of the Wigan players; the big blonde-haired bastard who scored that try just before half time. So I took the other gal off for a meal and then back to my place."

"Surprise, surprise," said Alan somewhat cynically.

John didn't pick up on the innuendo and gave Alan a wink.

"Phew," he said, blowing through his lips, "she wore me out, and what a body; phwoar."

He gestured a curvaceous outline, over-exaggerating the contours of the breasts somewhat, then turned his head from left to right and back again, admiring his reflection in the mirror as he straightened his tie.

"In fact," he continued, now arranging his hair, "she stayed last night as well. I had to take her home this morning to get changed before I dropped her at work. I don't mind telling you, I'm bloody knackered."

"Two nights with the same girl!" said Alan sarcastically. "She must have been good. It'll be wedding bells next."

John looked at Alan curiously, shaking his head.

"Bloody hell Al, you sound just like Diane. You've been married to her for so long now you're starting to think like her."

John went back to admiring his reflection in the mirror as Alan thought that his observations were getting just a little too near the truth for comfort; so he made a move towards the door. But he couldn't help having just one more cheap shot at John before leaving:

"I'll have you know that I'm very happy with Diane and you of all people should know why. In fact, she once told me that you said she was the best lover you'd ever had; and having been married to her for so long now, I can tell you, you were right. In fact, she's even better now."

John ceased his preening and stared at Alan open-mouthed.

"She told you that?"

"Of course," said Alan, "and lots more besides. Remember the time you couldn't get it up for a week?"

"Bloody hell," exclaimed John loudly. "She promised she'd never mention that to anyone."

He looked back at the mirror.

"Anyway I was ill," he said defensively.

"Oh I'm sure you were Johno. Well, thanks for the chat but I must get back to my work. See you around," he called, smiling smugly to himself as he left the washroom. John frowned at himself in the mirror.

"Johno?" he said to his reflection, "Diane was the only one who ever called me that!"

Back at his desk Alan picked up the phone and dialled home. After two rings the machine answered, playing Diane's recorded greeting before issuing a long beep.

At the farmhouse Diane was now dressed and again she rushed into the study to answer the phone, trying madly not to spill a coffee she was carrying. As she got to the desk Alan's voice was coming over the machine.

"...Come on, answer the phone Alan?"

Diane pushed the button to connect them.

"Hi love, sorry about that, I was just in the kitchen making a coffee when the phone went. How's it going?"

Alan exhaled audibly.

"Okay I suppose. I've got the files here but I just had to go to the loo and I bumped into John but..."

"What did he say," interrupted Diane, "did you fool him?"

"If you'd give me a second," asked Alan a little tersely, "I'll tell you."

"Sorry love, carry on."

"Thank you. Anyway, it was fine. He was going on incessantly about some blonde that he pulled at the rugby on Saturday."

Diane answered nonchalantly.

"Oh, good. Was that all?"

"Yes," replied Alan, "more or less. Anyway let's get these files done and then I can get home."

Diane sighed with relief as Alan started to go through the files.

"Okay, first one is..."

22

Alan was sitting at his desk hunched over the telephone, which was now on hands-free mode, so he could use both hands to go through the files with Diane.

"Okay," he said, "that's the last one finished."

Diane's voice came over the speaker.

"Good, now give the notes and files to Julie and get yourself home"

"What if she asks me any questions about the work?" asked Alan apprehensively.

"She won't love, not if you tell her exactly what I just said. Now get your things together and leave. We've got to get together and try get our bodies own back."

"Okay darling, I'll see you in about an hour. Bye."

"Bye love."

Alan punched the phone's disconnect button and scooped the files and notes together in his arms and quickly scanned the office before heading out. He opened the door and approached Julie who looked up smiling.

"Right Julie," he said as confidently as he could under prevailing circumstances. "I'd like you to do the usual 'get back to you soon' letters for all these clients and I'll sign them in the morning."

"Okay Alan," she said taking the files and placing them on her desk. "In fact I was just about to buzz you. The boss has just asked all partners, both junior and senior, to be in the boardroom at eleven-thirty. Some sort of important short-notice meeting I think."

Alan felt his heart rate increase immediately.

"But I've got to be at my meeting … near Bradford … at noon," he said looking at his watch.

"And it's nearly eleven twenty-five already."

Julie looked at the papers she'd been handed and looked back at Alan with a puzzled expression on her face.

"Alan, are you practising a new style of handwriting or something?"

"What do you mean?" said Alan, a frown creeping over his face.

Julie handed one of the papers back to him, pointing at the penned notes.

"This doesn't look like your usual handwriting."

Alan looked at the papers and started to turn red with the realisation that the writing was in Diane's hand, and not that of Alan.

"Oh … yes … right … I'd forgotten," he said, stalling while his mind searched for a plausible explanation. "That's actually Diane's handwriting," he said falteringly, "she wrote these out for me last night, while I was … um … in the bath."

He managed to force a smile but instinctively knew that it was a poor attempt at a cover up.

"My memory must be good," he added, "I didn't have to change a thing this morning."

Julie looked at Alan sideways.

"Oh, I see," she said, sounding less than convinced.

Then they both turned as a voice boomed from the door by reception.

"Come on Al," shouted John, his head poked around the door, "you'll be late for the meeting."

Alan gratefully seized this opportunity to curtail the discussion with Julie.

"Okay," he shouted back, "coming."

He turned to Julie and shrugged.

"Got to go. I'll see you tomorrow."

He turned and hurried to the door that John was holding open for him.

"Come on there's an elevator on its way up," said John.

They walked briskly across the lobby but Alan grabbed John's arm, slowing him down.

"Hang on."

John slowed and turned to Alan.

"What's up?"

"What's this meeting about?" asked Alan.

"Oh it's nothing really. The big-boys want to counsel everyone prior to the Mega-Software float. They're about to announce the issue date."

John leaned his head closer to Alan's and whispered:

"It's going to be four weeks today," he said, giving Alan an all-knowing wink.

"So what do they want from me, what can I contribute, I'm not even on the Mega team?"

As they got into the lift John looked at Alan curiously.

"Oh come on Al," he said as the doors closed, "you were one of those who wanted this open-door management thing. Remember, at that partner's meeting you came up to from London for a couple of months ago? You said," he waved his arms in the air and assumed a Churchillian voice: 'We should have openness and consultation on all matters that could impact the future of the firm.' Well that's what you're getting," he continued, reverting back to his own voice: "an opportunity to say your piece before the announcement goes public."

Alan felt a sense of foreboding sweep over him.

"Oh, right," he said resignedly.

The elevator-sounder went for their floor and as they came to a halt the doors opened and they stepped out into a bright atrium, dotted with large plants and small trees. Alan, who was totally unfamiliar with this particular part of the building, was quite happy to let John lead the way; and eventually they ended up in the boardroom, which was already full of the law-firm's partners.

They found their seats just as the Chairman, Peter, the most Senior Partner in the Leeds office, stood to speak. Alan looked down the long table as Peter addressed the packed room:

"Ladies and gentlemen, thank you for coming at such short notice," he boomed, "but we felt that everyone should be here for a final short discussion on the Mega-Software floatation; the largest transaction in the history of this firm. Especially as it originated right here in Leeds, not in London."

Peter gave a lingering smug smile before continuing.

"On behalf of the Mega-management, we plan to float this issue exactly four weeks today and this meeting is to basically see if anyone has any germane comments," he said, purposefully looking down the table towards Alan and one or two of the other Junior Partners. "So, before we announce the issue date to the press, are there any comments or questions?"

He looked around the room for prospective contributors but no one was prepared to make the first move.

"Well, come on, anyone?" he enquired firmly.

One of the other Senior Partners raised his hand. The Chairman nodded his head and took his seat as the man rose from his chair and started to speak:

"I'd just like to take this opportunity to thank…"

Suddenly Alan's head was flooded with images. He saw the Sony shop-window, filled with televisions, all showing the newsreader talking about the stock market crash and the Mega-Software deal's collapse. He saw Alan's face and heard his voice saying how they could use the information gleaned on the time-trip, to maybe save the deal. His head was spinning when the senior partner who was speaking concluded and sat down. Alan slowly lifted his hand and everyone around the table turned to follow the eyes of the Chairman who smiled and gestured for him to rise.

"I think you all know Alan Harris who joined us recently from the London office. Alan?"

Alan slowly rose from his seat. He stood there momentarily, gazing at all the faces staring back at him and then started to speak, falteringly:

"I just wanted to say…"

He paused and coughed to clear his throat and was totally unaware of a casual but very expensively dressed man who discreetly entered the room and leaned against the back wall. The stranger quietly observed the proceedings as Alan finished clearing his throat and continued:

"Well, actually," he said, still unsure as to what he was about to say, "this may sound a little off-the-wall but I had a dream the other night!"

A whisper went round the room and John, who was sitting next to Alan, tugged at the bottom of his friend's jacket.

"Sit down you plonker," he hissed.

Alan ignored him but John tugged Alan's jacket again.

"Sit down you stupid prick."

Alan brushed his hand away and continued:

"Now I know that those of you who've worked with me before will think this statement a little out of character and you'd be right but…"

Peter, who had just caught sight of the stranger at the back of the room, leapt up from his well-padded Chairman's seat, interrupting Alan's words sternly:

"Alan, I think that you should sit down now and maybe come and see me after the meeting."

The stranger by the door looked at Peter and wagged his finger gesturing for Peter to let Alan continue.

"Erm, on second thoughts," mumbled Peter, "maybe you should continue. Yes, let's hear what you have to say. Alan?"

Alan looked surprised but nothing like as surprised as the rest of the gathering; some of the senior partners looked incredulously at Peter.

"Thank you Mister Chairman," continued Alan. "I was saying that you might find this a little out of character, to recount a dream in the boardroom, on such an auspicious day for this firm. However, as the content of my dream is extremely relevant to today's meeting, I believe that it's worth risking my reputation, for what that's now worth, by relating it to you."

He gave a nervous laugh as he looked around the room and saw everyone's eyes riveted on him. He picked up a glass of water from the table and took a drink before continuing:

"In this dream I saw a TV news broadcast that was, according to the newsreader, being transmitted exactly four weeks hence from today. The newsreader said that due to a massive downturn in world stock markets, the Mega-Software floatation had collapsed."

There was a low muttering around the room.

"The newsreader's words in the dream not mine," explained Alan.

He laughed nervously and everyone around the table looked with raised eyebrows at those sat beside them, but no one said a word. The Chairman kept glancing nervously at the stranger by the door but the man looked on impassively. Alan took another drink of water and persisted:

"Now I'm aware that most, if not all of you here, probably think that I'm a slice short of a loaf, to coin a good old Yorkshire expression…"

A few people round the table raised their eyebrows again, silently concurring.

"…But I can assure you that I'm totally sincere in this revelation. I don't know why I had this dream but I did, and I couldn't live with myself or you, my fellow colleagues," he gestured around the table, "if I said nothing and it subsequently became reality," he said, pausing briefly to study the silent, staring faces around the table. "Thank you for your patience," he concluded and slumped back down into his chair as the stranger immediately beckoned the Chairman over to him.

Peter rose from his seat and walked over to the man where they exchanged a few whispered words. He then went back to his place at the head of the table and addressed the room:

"Ladies and gentlemen, we're going to take a short break, so please accept my apologies for this delay and would you all convene back here in..." he looked at his watch, "...say, thirty minutes."

He glowered down the table at Alan, who had stood up and was just about to leave with the rest.

"Alan," he called out.

Alan looked up and Peter beckoned for him to approach, and he advanced towards the Chairman with a worried look on his face.

"Yes Peter," he enquired nervously.

"Alan, would you be so kind as to come to my office in about five minutes?"

"Yes, of course," he quickly agreed.

The Chairman forced a smile and turned to leave the room by the executive door, exiting with the stranger. Alan left the boardroom to find John waiting outside the door. John looked exasperated.

"You fucking idiot," he said vehemently. "What the bloody-hell did you think you were doing in there?"

Alan looked at him blankly without comment.

"You do realise that you've probably just blown your sodding career in the last five minutes?"

23

Back at the farmhouse Diane was in the kitchen, dressed in her usual casual attire of designer denims topped off with a navy-blue Nike sweatshirt. She glanced up at the clock and then out the window.

"Oh what a great day," she said out loud, "I think I'll go for a little stroll. This working-from-home lark sure has its benefits."

She put on a thin chamois blouson-type jacket and left the house, heading for the village; and as she reached the main street she saw Becky coming out of the little corner-shop Post Office. Becky also spotted Diane and waved.

"Hi Diane, how are you this bright sunny morning?" she shouted.

Diane walked towards the shop, halting in front of Becky.

"Fine thanks Becky, how are you?"

"Oh I feel really great," she said with a big smile. "That dinner at your place on Saturday night was such fun, it was a real pick-me-up. I'd just about forgotten what it's like to have a good time with grown-ups."

"I'm glad you enjoyed it," said Diane. "We did too."

"How's Alan?" asked Becky, flashing a big smile again, showing her immaculate white teeth.

"Oh he's fine, he's at work in the big city today."

"You know, he's a real laugh is that man of yours and so good looking. I can see why you picked him," she said, laughing again and raising her eyebrows cheekily.

"Yes, he has his moments," said Diane, pausing in thought for a second. Then cocking her head nonchalantly to one side casually remarked: "Do you really think he's good looking?"

"Oh come on Diane, you know he is," exclaimed Becky. If he were mine I'd keep him on a very short leash in female company."

She laughed again and then put her hand on Diane's arm.

"Present company excepted of course. Anyway, what are you up to this morning, fancy a coffee?"

Diane looked at her watch.

"Well, I'm expecting Di…"

She put her hand to her mouth and coughed, trying to cover up her near-slip.

"…Excuse me Becky just a little frog."

Becky laughed and patted Diane on the back.

"What I was about to say," said Diane regaining her composure, "was that Alan may be coming back home from the office early, to do some paperwork in peace and quiet. Still, he could be an hour or so yet, so what the hell, let's coffee."

Becky took hold of Diane's arm.

"Great, let's go then."

The two girls walked down the street arm-in-arm, chatting like old school chums.

Meanwhile, Alan was back at his own desk, on the phone to home. He frantically looked at this watch.

"Two minutes and I'll have to be upstairs again," he thought to himself.

The phone at home answered with Diane's message and then beeped. Alan spoke urgently:

"Alan, are you there."

No response!

"Come on Alan, for God's sake answer will you."

He paused but there was still no reply and he let out a sigh.

"Okay, if you get this message in the next few minutes call me at your office. Otherwise it looks like I'll be a bit late getting home. Something's ... um ... cropped up here and I can't get away yet. Bye."

He put the phone down and cradled his head in his hands, looking up only when someone knocked on the door. Julie poked her head round.

"Oh, you are here Alan! The boss just called down for you to go to his office. He didn't sound too happy."

Alan looked at his watch and jumped up from his chair.

"Oh shit, I'm late."

He looked at Julie with a worried expression.

"Okay, I'm on my way."

Being the most senior of the senior partners, Peter's office was quite splendid, with an abundance of dark-oak panelling, leather furniture, thick mushroom-coloured carpets; and being a corner office, two windows with different views of the city.

Peter was standing in the centre of the room as his secretary escorted Alan in. Sitting in one of the six large armchairs around the coffee table was the stranger. Peter looked at his watch.

"Thank you for joining us Alan. I'd like to introduce you to…"

He gestured towards the stranger who rose from his seat.

"Mister James Alexander. Founder, Chairman and Chief Executive of Mega-Software."

He turned to James Alexander.

"James, this is Alan Harris, who you heard … erm … speaking, earlier."

James Alexander was a younger, British version of Bill Gates, the Microsoft multi-billionaire; crossed with a tinge of Richard Branson the Virgin boss. Starting his business,

Mega-Software, in his father's garage at the tender age of only seventeen, James has built up the company over the last twenty years into the premier European software corporation; with many of its latest products addressing the rapidly-expanding Internet markets.

Believing that it was now time to grow the company into new territories and develop newer and better versions of their bread-and-butter products, James was raising a huge amount of money by floating his company on the London stock exchange, with the assistance of the Leeds law-firm.

He had chosen the Leeds firm in the face of strong opposition from his London advisers, who weren't keen on using anyone outside the City of London. However, thus far, James' choice had proved to be not only a great time saver – he didn't have to keep going down to London every other day to meet with City lawyers – it was also extremely cost effective, as the Leeds law-firm's billing was substantially less than that of a top London firm.

James believed that it was this type of decision-making – using local services wherever possible and generally supporting northern enterprise – allied to his casual, laid-back style of management, which had ultimately led Mega to its current, extremely enviable position in the UK software industry; as the number one company in its field.

Alan and James shook hands firmly.

"Good to meet you Alan," said James sincerely.

"Nice to meet you too Mister Alexander," said Alan, mirroring the sincerity.

"Please, call me James," he said smiling warmly at Alan.

"Right, thank you James."

Peter gestured to the group of armchairs.

"Why don't we sit down?"

They each took a seat in the armchairs around the coffee table.

"Now Alan," asked Peter in a fatherly tone, "what's all this nonsense about having…"

James quietly interjected:

"If I may Peter?"

"Oh, of course James," said Peter deferentially, "go ahead."

James looked at Alan inquisitively, which was probably something to do with Alan's demeanour; sitting in Diane's favourite attentive pose, on the edge of the seat with his legs crossed wrap-over-style and hands clasped on his knee.

"Alan, I heard what you said in the boardroom, about your dream. Tell me, have you ever had a dream like this before?"

"No Mister … sorry … James," he said falteringly, "I haven't."

James smiled at Alan's nervousness and paused to study him again.

"So, if I interpret what you said earlier correctly, you just wanted to let everyone know of this dream, in case it did turn out to be true and the imminent floatation of my company," he looked up in thought, "how did you put it, 'collapsed'."

James looked at Peter and gave a little chuckle.

"I assume," he said, "that's a City-technical-term for failed miserably?"

Peter smiled nervously and fidgeted.

"You could say that James."

Alan spoke-up:

"I'm sorry to interrupt but those were the words used by the newsreader in my dream, not my own choice of words. I was just trying to relate the dream verbatim."

"So you said Alan," remarked James. "But tell me something. If the meeting this morning hadn't been called, would you have told your senior partner here," he gestured towards Peter, "about your dream?"

Alan looked James straight in the eyes.

"To be perfectly frank," he said firmly, "I don't honestly know. In fact, since having had the dream, until this morning, I hadn't given it much thought. It was only when we were all sat in the boardroom that it came back to me really strongly; and even then I didn't think that I would get up and say what I did. It sort of just happened. One moment I'm sat listening to my thoughts and the next thing my arms in the air and I'm standing there. It just seemed the right thing to do at the time."

James looked very thoughtful.

"I see," he said sitting back in his chair. "So what do you suggest that we do now? Personally I can only see three options."

Peter looked worried and sat forward in his chair.

"What are those James?" he asked nervously.

Without looking at Peter, James addressed Alan:

"What do you say Alan?"

Alan looked at Peter who was scowling at being so overtly ignored.

"I think that there are four options," Alan said confidently to James; "depending on how you view this type of situation that is."

"Go on then," said James a little impatiently. "Fire away."

Alan sat up straight in his chair.

"Well, firstly, and probably most people's choice, would be to totally ignore what I said, send me to the firm's psychiatrist for an evaluation and then…"

He shrugged his shoulders, pursing his lips.

"…Who knows?"

James still looked interested.

"And secondly?"

"Secondly," said Alan, "I would say that the floatation date be postponed until some period after the proposed date of four weeks from now and see if my dream actually happens."

"Initially, that was my second choice too," intervened James. "But on reflection, if you're dream's right, then we would have to adjust our issue price downwards, to take account of the lower market prices that would certainly prevail after a market-crash."

He looked at Alan tilting his head slightly.

"And thirdly?"

"Thirdly," said Alan, "you bring the floatation date forward of the proposed date, say two weeks from now…"

Peter nearly flew out of his chair.

"Good God man," he barked, "we can't finish everything in two weeks."

James held his hand up to subdue Peter's comments.

"Hold on Peter," he said firmly, "let Alan finish."

James looked back at Alan.

"Go on Alan, carry on."

"Right, yes," continued Alan. "Bring the date forward two weeks, which…" he paused, looking James straight in the eyes, holding the other man's stare, "…using your philosophy would leave the issue price the same as it is currently. The issue would then, hopefully, be fully subscribed and still leave a couple of weeks for things to pad out before the markets crash. Assuming that my dream was correct of course."

James smiled with a slight nod of his head.

"Of course," he concurred. "And, assuming that I did believe you ... sorry Alan, I meant believed your dream, then that's the option that I would go for; for all the same reasons. What I don't believe though," he said, turning to look at Peter, "is that your most exceptional law-firm and its accomplished staff couldn't get this deal finalised in two weeks."

Peter puffed himself up pompously.

"Well, if you were going to ... I mean really had to bring the date forward two weeks, we could probably get things done; but the institutions wouldn't like it," he said, raising a cautionary finger.

"Fuck the institutions," roared James as he leapt out of his chair."

Alan and Peter recoiled slightly at this sudden overt reaction and watched warily as James paced up and down the centre of the office.

"All that those bloodsucking institutions are interested in doing is making a quick bundle of money on the back of my company," he ranted. "If one of them comes in the rest will follow. They're just like bloody sheep."

He looked at Alan and Peter's blank faces and laughed out loud.

"Sorry about that little outburst," he said sitting down again, "but ever since I started this floatation I've had more institutional analysts crawling around my offices than I care to remember. They really piss me off with their inane questions. Anyone would think that Mega was a new company with no track record. With the benefit of hindsight I think I'd have stuck with my banks for the finance. It may have been more expensive in the short term but at least I wouldn't have had to answer to the whole world."

He smiled at Alan and seemed to relax as quickly as he had blown up.

"Anyway, I digress, he said. "You had a fourth option Alan?"

"Well, this was certainly going to be my last choice but having heard you just now, I'm not so sure that you'll concur."

He paused momentarily.

"Well, go on then," said James, sounding a little impatient.

"Forget the whole thing and cancel the floatation!"

James smiled but Peter scowled.

"You're right," said James with a sly grin, "and as much as I like the idea, I think we've come too far to branch off down that road without doing irreparable damage to the Mega name. Anyway, we have to decide what to do, so I'll make a quick call to my office and talk to Peter here and we'll see you back in the boardroom in," he looked at his watch, "about five minutes."

They all stood and James shook Alan's hand.

"Thank you again Alan; I think! It took a lot of courage for you to speak your mind out there and whatever we decide," he glanced at Peter, "I'm sure that your job's safe, eh Peter?"

Peter forced a smile.

"Of course," he said, just a little too quickly for Alan's liking. "Now, shall we get on, time's pressing?"

Exactly thirty minutes from the boardroom emptying, it was full again, apart from Peter and James. Alan was back sitting next to John.

"So, when do you clear your desk?" asked John sarcastically.

"Oh piss off will you, I did what I did and that's it."

John was taken aback at his friend's uncharacteristically severe response but persisted in his sarcastic mode.

"Sorry old buddy but I mean, Martin Luther-King's 'I had a dream', in the boardroom, in front of all the partners and the firms biggest client; who just happens to be one of the top-twenty richest men in the bloody country. What did you expect, promotion?"

At that moment the executive door opened and Peter, looking a little harassed, and James

Alexander, with no give-away facial expression, entered the room. Peter went to his Chairman's seat at the head of the table and James wandered over to lean against the back wall again. Peter looked up and down the table as the chatter subsided.

"Thank you for coming back in," he said glancing up from his notes. "After some discussion with Mister Alexander and the Mega-Software management team, it has been decided that the Mega-Software floatation date will now be..."

He paused momentarily for effect, looking around the room at all the expectant faces.

"...Exactly fourteen days from today."

A buzz went around the table and all eyes looked towards Alan as Peter held his hands up to get everyone's attention.

"Now I know this means plans will have to be changed," he said firmly, "and that there'll be limited time off for everyone associated with the floatation for the next two weeks; but this is the client's final decision and that's what's going to happen. So..."

Alan looked around the room as everyone hurriedly got their pens out and started to write. He glanced round to look at James Alexander but he was no longer there. People started to get up from the table, rushing off to grab their staff before they left for lunch. Alan felt a bump as John got up from the seat beside him and he quickly snapped out of his contemplation.

"You off then?" he asked in a much too matter-of-fact tone for John's liking, whose face was as grey as thunder.

"Off then! I'll be living in this bloody place for the next two weeks thanks to you. And I had a date with that blonde gal tonight. Thanks a bunch old buddy," he concluded vociferously.

And with a flourish he pushed his chair back and stomped off angrily.

Alan sighed to himself and got up from the table, heading for the door; noting the quick glances he attracted from everyone he passed.

24

Diane walked into the house feeling quite up after having had a quick coffee and chat with Becky; but having noticed on her way in that the car wasn't yet back, she looked nervously at her watch.

"Where the hell's Diane got to?" she wondered out loud.

Springing up the stairs two at a time, she went into the study and saw that the answer-machine message light was blinking. She quickly hit the play button on the machine and Alan's voice emitted:

"Alan, are you there. Come on Alan, for God's sake answer the phone."

There was a slight pause and she heard Alan sigh. The message continued:

"Okay, if you get this message in the next few minutes call me at your office. Otherwise it looks like I'll be a bit late getting home. Something's … um … cropped up here and I can't get away yet. Bye."

Diane's face dropped. She looked at the time of the call and then at her watch.

"What the hell's gone wrong now?" she groaned to herself.

She pressed the speakerphone button and dialled Alan's direct line. After a couple of rings Julie answered.

"Good afternoon, Alan Harris's office."

"Oh hi Julie, this is Diane Harris, is Alan there please?"

"Oh hi Mrs. Harris," said Julie in her usual friendly manner. "No, I'm afraid Alan's out for the rest of the day."

"Could you tell me when he left?" asked Diane, a little too abruptly.

"Well, not really," said Julie somewhat falteringly. "You see he went up to the boss's office for a meeting at about noon-ish and then he was going off to see a prospective client."

Diane's voice went up an octave and a few decibels:

"Went for a meeting with the boss?"

"Er … yes. Is there a problem?" enquired Julie, sounding a little concerned.

"No, sorry Julie," replied Diane apologetically, "I didn't mean to shout, It's just that I need to speak to him urgently."

Not waiting for a response Diane continued:

"Look, if you do see him or talk to him, would you ask him to call me as soon as possible?"

"Yes Mrs. Harris, sure," said Julie promptly.

"Okay then, thanks, bye."

"Bye Mrs. Harris."

Diane disconnected the call and looked at the telephone with bewilderment and unconsciously scratched her head.

"What the bloody-hell's happened now?" she shouted out in frustration.

She hit the phone button again and called the mobile-telephone number. After two rings there was a recorded message:

"The mobile you have called may be switched off, please try again later."

"God damn it, it's bloody well switched off!" she exclaimed, as she slammed the telephone off-button with her fist.

An hour or so later Diane was in the kitchen staring out of the window, cradling a mug coffee in her hands, when she heard a car pull into the courtyard. She put the coffee down and rushed to the front door, nearly dragging it of its hinges as she opened it. Alan was just getting out of the car but his face gave nothing away.

"What's happened?" asked Diane urgently, as Alan walked up to the doorway and kissed her on the cheek.

"Come on inside and I'll tell you. God I could do with a drink."

Diane felt a sense of impending doom as the couple went into the kitchen and Alan sat down at the kitchen table. Diane stood opposite him leaning with both hands on the table but she didn't speak.

She sensed from Alan's demeanour that she shouldn't push too much and after a few seconds innocuously broke the silence:

"What would you like to drink love?"

"Oh, I suppose a coffee will do," said Alan dejectedly. "It's too early for a real drink, it'll make me sleepy at this time of day."

"Okay," said Diane, "a coffee it is."

She went over to the Aga where the coffeepot was bubbling away and poured out a mug-full for Alan. She put the hot drink on the table and Alan looked up with a wan smiled.

"Thanks darling."

Diane waited patiently for him to speak as Alan took a sip of the steaming coffee before letting out a long sigh.

"Well, I really don't know where to start," he said taking another sip from the mug. "I suppose that things started to veer off plan when I was summoned, along with everyone else I might add, to a meeting in the boardroom; to have a final chat before your boss announced the date of the Mega-Software deal to the press."

He paused and looked up at Diane.

"Darling," he said incredulously, "it was the same date that I went forward to, four weeks from today!"

"Oh shit," exclaimed Diane, then looking at Alan's anguished face, apologised: "Sorry love."

"It's okay," said Alan sympathetically. "I know you must be stressed out, sat here with nothing to do."

He took another sip of his coffee and continued:

"Anyway, as one of your senior partners was waffling on congratulating everyone, I started to get these pictures in my head, like a really vivid daydream. First I saw the TV news in Sony's shop-window, and then there you were," he looked down at himself, "or should I say there I was, going on about how you ... me ... we, should use the knowledge we had about the deal failing. That we could put it to some use."

He paused and looked Diane straight in the eyes.

"So I told them about it."

Diane gawked incredulously at Alan.

"You what?" she exclaimed. "You told all my partners that you ... I ... whatever, had travelled into the future and seen a financial news report."

Alan snapped back instantly:

"No, of course not you pillock."

Diane exhaled loudly with relief.

"Oh, thank God for that."

"What I told them," said Alan, speaking more calmly, "was that I'd had a dream about the deal collapsing."

Diane slumped down onto one of the chairs.

"A dream?"

She threw her hands in the air.

"Oh well, that's alright then," she said sarcastically. "They probably think I'm only halfway round the bend."

She put her head in her hands and slumped on the table.

"I'm finished. We'll have to move to Scotland, or Wales; no, further, Canada, somewhere no one knows us."

"Don't be so melodramatic," said Alan assertively, "and please be quiet until I've finished telling you everything that happened."

Diane raised her eyebrows at Alan's unusually commanding tone but said nothing.

"After I told everyone about the dream," he continued, "I had a meeting with James Alexander."

Diane's jaw dropped.

"You, had a meeting with James Alexander, the boss of Mega-Software?"

"Yes," said Alan. "And he, James that is, is a very nice man. Anyway, I met with him in your boss's office and…"

Alan related the whole day's events while Diane listened attentively.

"So the date's been changed," he concluded, "and everyone knows. And that little chat we had on the way to get the papers on Sunday came in very useful when I had that meeting this afternoon … remember, when you came up with all the possible options for Mega-Software, if the markets were about to crash? Well James agreed, with all of them."

Then he suddenly laughed as he recalled John's final outburst in the boardroom.

"I don't think John was too enamoured though, with having to work this evening. Remember, I told you he'd scored with some blonde tart he met at the rugby? I suppose he wanted to break his leg-over record. Did you see her, was she attractive?" he added as an afterthought.

Alan looked at Diane but she was obviously miles away.

"Are you with me?" asked Alan loudly.

"What, sorry," she said shaking her head, "I was just thinking about what the outcome of this fiasco might be. You know," she said a little more enthusiastically, "if what you saw about the stock markets taking a plunge on that Monday turns out to be right, then I could come out of this smelling of roses."

Alan looked at Diane and this time it was his turn to shake his head.

"I'll take that as a backhanded compliment then shall I; for saving the firm and maybe helping to get you considered as a senior partner?"

Diane looked at Alan and frowned, still deep in her own thoughts.

"Sorry love, I was miles away again. What did you say?"

"Oh nothing important darling," sighed Alan, "I was just wondering what was for dinner tonight; what had you planned to cook?"

"Cook?" said Diane enquiringly. "Oh dinner, right. I think we should go out to eat tonight, you know, a little celebration."

"I don't know, men!" said Alan shaking his head again.

The dining area of the village local was very quiet. Apart from two other couples and a family of four, Diane and Alan were the only customers. The waiter, a spotty-faced lanky youth with a greying-white nylon shirt and crooked bowtie had just given them the menus and was running through that evening's specials:

"Specials toneight is," said the waiter, "Jumbo Addock wi' 'ome med chips – A large Yorkshire puddin' wi' spicy sausages an' onion gravy – Lasagni – Yorkshire-'am salad, an' finally mixed grill; which 'as a piece of every meat y' could think o' plus black puddin' an' chips an' onion rings. But y'd 'ave t' bi starvin' t' finish it all. Even t' local rugby team ca't finish that plateful," he said, scratching his head with his pen. Well, all except fo' one o' t' prop for'ards, bur 'e's nineteen stone an' 'as three shredded-wheat fo' breakfast."

Alan and Diane looked at each other and burst into laughter.

"I wonder if you could you give us a couple of minutes to decide please?" asked Diane.

The waiter closed his order pad.

"No problem, just giv' us a wave when y' ready."

He left the table and went back to chatting-up one of the young waitresses as Alan perused the menu.

"I think I'll give the mixed-grill a wide berth, I don't want to give you're body anything that a rugby team can't tackle!"

Diane laughed at Alan's apt choice of words.

"I think that had I been sitting where you are," she said, "I'd have ordered the Jumbo Haddock and Chips. But, I don't think that your little stomach could handle that, so I'm going to have the Yorkshire-ham salad."

"Okay then," said Alan, "that seems fair; and, as you think you're figure can handle it, I'll have the Jumbo Haddock."

He leaned back in his chair and smiled.

"This is, without doubt, the only way to diet. Eat your fill for a few days and then return the slightly bloated body for a slimmer model. Oh yes, I could sell that concept."

Diane snatched the menu out of his hand.

"Hey you, don't eat all the chips or I'll have to work out for weeks when I get my body back. And as you brought up the subject of our little predicament, are we going to try for an OOBE tonight?"

"Sure," said Alan, reflecting for a moment. "As nice as it was finding out what it's like to be in a man's body, and everything that entails," he said, abruptly tugging at the bulge in his trouser crotch. "I don't know, I only have to think about my own body and this thing starts to rear its ugly head. Does it do this all the time?"

Diane smiled seductively.

"Yes, especially when I think of you."

She casually stroked her right breast with her outstretched index finger and within seconds her nipple started to show through her blouse. Alan glanced around the restaurant to see if anyone had noticed her antics.

"Will you stop that," he said trying to kick Diane under the table. "You'll get me a reputation in here."

"Sorry love but I can't help it, it feels so good, especially when you play with yourself like that."

"Look," said Alan sternly, "we're supposed to be talking about getting our bodies back, not how to get them aroused."

He looked around the room again and leaned towards Diane.

"Seriously though, I think that I'll be able to have an OOBE tonight, but I'm not sure about you. I don't know if you remember but Arthur and me had to pull your spirit out last night and it wasn't an easy task. It felt like you were stuck with Velcro or something."

"Well maybe now I've got your body, it'll be easier tonight."

"Maybe," said Alan, "but we'll have to try to be very relaxed. You know, no stress."

"Okay then," said Diane, "let's get the waiter back and order the food and a bottle of wine. That'll help us relax a bit."

She waved her hand at the waiter and he made for their table."

25

Diane barged through the front door of the farmhouse laughing loudly, swiftly followed by Alan. As they entered the hallway Diane stumbled over the doormat and Alan caught her by the arm just in time to stop her from falling.

"Oh bloody hell love," said Diane, "I shouldn't have ordered that second bottle of wine, this body of yours can't take it."

Alan kept a firm grip on Diane's arm.

"You're right," he said, "but it's the reverse with me. I don't think I've ever had so much wine before and not felt drunk. Come on, I'll help you upstairs."

Once in the bedroom Diane staggered across the floor and twirling round with arms outstretched fell backwards onto the bed. Alan stood in the middle of the room with his hands on his hips, surveying the scene. Diane beckoned him over seductively.

"Come here you," she slurred.

Alan walked over and sat on the bed as Diane struggled with the catch on her skirt.

"You'll have to help me off with these clothes, I can't seem to manage when they're on me."

"So it seems," said Alan with a wry smile. "You don't normally have this trouble when they're on me."

He reached down and unfastened the skirt, pulling it down over Diane's stocking covered legs.

"I didn't know you put on my best Janet Reger underwear," he said, raising his eyebrows at the enticing sight.

"Well I've bought you so much in the past, I thought I'd see what it was like to wear."

"And?" said Alan, leaving the word hanging.

"I like it," she said lustily, "I like it a lot. It makes me feel..."

She ran her hands from her knees slowly up her legs, across the top of her stockings and down the inside of her bare upper-thighs, gently caressing her silk- covered pubic mound with her fingertips. Then she seductively flicked a suspender with her thumb.

"Mmm, horny."

Alan looked down at the bulge growing in his trousers.

"No darling, it makes me feel horny."

Alan slid over to Diane and kissed her passionately. Diane responded immediately and the couple started to undress each other eagerly.

"Oh Alan," moaned Alan.

"Oh Di," groaned Diane. "Get this bra off, quick!"

Alan removed Diane's blouse and put his hand under her back, expertly unhooking the bra and pulling it over her shoulders to reveal her firm breasts. Her nipples were swollen and hard, and as Alan stroked them tenderly Diane moaned again and slowly pulled his head down onto her. Alan placed his lips over one of the pinkish-brown nipples and gently sucked, flicking it with his tongue. Diane pulled his head down more firmly as she clumsily tried to remove her silk pants with one hand.

As Alan struggled to get his belt undone Diane pulled his shirt off over his head, reluctantly detaching him from her nipple. Having now extricated himself from his trousers and Jockeys, Alan looked down amazed – not just at the sight of his erect penis, which, as Diane, he'd never viewed from that particular perspective, but the feeling too – it was as if it was about to burst out of its skin! He looked over at Diane, who was lying with her eyes closed, the tip of her tongue slightly protruding from her pouting lips – seemingly oblivious to his presence – simultaneously fondling her breasts and massaging her vagina.

Alan's penis twitched involuntarily and he cautiously grasped it with his right hand, surprised at how sensitive it felt at its tip. He slowly started to move his hand up and down the rigid shaft and felt a tightening sensation somewhere deep at its base as the skin of his scrotum started to contract. Suddenly Diane's hand grasped his.

"Don't do that," she murmured, "it'll go off; put it inside me, I want to feel what it's like for you."

Alan moved his body between Diane's wide-open legs and looked down at her vagina, which she was still gently massaging, and was now extremely pink, with the labia folded back like the open petals of an orchid. He lowered his body onto Diane and could feel the roughness of her pubic hair against the head of his extremely sensitive penis.

Diane had to close her eyes, as the sight of Alan's face – in reality his own face – staring down at her, was somewhat off-putting. She grasped Alan's penis firmly and steered it to the wet opening of her vagina, rubbing it gently over her clitoris a few times before guiding it inside her.

Alan was now past the point of want and was overtaken by need. He slowly slid his throbbing shaft into Diane as far as it would go and was both surprised and extremely aroused at how warm and soft it felt inside. Diane let out a groan that sounded like a cross between pain and pleasure and then, unexpectedly, raised herself up off the bed. Grabbing Alan around the neck with both arms she unfolded her legs from around his back and twisted him over, so that he was now on his back and she was on her haunches, squat over him. Grasping his penis, which had inadvertently slipped out during the manoeuvre, she re-inserted it between the lips of her vagina before gently lowering herself down over it with a low moan.

As Diane mounted him and started to rub her clitoris slowly backwards and forwards against the pubic hair at the base of his penis, Alan felt a strange sensation welling-up, somewhere deep down in his loins. He lay back and looked on as Diane straddled him, fondling her own breasts and riding him more and more aggressively – her labia now sliding up and down over his glistening shaft like two caressing lips – another sight he'd never seen before as Diane, but found very arousing nonetheless.

Suddenly Alan felt a strong desire to be in control and grabbed Diane, rolling her over onto her back. He knelt between her open legs, grabbed her under her knees and pushed her thighs towards her body, raising her buttocks slightly off the bed; which fully exposed the now damp and matted pubic hair surrounding her wet vagina. Grasping his penis in one hand he pushed its full length straight into Diane, who winced visibly for a moment, then said urgently:

"Go on, do it hard, fuck me now!"

Still kneeling between her legs, Alan started to thrust rapidly in and out of Diane; who was by now holding on to her own legs, pulling them tightly towards her.

Alan was mesmerised by the sight of his penis sliding in and out of Diane's vagina and this visual stimulation, along with all the other new sensations, took him quickly over the edge. Suddenly he felt a million tingles up the entire length of his shaft and before he realised what was about to happen he felt an explosion that started somewhere near his rectum and shot all the way to the tip of his penis. It racked his body so hard with a mixture of pleasure and pain that he collapsed over Diane with a loud groan, as he felt his sperm erupt deep inside her.

Meanwhile, Diane was having her own experience! As soon as Alan had turned her on her back and fully penetrated her in one thrust, she recognised, from her recent episode in the bathroom, that warm glow that emanated from inside her lower abdomen; and it slowly started to spread outwards and upwards. She hooked her hands behind her knees and pulled her legs tighter in towards her chest, so that every thrust that Alan made was as deep inside her as possible. Momentarily she felt Alan's penis swell inside her vagina as he was about to orgasm; and then, as he did, he collapsed on top of her moaning.

She was amazed that she could feel his sperm hit the neck of her womb and as his penis continued to throb inside her, she wrapped her legs tightly around him, holding him inside. Then, with the last shudders of Alan's body lightly stimulating

Diane's clitoris, she too erupted with a series of spasms that lit up her whole being.

And there they lay for quite some time, motionless and silent in each other's arms, savouring a truly unique experience!

26

Early next morning Alan was standing by the Aga pouring tea when Diane came into the kitchen, looking a little worse for wear. She walked over to Alan and gave him a kiss on the cheek, wrinkling up her nose as his stubbly growth spiked her. She slumped into one of the chairs at the table with a groan.

"When I get my body back," she said looking up at Alan, "I promise to shave more often. It's not very nice having to kiss a welder's file first thing of a morning, is it?"

Alan brought the tea over to the table and sat down opposite her.

"It's just like anything else, you get used to it after a while."

There was a short pause as they both sipped the steaming brew.

"That was some evening, I can't believe I got so drunk on less than a bottle of wine," said Diane.

"And I can't believe that I drank more than a bottle of wine and didn't get drunk," riposted Alan.

"Just goes to show doesn't it?" said Diane reflectively.

"Show what darling?" asked Alan.

"That one's body-mass is extremely relevant to the amount of alcohol one can safely consume."

"Oh, right," he said looking up from his tea.

He reached out to rest his hand on Diane's.

"Actually darling," he said, sounding a little troubled, "I feel a bit guilty about last night. I feel I ought to apologise for acting the way I did."

Diane looked up with a puzzled expression on her face but said nothing.

"Oh, come on, you know what I mean," said Alan bluntly. "We made love like a couple of animals last night and it was me that instigated it, took advantage of you being drunk."

Diane took Alan's hand in hers.

"Do you hear me complaining? Anyway, I wasn't drunk, just slightly tipsy." she said defensively.

"That's not the point though," said Alan.

"Well what is the point then?"

"I suppose the point is," he said hesitantly, "although I'm really a woman and it was my own body that I was making love to, on reflection It seemed that I was being driven by something that was very difficult to control and it frightened me. I mean, when I got that strong sexual urge last night, even though I knew deep down I shouldn't respond to it, I just couldn't stop."

"Don't be silly," said Diane. "I was giving you the come-on as well. Don't forget, we both know what the biggest turn-on's are as far as our own bodies are concerned, and because of our current state of affairs, what happened was, I would imagine, what any sexually-healthy couple would do under similar circumstances."

"I don't disagree with any of that darling," said Alan, "In fact it was great to experience what you normally feel."

Diane frowned.

"Well what do you mean then?"

Alan took a deep breath.

"What alarmed me was that I didn't feel that I had any real control over your body. It was like it was on autopilot, and no matter how long it took it had to come, if you'll forgive the pun, to the final outcome, no matter what. Now I know for a fact that when I was in my own body there have been times that you were feeling extremely horny but I wasn't; but you always managed to control yourself."

He sighed deeply with frustration at not being able to verbalise his feelings.

"What I mean is I can't remember a time that you ever tried to force yourself on me. But honestly, last night, I don't think that I could have stopped myself. I think I might have been guilty of marital-rape if you'd tried to stop me ... you know ... doing it."

"Look love," said Diane sympathetically, "don't loose sight of the fact that under normal circumstances we grow up with our own bodies, and learning to control them is a gradual thing; achieved over many years. And most of the time we do control them. Last night was unique, a one-off, and you probably just got a little over-excited."

She paused in thought momentarily and then laughed.

"Well as far as I'm aware it was unique. So, don't take it out of context, just put it down to experience and stop worrying about it."

"I suppose you're right," agreed Alan with a resigned expression. "Thanks for understanding anyway."

Diane glanced up at the kitchen clock, which was now showing seven thirty.

"Bloody hell look at the time, you have to leave in half-an-hour and you've got to shower and shave."

Alan got up from the table. "I always thought it was the three S's that men did in a morning!"

"They looked at each other and burst out laughing as Diane put her arm around Alan's shoulder and they headed out of the kitchen."

Thirty minutes later and the couple were standing in the hallway by the front door. Diane was still in her dressing gown but Alan was now dressed for the office, in a dark-blue wool suit, white shirt and a blue and red patterned silk tie. Diane made a final adjustment to the tie, patted down the lapels on Alan's jacket and opened the door. They walked outside into the bright morning sunshine.

"Are you sure I look good enough for you darling?" enquired Alan frivolously.

He put his arms out and did a twirl.

"You look great but not as good as this," said Diane cheekily, opening her dressing gown to reveal her naked body.

"Sorry darling," said Alan shaking his head, "but I'm thoroughly sated in that department. Anyway, put my body away, the postman might come around the corner any minute."

Diane wrapped her dressing gown around her and crossed her arms.

"Alright let's get serious," she said. "We'll just go through the checklist one more time. Got the mobile phone?"

Alan held up the phone.

"And it's switched on," he remarked sarcastically.

"Good, and don't forget to keep it with you at all times," said Diane firmly, "no matter where you are."

Alan feigned a salute.

"Yes sir … oops … sorry, Ma'am."

"Come on love, don't mess about, this is serious. Now don't forget," she continued, "show your face in the office, collect my messages and tell Julie that you're going to the meeting you were supposed to have yesterday; and I'll meet you at around eleven at Harvey-Nichols' coffee shop in

The Victoria Quarter, the one in the covered street."

Alan got into the car.

"Okay boss," he said slamming the door and lowering the window. "Is that it?"

"I think so," said Diane. "Just don't get sidetracked by anyone!"

She kissed Alan through the open window and waved as he pulled away.

In the office later that day Alan had just sat down at his desk when there was a knock on the door. Julie entered with a mug of coffee and a handful of messages and passed them over to Alan.

"Oh, thanks Julie, just what I needed," he said, taking a swig of coffee.

"You're welcome," said Julie, sitting down and elegantly crossing her long legs. "Most of the messages aren't that urgent," she said, "apart from the one from the big boss and one from Mister Alexander. He specifically asked that you ring him before nine-thirty if possible."

She looked at the face of her large 'Storm' stainless-steel designer watch.

"And it's just gone nine-fifteen."

Alan frowned as he read the messages.

"I wonder what he wants?" he said thoughtfully.

Julie looked at Alan with a slight frown. She was starting to notice that he wasn't quite himself lately.

"I don't know, he didn't say," she said unconsciously.

"Okay Julie, thanks," said Alan, still perusing the message slips.

Julie got up and walked to the door.

"Oh by the way," Alan called after her, "I'll be going out about ten-thirty, to that meeting I missed yesterday. I'll call you," he held up the mobile phone, "and let you know what's happening this afternoon."

"Okay boss," she said, smiling warmly before exiting the room.

Alan looked again at the messages from James Alexander and Alan's boss, Peter, and hit the speakerphone-button on his telephone. A dial tone emitted and he punched in the number on the message slip. He sat back in his chair and put his hand down the front of his trousers to rearrange his tackle as the phone rang-out. A voice issued from the speaker.

"Alexander."

Alan sat up quickly, surprised that he had gone straight through to James' direct line, and he struggled wildly to extricate his hand from his trousers.

"Oh hi … um … James. This is Alan Harris, at the law firm."

"Oh, hi Alan," said James warmly, "thanks for calling back so promptly. Just hang on a second would you?"

Alan heard muffled sounds from the phone before James' voice came back on.

"Sorry about that, just giving my secretary some papers. Right, I was wondering if you could meet me for lunch today?"

Alan was briefly taken aback by the request and a short silence ensued.

"Hello, Alan," queried James' voice over the speaker.

"James, sorry," said Alan, "I was just looking at my diary."

He rustled some papers on his desk.

"Um, what time did have in mind?"

"Oh, about one if that's okay with you," requested James respectfully. "At that little Italian restaurant, just around the corner from Harvey Nichols. Do you know it?"

"I think so but don't worry I'll find it."

"Great," replied James, sounding genuinely pleased. "I'll see you there then, at one."

"Right, thanks."

The phone went dead and Alan looked up at the ceiling blowing out his cheeks.

"Alan's not going to like this one little bit," he said out loud. "Oh well, c'est la vie. Now, let's see what 'Sir Peter' wants," he thought to himself sarcastically.

He leaned back over the desk and punched in Peter's three-digit, direct internal number. Before the phone completed one ring a voice boomed out over the speaker.

"Yes?"

Alan was caught-out again by the speed of the response.

"Oh, hello, this is Alan Harris."

Peter responded, just a little too smugly for Alan's liking.

"Ah, yes, Alan. I just wanted to let you know that James Alexander might call you this morning, about a luncheon appointment. Now whatever it takes," he said, assuming a firmer tone, "you must re-arrange your diary and fit him in. I don't need to tell you how important his business is to this firm, and even if he wants a hot-dog in the park, you must ensure that you are there, and on time!"

Alan was quite matter-of-fact in his reply.

"Thank you for letting me know Peter," he said calmly, "but I've already spoken with James. I'm meeting him at one today; fortunately not in the park!"

Peter sounded a little frumpy in his response:

"Oh, right. Well just mind what you say. No more talk of dreams and the like. Stick to business. Right then."

The phone went dead before Alan could say…!

27

Diane walked confidently through the crowded streets of Leeds, on her way from the railway station to The Victoria Quarter – a recently refurbished shopping area of central Leeds that has attracted the very crème-de-la-crème of the retail world to it's ornately covered Victorian streets. Dressed very conservatively yet elegantly in a light-grey silk Jacques Vert two-piece suit with a short-ish skirt and fitted jacket, with a contrasting Grès silk scarf around her neck, Diane stood out somewhat amongst the mainly workaday throng currently walking the City streets. Her outfit was topped off with matching shoes and handbag that Alan had bought Diane from the 'Bally' flagship-store, in Zurich, when she accompanied him there on a business trip last year.

As she strode out purposefully, Diane couldn't help but notice the admiring glances she attracted, especially from male passers-by; and as she turned the corner of a building that was fronted by scaffolding, she was the target of a wolf-whistle from one of the workmen atop. She smiled inwardly at this 'not so PC' admiration.

She decided to take a short cut she knew through a fairly narrow cobbled street that connected two of the major shopping streets; and as she reached just about halfway distance she felt a heavy bump on her right arm. Diane turned quickly as a scruffy young man with matted hair and three days facial growth grabbed hold of her handbag and started tugging at it. Not thinking straight for a moment she shouted out loudly:

"Hey, what do you think your doing?"

"Give us the fucking bag bitch," barked the youth as he pushed Diane roughly but still kept a vice-like grip on the handbag.

Without a second thought Diane gave the youth, who was now directly in front of her, a hard straight jab to the bridge of his nose, visibly wincing at the loud crack that accompanied it.

"Oh fuck!" exclaimed the youth, clutching his broken nose with both hands as the blood spurted out between his fingers.

"Oh shit!" exclaimed Diane loudly, nursing her hand. "I think I've broken something."

"Yes, my fucking nose you bastard," screamed the youth.

Now this young man, who was either somewhat less than bright or on some illegal substance, thought that Diane's overt show of distress gave him another opportunity to steal the elusive bag; and with the blood still flowing profusely from his broken nose, he made a move forward. That was his second mistake inside half a minute! His eyes nearly popped out of their sockets with the excruciating pain that immediately followed as

Diane's foot connected heavily with both his testicles at the same time; and he fell to the floor screaming, this time clutching his groin.

By now the commotion of the attempted mugging had brought several male bystanders rushing to Diane's assistance, but as the assailant was no longer a threat, writhing on the ground sobbing with blood streaming from his nose, they just stood around muttering in awe.

"Did you see that?" said one middle-aged man to an elderly chap stood by his side.

"Aye lad a did. Last time I saw a kick like that, wa' w'en England beat Australia in t' last minute at Twickenham wi' a Rob Andrew drop-goal!"

"Are you alright miss," enquired one of the other onlookers of Diane, who was now standing by the stricken youth holding her injured hand.

"Yes thanks," she said, "I think it's just bruised."

Diane started fishing around in her handbag, looking for her mobile phone to call the police, when a young policeman and policewoman ran up to the small crowd that had now formed, pushing their way through to the centre.

"What's goin' on then?" enquired the young male officer.

The elderly chap chirped up:

"That young fellow-mi-lad just tried to mug this young lady," he said, gesturing towards Diane.

The policewoman knelt down by the side of the moaning youth, who was still in a very tight foetal position, and surveyed his bloody face.

"Looks like he picked on the wrong woman then," she said with a wry smile.

"A' you all right madam?" asked the policeman of Diane.

"Yes thanks, I think I bruised my hand when I hit him the first time; and my foot's throbbing a bit, but I'll live."

The officer looked Diane up and down and then looked at the youth; who, even though curled up on the ground, was obviously much larger than she.

"So you whacked him on the nose and then kicked him in the..."

"Bollocks," shouted someone in the crowd, and the rest of the gathering roared with laughter.

The female officer looked at her male colleague with raised eyebrows.

"Ambulance or van," she queried.

"Much as I hate to pamper this sort," said the young bobby, looking disdainfully at the youth, "the book says that if they're injured and they can't walk, then it's an ambulance."

The policewoman nodded and started to talk into her radio as the male officer addressed the crowd:

"Okay, if you didn't actually see the assault, then please move along. If you were a witness, then please make yourself known to me or my partner here."

Most of the crowd dispersed quickly, leaving four people who were eyewitnesses. Diane looked at her watch.

"Is this going to take long," she politely enquired of the policewoman, who had just finished talking to her H.Q.

"I don't think so madam, once we've taken your details and a brief statement from you and the other witnesses you should be on your way."

"Oh, good," said Diane, still rubbing her hand, I've got to meet my husband shortly."

"Tell me," said the policewoman with an evil-looking smile, "did it feel really good when you kicked him in the…?"

Eventually Diane arrived at the Victoria Quarter about twenty minutes late, and as she entered the covered area saw Alan, already sat in the café area. She walked on and waved as she caught his eye. Weaving her way through the small crowd of morning shoppers she went into the tabled section and sat down next to him, letting out a little groan as she plonked down on the chair.

"I'll tell you what," she said kicking off one of her shoes and rubbing her foot, "these shoes weren't designed for walking and they're the shortest heels I could find."

Alan looked Diane up and down with raised eyebrows.

"Are you going somewhere later?"

"What do you mean?" she asked, looking down at herself. "I'm no more dressed-up than you are. "Suit…"

She felt the lapels of her jacket.

"Tie…"

She nonchalantly flicked her scarf.

"Nice shoes…"

She waggled her one shoe-clad foot.

"Briefcase…"

She held up her handbag.

"Okay, okay, point taken," conceded Alan with a smile.

He looked at her again, this time more admiringly.

"I must say, seeing that outfit thus," he gestured, "it looks just great on me."

Diane put her index finger to her chin and fluttered her eyelashes.

"Thank you kind sir, not bad for someone who's just been mugged, eh?"

"Mugged?" cried Alan, staring wide-eyed.

"Yes, mugged."

Diane related the whole story to Alan as they sipped their frothy cappuccinos.

"...And I've got to go in and make a full statement some time in the next few days. The police said they they'd ring me."

Alan shook his head in disbelief.

"So how's my hand now?" he joked.

"Oh it's okay," said Diane. "It's just a little sore but I'm sure it'll be okay by the time you get it back."

"Anyway, as long as you're okay," said Alan, shuffling nervously in his chair and pausing momentarily. "Look, I got a message to call James Alexander this morning," he said pensively.

Diane sat up in her chair and cocked her head to one side.

"He called you, what did he want?"

"He wants to meet me for lunch, at some Italian restaurant near here."

Diane looked gobsmacked.

"Lunch!" she exclaimed. Bloody hell, I don't know; you kidnap my body for a few days and already you're invited out for lunch with the firm's biggest client.

I suppose the boss is going too? He wouldn't miss a free lunch if it coincided with the end of the world!" concluded Diane sarcastically.

"Well, actually no," said Alan hesitantly. "He's not. In fact I got a summons to call him too this morning and he made it quite plain that I had to go and meet James, but very firmly insisted that there was absolutely no talk about anything but business."

"Well, well; I wonder what Mister Rich-and-Famous Alexander wants," she said with a slightly jealous intonation to her voice.

"Well, it can't be my body now, can it?" said Alan sarcastically.

"Ha, ha, very funny," mocked Diane.

"Oh, come on darling lighten up there," pleaded Alan. "He probably wants to psychoanalyse me; or should I say you? After all, he's changing the date of his company's floatation, at God knows what cost knowing you're firm's billing criteria; and all because I, supposedly, had a dream. I think lunch is the least he could expect under the circumstances, don't you think?"

"Yes, you're right of course," conceded Diane. "If I were him, I'd have had you carted off to the psychiatry wing at Jimmy's Hospital."

She paused in thought for a moment, recalling something she had to tell Alan.

"Oh, by the way, before I forget; your office left a message on the answer machine at home this morning. They want you to go in and proof some article urgently. Something about, hang on…"

She fished in her handbag and brought out a piece of paper.

"…'If you're in town and it's at all possible," she read, "please come in and sign- off on the proof for the Johnny Bizarre article. Going to press tomorrow.' And they sent a copy of the proof to your computer as well," she said, looking up from the note, "but I couldn't get the damned thing to print out."

"Bloody hell," said Alan, looking slightly miffed. "How am I going to handle this one? There isn't time to go back home and send a reply and I don't know how long lunch with James will last; so it could be too late if I wait until this afternoon."

Diane smiled, pointing a finger at herself. Alan shook his head vigorously.

"Oh no, not that."

"Why not!" said Diane indignantly? You've spent the last two days doing my job. It's only fair that I reciprocate. Anyway I'm bored."

"I know you are darling but you haven't a clue about pre-press proof-reading."

Diane sat back in her chair, clasped her hands and looked up, admiring the architecture of the covered street.

"So tell me," she said nonchalantly, purposefully not looking at Alan, "when exactly was it you got your law degree?"

"Okay, you win," said Diane smiling, "but all you do is look over the proofs and initial them, and then give them back to the copy department. And make sure that they look like my initials; remember how I made that handwriting mistake with Julie? And don't get into any conversation with anyone else about anything."

"Finished?" asked Diane abruptly. "I'm sure that I can remember all that, It's just about, to the word, what I told you when you went to my office on Monday; and look what happened there!"

"Touché Madame," acknowledge Alan. "But that was the first time we'd done this. We should try to learn from our … sorry … my mistakes."

"Don't worry love, I'll be in and out in less than half-an-hour."

"Hmm," muttered Alan looking at his watch.

"Okay, we've got over an hour-and-a-half yet, and as I've got the perfect model with me, and we're in the heart of the Leeds fashion district, let's finish our coffee and go shopping!"

"Oh no, not that love," groaned Diane. "Anything but clothes shopping!"

The couple visited several women's clothes shops and Diane tried on an assortment of outfits for Alan. And although Diane didn't particularly like getting dressed and undressed every two minutes, being a red-blooded-male, at least on the inside, she saw some noteworthy scenes in the various women's changing rooms. But some of the shop assistants just couldn't quite get to grips with the fact that the husband seemed far more interested in the clothes than the wife! So after what seemed like an eternity to Diane they walked out of Harvey Nichols' main entrance laden with several large bags. Alan turned to Diane and kissed her on the cheek.

"Thank you for being my model darling. It's much better than using a mirror."

"Actually, I quite enjoyed it," said Diane with a cheeky grin. "It's amazing what you catch sight of in some of those changing rooms."

"Pervert," exclaimed Alan flippantly, glancing at his watch.

"Okay, I've got ten minutes to get to the restaurant, can you take the bags?"

"Me?" said Diane looking peeved at the request."

"Look darling, I know that you're currently the fairer-sex but I think it might look a little strange if I walk into that restaurant for a business meeting loaded down with women's clothes shopping. It could dent your reputation with James Alexander somewhat. He might think you're a cross-dresser or something!"

"Alright, alright," conceded Diane, "point taken, give them here."

"Okay, must dash or I'll be late," said Alan. "Call me on the mobile when you've finished the proof-reading at my office," he said as he turned and hurried off up the street.

"Bye love," said Diane, more to herself than the disappearing form of Alan, who had already blended into the ever-increasing lunchtime crowd; and waving her injured hand in Alan's general direction, Diane turned and walked off down the street, loaded down with bags.

28

Alan was only two minutes late for his appointment as he walked into the restaurant; which although not very large, had a cosy and very Italian feel to it. He looked around spotting James sitting at a table about halfway down one side of the room, in discussion with one of the waiters. He walked towards the table and James stood up as he approached, offering Alan his hand.

"Hi Alan," said James with a beaming smile, grasping Alan's hand firmly. "Thanks for coming at such short notice."

"That's okay James, thanks for the invite. It's nice to get out for lunch for a change."

They both took their seats and the waiter handed them each a menu before retiring.

"So, you don't get out to lunch much eh?"

"Not really," said Alan, searching his mind for a good reason as to why not. "You see, although I'm a partner," he prevaricated, "I'm classed as a junior until I've completed a full year as a partner. The seniors, like Peter, seem to get all the best business lunches."

"I see," said James, accepting Alan's story at face value. "Well, you'd better make the most of this one then."

The waiter returned with a bottle carefully cradled in both hands and handed it to James.

"I took the liberty of ordering the wine," he said, turning the bottle to show Alan. "This is the only restaurant in town that stocks this particular Italian wine. Personally I love it; it reminds me of a little seafood restaurant I go to in Italy; down near the harbour in Sorrento. Every time I drink it I can hear seagulls and the sound of fishing boats making out to sea; but we can change it if you'd prefer something different?"

"How could I after such a glowing recommendation," replied Alan.

"Right then," said James, giving Alan an engaging smile and looking up at the waiter, who could easily have been a stand-in for a henchman in 'The Godfather', with his barrel chest and thick, hairy forearms. "That's one bottle sold then Tony."

Tony nodded courteously and took back the bottle.

"Let's get the ordering out of the way," suggested James, "then we can talk."

They perused the menus while Tony uncorked the wine and poured a taster for James. James took a sip and nodded his acceptance as Tony poured the wine for the two men and then took out his order-pad and stood poised, with pen in hand.

"I think I'll have my usual Tony," said James," handing his menu back.

Tony nodded with a knowing and appreciative smile.

"What about you Alan?" asked James.

"I like a nice surprise, so if it's okay, I'll have what you're having; but please don't tell me what it is."

"Okay Tony, that's two of the usual then, thank you."

Tony took Alan's menu and left the table.

"I hope you like traditional Southern-Italian food Alan."

"I like all things Italian," he replied effusively, "their food, clothes, shoes, cars, you name it."

"Ah, then I was right, I just knew we had something in common.

Alan smiled politely but remained cautiously silent.

"Anyway," said James, getting down to business, "thanks again for coming along today. The main reason I wanted to see you in private was to discuss your dream."

Alan made to say something but James puts his hand up haltingly.

"Look, I know your boss, Peter, very well and I'll bet he's told you not to discuss anything with me that's not to do with your firm's legal input into the floatation. Right?"

Alan pursed his lips and James immediately laughed out loud.

"Aha, I knew it," he exclaimed. "Well, in my book, as we've already changed the company's issue date because of your revelation, I think I have the right to ask a few simple questions. Don't you?"

"Yes James, I do," agreed Alan sincerely.

"Good, thank you. You know, you're one of the few corporate lawyers I've ever met that seems to have a conscience. Now, if you don't mind, I wonder if you could tell me exactly how your dream went, from start to finish; and don't leave anything out."

"I don't mind at all," said Alan with a wry smile.

He paused momentarily to get his thoughts straight and then began:

"It all started when, in my dream, I was flying over Leeds like something out of a Superman movie and…"

Diane walked around the Magazine's office complex until she eventually found her way to Diane's office. She went up to her desk and saw the article that had to be proofed in a buff-folder in Diane's 'In' tray, and putting her bags down was just about to sit down and read it when Susan Turner walked in.

"Hi there Di, everyone was looking for you earlier."

Diane looked up startled.

"Oh, hi Susan, yes, I was on my way in here but I got held up at a meeting."

"You're not going for job interviews already are you?" asked Susan, looking Diane up and down with a puzzled expression.

"Interviews?"

"Yes, interviews," laughed Susan. "Either that or you're having an affair," she asserted flippantly.

It was Diane's turn to look puzzled.

"What are you going on about Susan?"

"Well, look at you, dressed to the nines on a workday. Come on, you can tell your Auntie Sue."

Diane became more than a little defensive.

"Bloody hell, can't a girl get dressed-up every so often?"

"Whoa there sister," said Susan sternly, "don't be so tetchy. What's up, have another bad night with that OOBE thing?"

"Yes ... no ... sorry Susan, I'm just a little pressed that's all, everyone's at me to get this article proofed and I've got to meet Alan in town later this afternoon."

"Okay," ceded Susan, "I'll let you get on, but give me a shout before you leave, I want to discuss that OOBE thing with you."

"Sure, no problem," fibbed Diane, "I'll call you."

Susan left the office and Diane sat down at the desk and started to read the proofs, basically checking for typos. She flicked through the article and pictures and initialled DH on each page, remembering to copy Diane's writing style.

"This is a doodle," she thought, and after about ten minutes had completed her task and left the office, making for the elevators.

As she was passing the reception desk the receptionist put up a halting hand, giving her an envelope with her name on it. Diane gave it a quick glance then slipped it in her handbag. She smiled at the young girl and was just about to head for the elevators when she heard a shout.

"Hey Di."

She looked round and saw Susan approaching at pace.

"Where are you sloping off to?"

"Oh, I'm sorry, I forgot to call you. I was just going to get a spot of lunch.

"Hmm," said Susan frowning, giving Diane the once-over for the second time. "You're a strange one today. Look, I'm going for lunch too, so let me pay you back for the other day. Come on, we'll eat and chat."

"But!"

"No buts," said Susan resolutely, "I insist."

And before Diane could argue further, Susan had her firmly by the arm and waltzed her off towards the elevators.

Back in the Italian Restaurant Alan and James had just finished their meal and the waiter, Tony, was clearing the table.

"As usual, Tony, that was fabulous," said James sincerely. "Give my thanks to your Mum and Dad in the kitchen."

"Yes, mine too," requested Alan, that was the best seafood pasta I've ever had."

Tony nodded his head and smiled.

"Mille-grace signors," he said with a very strong Italian accent. I'lla pass ona youra thanks to Mama and Papa. Can I geta you anythink else?"

James looked at Alan who shook his head and patted his stomach.

"No thanks, I'm FTB."

"We're fine Tony," said James.

"Si, signor James, grace."

Tony picked up the stacked dishes and left the table. James looked across at Alan.

"So Alan, I can tell from the way you recounted your dream that you're convinced that the market crash is going to happen. I suppose that you've already been on to your stockbroker," he said with a little grin, "to instruct him to sell your portfolio before the fateful day?"

"Well, actually, no, I haven't," said Alan with a somewhat perplexed look. "As I said to you yesterday, it was only when I had those flashbacks in the meeting that I actually realised that my dream was for real."

James studied Alan silently for a moment.

"I like to think of myself as a good judge of character," he said, "and before this lunch my only real preconception of you was that you seemed to believe your dream. But now I've spent some time with you and heard your revelation for myself I think that you're also a sincere chap; and I'm coming round to a certain belief of your dream too. That's why I'm pleased I've already set the wheels in motion to bring forward the Mega-Software issue. But I'm sure you're aware there are other options open to me, as far as my personal investments are concerned that is?"

He looked at Alan waiting for a response but didn't get the one he expected.

"I'm sure there are," replied Alan dryly, not really knowing what to say.

James laughed out loud.

"Oh Alan, Alan; you're either a very modest lawyer, if there is such an animal, or an extremely clever one," he said, looking Alan square in the eyes, trying to evaluate the man's true self. "On reflection though, maybe you're both. I know we've only had a short time to talk but I feel … I don't know … an empathy with you. I also tend to follow my gut instinct and right now it's telling me to listen to you."

"Look James," said Alan, wondering where all this was leading, "all I've done is let you, and everyone in the office of course, know about my dream. Because, well, because at the time it seemed the right thing to do."

"Exactly," said James, echoing Alan's words, "because it seemed the right thing to do. I don't know of another person in your firm, or even in my company for that matter, where we have a long-standing policy of open-door management, who'd have had the balls to stand up and say what you did yesterday. Especially in front of their peers, with the risk of being ostracised, or worse!"

He paused momentarily, still gazing directly at Alan.

"I don't think you've really thought through the implications of this dream of yours, have you?"

"In what respect?" asked Alan cautiously, beginning to feel a little uneasy.

"Several respects," said James. "For instance, let's assume for a moment that everything you saw in your dream turns out to be correct. That would mean that stock markets worldwide are going to take a big tumble in less than a month. Yes?"

"Yes," said Alan, still puzzled.

"Well that information alone could make or break millions of people," remarked James. "Including me! Never mind the harm it could have done to Mega-Software. And as I'm sure you know," he said grinning sheepishly, "I'm worth a few bob, as they say in these parts; and most of that wealth is tied up in investments in world stock markets. So if they loose twenty-five percent of their value, I loose twenty-five percent of my wealth. However, if we factor in the assumption that your dream is right, then I have the option of switching my investments before the crash, into let's say gold, which would probably go up in value in the short-term, when the markets nosedive; and then switching from gold back into the markets when they've bottomed-out. That would turn a potential twenty-five percent loss into," he looked up for mathematical inspiration, "oh, a possible forty percent gain in the medium term."

It was Alan's turn to look James straight in the eye.

"And what if my dream was wrong and the markets don't take a dive?"

"Then I'd blow money," said James with a little shrug of his shoulders. "Maybe a million in commissions and admin charges with my brokers and probably the same amount in interest charges on my margin account with my bank."

"Oh, well," said Alan, "then I suppose it all depends on what percentage of your net-worth those costs are."

"Exactly! In fact they're probably currently only about a tenth of one percent," said James in a matter-of-fact tone.

"So why are you sitting here talking to me?" Call your broker," quipped Alan.

"I already did," said James, laughing loudly. "I'm going to see him later this afternoon. But I wanted to meet with you first, just to reinforce my gut-feel."

He leaned closer over the table and lowered his voice.

"Look Alan, when the floatation's finalised, no matter what the outcome, I'd like you to come over and take a look at my set-up at Mega. I think you'd like what you see. I'm always on the lookout for special individuals like you, and you wouldn't be a junior in my company, that's if I can still call it mine after the floatation! So please, give it some thought," he said, smiling warmly at Alan.

"I really don't know what to say," said Alan, with a look of genuine surprise.

"Don't say anything, just promise me that you'll think about it."

"Okay," agreed Alan firmly, "I will."

"Good," said James, glancing at his watch. "Well I'd better be off, I don't want to be late for my broker. He's going to think that I've gone completely off my rocker," he joked with a laugh. "Anyway, it was great meeting you again Alan, and I'd be grateful if you didn't tell anyone about the content of our little tête-à-tête; especially Peter!"

He stood up and put out his hand. Alan stood and the men shook hands warmly.

"I won't say a word," said Alan assuredly, "and it was nice to meet you again James; oh, and thanks for the great meal."

"You're more than welcome."

As Alan and James stepped out of the restaurant into the busy street they bumped smack into Diane and Susan, who were just on their way in, for their lunch. Alan and Diane exchanged nervous glances, slightly taken aback by the chance meeting; but Susan was effusive.

"Oh Alan, hi, how are you", she exclaimed enthusiastically, throwing her arms around Alan's neck and kissing him firmly on both cheeks, Euro-style.

"Sue, how are you," he asked, still looking embarrassed and somewhat flushed. "You look great."

"Well, thank you kind sir," said Susan with a little mock-curtsy.

Alan approached Diane nervously.

"Hello darling," he said, as he leaned over and kissed her hastily on the lips. "You look good too."

"Thanks love, Susan here just dragged me out of the office for lunch," said Diane with a somewhat contrite air.

Alan hastily turned to James.

"Oh, I'm sorry James," he said apologetically. "This is my wife Diane and her friend and colleague Susan Turner."

James nodded at the girls, giving them a Hollywood-type smile.

"Girls, this is James Alexander."

Diane moved closer to shake James' hand.

"Good to meet you Mr. Alexander," she said, a little reverently.

"And you too, Diane; and please, call me James."

Susan also moved in closer, much closer, with her hand at the ready.

"Not The James Alexander, of Mega-Software?"

James took Susan's hand and laughed.

"I'm afraid so," he said, flashing that winning smile again, "for my sins."

"Oh my," said Susan, "your pictures don't do you justice at all."

"Well thank you, I'll take that as a compliment," replied James.

They all laughed, Alan and Diane a little more nervously than the other two. James looked at his watch.

"Well, I must get off," said James, "it was good to meet you ladies."

He shook Alan's hand warmly again.

"I'll see you soon Alan. Take care."

"Yes, thanks James. See you soon."

He briefly nodded once more and the trio stood by the doorway and watched as he walked off up the street and disappeared around the corner.

"Well, well, James Alexander," said Susan rubbing her hands together with a me-want-him grin all over her face. "I didn't know you knew him."

"Really," said Alan nonchalantly. "My firm's working on his company's multi-billion-pound floatation and we were just having a working lunch; you know, going over a few loose ends?"

Susan looked suitably impressed.

"All the magazines say he's one of the top-ten most eligible bachelors in the UK. I can see why now," she said with a twinkle in her eye. "He's very charming, and extremely handsome."

"Yes he is," concurred Alan," just a little too enthusiastically for a supposed red-blooded male. "He's also very, very wealthy."

"Oh, really, I didn't know that," said Susan with mock surprise.

Alan and Susan laughed.

"I don't know," said Diane disdainfully, women!"

29

It was five-thirty by the hall clock when Alan and Diane got back home from Leeds. They went into the kitchen without speaking and Diane put the kettle on as Alan stood in Diane's favourite place, with his back to the Aga. They continued the conversation that they'd left off in the car:

"I just don't know why I said 'women'," reiterated Diane. "No, that's not true, I do know why, I'm a man, and men say that, don't they?"

"Forget it darling," said Alan. I don't think Sue spotted anything too untoward, and even if she did, she soon forgot about it, especially after she'd had her first glass of wine and started chatting-up Tony."

"Maybe," replied Diane, "but she kept on giving the both of us such strange looks."

"True, I noticed that too," said Alan, "but I think I've sussed out why."

"Really?"

"Yes, didn't you notice that she seemed to give us that look every time we used her name? I mean, I've always called her Sue, have done ever since we first met, probably because she's always called me Di. And you, being the correct gentleman, have always called her Susan."

Diane raised her finger as the penny dropped.

"Aha!"

"Aha indeed," said Alan. "The only thing that worries me is why she didn't mention it. I mean, you know Sue, she's not exactly backward at coming forward now is she?"

"Well, maybe it wasn't that."

"No, I'm sure it was but maybe not just that."

"What do you mean love?"

"Well, we all have our own little mannerisms and ways of talking, don't we? When we don't use our names, you tend to call me love; you just said it then, that little Yorkshire-ism of yours, and I call you darling...

"Yes," butted in Diane. "That little 'Southern-Deb' thing that you picked-up in London"

"And we still do that," continued Alan, ignoring Diane's comment, "even though we're temporarily, I hope, in each other's body."

"Of course, that's right. It wouldn't mean anything to someone who didn't know us very well, but to Susan, or should I say, Sue, or someone else who knows us, they might well notice."

"Yes," cut in Alan, "like John, for instance."

"Right," agreed Diane. "We're going to have to be careful in future, until we get reversed. And talking of that, we must have a try tonight. No more drink or sex until we change back."

"Let's hope it's not too long then," said Alan grinning widely and grabbing hold of his crotch.

"You know how difficult it is for me to control this thing,"

"I hope you remember that when we eventually do get reversed," said Diane optimistically.

"Oh I will," he said with a laugh, glancing up at the clock. "Right then, I'm going to get changed, then I'll get us something light for tea."

Later that evening the couple was in the lounge. Alan was looking over the Johnny Bizarre article that had come in on the computer and Diane was reading an OOBE research book. The phone rang and Diane got up to answer it:

"Hello."

She paused, listening.

"Oh hi Becky, how are you? ... I'm good thanks, what can I do for you? ... Hang on a second let me ask Alan, he's right here."

She covered the mouthpiece before she spoke to Alan:

"It's Becky, she wants to know if we'd like to go over for dinner tomorrow night."

Alan shrugged his shoulders, and then nodded his agreement.

"Okay Becky, that'd be great, thanks ... Yes, I'm sure that'll be fine ... Okay, see you at seven tomorrow, bye."

She put the phone down.

"Oh well, and I was going to cook something special tomorrow. Never mind." Alan laughed and threw a cushion at Diane.

"Liar!"

The couple was in bed asleep as the clock on the nightstand showed three- twenty-five. Diane's spirit detached from Alan's body and floated upwards. She rolled over and looked down at the two sleeping forms.

"I wonder if you'll be able to get out tonight?" she said to herself as she floated down towards her own body. "You said you'd try but I can't see any signs of an outline. Oh please do try Alan."

She floated back up toward the ceiling and lay there pondering for a while.

"Well, there's no point hanging around here all night, I think I'll try Arthur's suggestion and ID you, then I can go off for a quick jaunt."

She screwed up her face in concentration and visualised Alan, locking the image away somewhere deep in her consciousness.

"Okay that's that done; I hope it works. Now, where shall I go tonight?"

That familiar white flash obscured the whole scene!

Diane knew that she was streaking through the darkness of the Ether but she'd never had the perception of travelling for such a distance as this.

"Where am I going, I didn't think of anyone or anywhere, I'm sure?"

Eventually she felt herself slowing down and saw in the distance a dawn-like light but bluer and much softer than an earth-type dawn she'd ever experienced.

As she came to a halt on the edge of the light she felt an overwhelming sensation of love and well being.

"Oh, that's so wonderful," she thought.

Diane bathed in the warm light and experienced a feeling that she could only liken to being lovingly massaged by a multitude of gentle fingers. She also had a compelling feeling of belonging, as if she'd been away on a long trip but was now back home.

"Oh, this is heavenly," she innocently thought.

Suddenly a soft, deep, God-like voice filled her head.

"Hello Diane, I believe you're having a little problem back on earth?"

Diane looked around and although she couldn't see anything, she was sure she knew that voice.

"Arthur, is that you" she asked expectantly?

"Yes Diane, it's me."

She looked around again but still couldn't see anything.

"But where are you, I can't see you."

"It's alright," said Arthur soothingly, "I'm on the other side of the light; I've gone over at last, but now I'm here I can't return but I can communicate with you; well at least for the time being."

"Oh, I see," said Diane, not doing a very good job at hiding her disappointment.

"Now, now, don't get upset," soothed Arthur. "I brought you here because I felt that I contributed somewhat to your little problem; you and Alan and the mix-up with your earthly-bodies."

"But it wasn't your fault Arthur, we just … well … we just got mixed-up on re-entry, so to speak."

"I know, but if I hadn't helped you to get Alan out in the first place then there wouldn't have been a re-entry problem, now would there? Anyway, I'm going to send you a little NVC package, you remember, the ones you like so much?"

"Yes," said Diane, still scanning the blue horizon for the source of Arthur's voice.

"It should explain everything, and hopefully help you to fix your problem.

"Oh that'd be great. I'm already fed-up with being a man."

Arthur's voice laughed softly.

"I'm sure that you'll put the experience to good use my dear. Anyway, I must be off, so goodbye for now and I'll see you over here, sometime."

"Don't go yet Arthur, there's something I want to ask you."

There was no response.

"Arthur, are you there?"

Silence!

"Oh no," she cried."

Suddenly Diane's back straightened stiffly and she started to receive the NVC from Arthur.

"Uh, ooh, oh yes, I just love that feeling. Oh yes."

Diane gyrated for a while as the NVC came through, and then went limp as soon as it ended. And immediately she understood the meaning of the message.

"Of course, why didn't I think of that? That should sort Alan out."

She took one more lingering look at the wonderful blue dawn in the distance.

"Oh well, I'd better get back," she said to herself with a sigh.

The white flash blocked out the view.

Diane was back in bed, staring up at the ceiling. Quietly getting out of bed she picked up her pad and pen from the bedside table and went into the bathroom to make her notes.

30

Alan was already dressed for the office, seated at the kitchen table eating his breakfast when Diane came in wearing dressing gown and slippers. She looked tired, dragging her fingers through her hair, yawning loudly.

"Morning sleepy head," said Alan brightly.

"Morning love," replied Diane, yawning again.

She traipsed over to the Aga and poured herself a mug of tea, holding the teapot aloft.

"Another?"

"No thanks, I've got to get you to the office."

"Oh stuff the office," said Diane testily. "Let my body take a day off."

Alan looked at Diane with an enquiring expression.

"What's wrong darling, you don't look well."

"I don't know, I just feel strange, sort of stressed and tired at the same time. And these things feel a bit tender," she said, rubbing her breasts gently.

Alan got up from the table and walked over to the calendar on the wall by the fridge. He turned the page to last month and smiled.

"Well, I'd say you're probably in the early stages of my PMS!"

Diane looked apprehensive and immediately put her hand between her legs.

"Oh no," she wailed.

"Don't be silly," said Alan, "you're not due on for another five days yet. This is just the…"

He made a gesture of quotes in the air.

"Getting you ready period. Oops, no pun intended," he laughed.

"Bloody hell love, how long will I feel like this?" cried Diane dejectedly.

"Oh only a few days, until the period starts. Look," said Alan, walking over to one of the kitchen cupboards and taking out two packets, "take one of these capsules and two of these tablets right now."

Diane looked warily at the medication.

"What is it?" she said screwing up her nose.

"The capsule is primrose oil, it's supposed to help the PMS. These white tablets are Paracetamol, they'll help if you get any cramps."

"Cramps!" wailed Diane.

"Yes, cramps. Look, don't be a cry-baby and take the tablets."

He handed over the medication and filled a glass with water from the tap.

"Wouldn't it be great," Alan speculated out-loud, "if every man had to experience this at least once in his life; preferably when he's about sixteen and impressionable? Then we women might get a bit more sympathy and understanding from our so-called 'better halves'!"

"Oh come on love that's not fair," said Diane with an injured tone to her voice. "I've always been sympathetic to your monthlies."

"True. Well to a certain extent," he said in reflection. "But I still think it would be good for all men to experience it. Most males think that women are making a big thing out of nothing, just because it's a natural occurrence and happens every month. Anyway, I've said my piece, so take your pills and go back to bed if you don't feel any better."

He looked at the clock, which now showed seven fifty-five.

"Look darling, I'm sorry but I really do have to go."

He kissed Diane on the cheek, picked up his briefcase and left the kitchen, shouting from the front door:

"See you later, I'll be at the office if you need me, bye."

Diane was left looking a sorry sight, standing in the middle of the kitchen holding the tablets and the glass of water.

"But Di, you didn't say if you had an OOBE last night. Di!"

Alan was sitting in his office looking through the thick Yellow Pages book when the telephone rang. He pressed the hands-free button and spoke:

"Hello, Alan Harris."

Peter's voice emitted loudly from the speaker.

"Ah, Alan, I wonder if you could come up to my office sometime before lunch, shall we say eleven-thirty?"

Alan looked at his watch.

"Yes, of course Peter, what's it…"

"Good," I'll see you then."

As usual, the phone went dead before Alan could question further. He shook his head and hit the phone button to disconnect.

"Now what hell does that pompous git want?" he though to himself.

Shrugging his shoulders he went back to looking through the Yellow Pages and eventually found what he was searching for.

"Ah ha, I bet they've got one," he said out loud.

He hit the speakerphone button and dialled the number. The call rang out and momentarily a voice answered.

"Good morning, Audiomation, can I help you?"

"Yes, I think you can," replied Alan, smiling inwardly.

Peter was sat at his desk as his secretary ushered Alan into his office. He waved for Alan to take a chair in front of his grandiose desk.

"Hello Alan," he said, in an uncommonly friendly tone. "Would you like a coffee or a juice?"

"No thank you," said Alan politely, "I've just had one downstairs."

Peter nodded to his secretary and she left, closing the door quietly behind her.

"Okay Alan, tell me what happened at your meeting with James Alexander yesterday?" he bluntly enquired, looking Alan straight in the eyes.

Alan returned Peter's stare.

"We had lunch," declared Alan nonchalantly.

"I guessed that much," snapped Peter, whose sudden mood-swing made Alan feel a little more comfortable. "What did he want to talk about?"

"Oh talk," said Alan, maybe just a little too glibly. "Well, basically, about dreams I suppose."

"Dreams" growled Peter incredulously. "Didn't I tell you not to discuss anything but business?"

"Actually, you said and I quote: '…no more talk of dreams and the like … stick to business'. But you also said: '…how important his business is to this firm,' and as he was the one asking all the searching questions, well, what could I do but accede to the clients request."

"Good God man," bellowed Peter, who didn't like subordinates trying out one-upmanship on him, "don't you know how to subtly change the subject in a conversation?"

"Of course I do," said Alan indignantly, "but even the most fluent of politicians has to answer a direct question if it's put to him ten times, or he might just annoy the questioner; and I most certainly didn't want to upset this questioner, he's our biggest client."

"Hmph, well," blustered Peter as his telephone rang.

He snatched up the handset and shouted into the mouthpiece:

"I thought I told you no calls."

A short silence ensued and Peter's face went slightly pink.

"Oh, alright," he said more calmly, "put him through. "Hello," said Peter, his face blossoming into a big smile. "I'm fine James, how are you? … Oh good, I'm so pleased. In fact Alan's here in my office right now, he was just telling me what a pleasant and stimulating luncheon he had with you."

Peter laughed at something James said and he looked at Alan through hooded eyes.

"Yes he does, doesn't he? … Okay then James thanks for calling, bye."

Peter hung up the phone, placed his elbows on his desk and looked at Alan thoughtfully over steepled fingers.

"It seems," he said, uncharacteristically quietly, "that he likes you."

"Oh good," said Alan smiling, "it's reciprocated. He's a very intelligent and pleasant man."

"And one of the wealthiest nouveau-riche men in the North of England, if not the country," said

Peter with a somewhat resentful inflexion in his voice. "So, from now on, as you two seem to get on so well, I want you to join John on the Mega-Software team, until the floatation's over."

"Fine," said Alan a little surprised. "I'll enjoy that."

Then he paused thoughtfully for a moment.

"Just one little thing though."

"Yes?" said Peter inquisitively."

"I know John's team is currently working flat-out on this deal, eighteen-hour days and all that…"

Peter jumped in, raising his eyebrows slightly.

"Is that a problem for you Alan?"

"No, not at all, well, except for tonight. We, my wife Diane and me that is, have a prior dinner engagement."

Peter sounded ominously mellow in his response.

"Don't worry dear boy, you can start on the team tomorrow. I'll inform John."

Alan was somewhat bewildered at Peter's understanding manner.

"Oh, right then, thank you," he said as Peter rose from his seat and looked at his watch.

"Must dash," said Peter, offering his hand to Alan. "I've got a meeting at noon."

Alan shook Peter's hand as the law-firm's pompous senior partner continued:

"This could be a big career enhancement for you young man," advised Peter in a fatherly tone, "make sure you grasp it with both hands."

"Yes, thank you, I will," said Alan forcing a smile.

Peter's phone rang again and as he started to talk Alan left the office looking just a little perplexed.

Becky Ayres was in her kitchen preparing food for that night's dinner with Diane and Alan when she heard a knock at the front door. Wiping her hands on her apron, she went to see who it was. Becky opened the door and was pleasantly surprised to see Diane standing there, looking a little dishevelled.

"Hi Diane, come on in."

"Oh thanks Becky."

Diane stepped up into the hallway and the two went straight through into the kitchen. Becky automatically went over to the sink and picked up the kettle, filling it from the tap.

"Tea or coffee?"

"Oh, tea please Becky, I'm parched. I must have walked five miles this morning."

"Five miles!" exclaimed Becky, with a look of astonishment. "Are you in training for something or just a little mad?"

Diane forced a smile.

"Neither," she said, "I'm just trying to walk off my cramps, you know, that time of month."

"That's a new one on me," said Becky with a laugh. "If I did a five-mile walk I'd end up with the cramps."

The kettle clicked off and she poured some of the steaming water into the teapot, swishing it around to warm the pot.

"Have you taken anything for them?" said Becky as she put several heaped teaspoons of tea into the pot and filled it with water.

"Oh just the usual, an evening primrose capsule and a couple of Paracetamol."

Becky went to one of her kitchen cupboards and took out a small packet.

"Here, try these."

She handed the packet to Diane.

"It's an herbal remedy for period pains, they seem to work for me."

"Thanks Becky," said Diane, glancing at the instructions on the packet. "I'll give them a try."

Becky poured the tea and the two sat down at the kitchen table.

"How's work?" enquired Becky.

"Oh, you know, not bad," said Diane. "I was in the office yesterday, editing the print-proof of an article on Johnny Bizarre. It'll be in the magazine next week."

"Johnny Bizarre," said Becky with a shake of her head, "there's a name to conjure with. Where do they get them?"

"I'm not sure," said Diane, "but he's not a bad bloke, quite articulate off screen."

"You've met him?" asked Becky with a look of awe.

"Yes, briefly. He came to the office; well, to Alan's office, last year. Alan's firm's London office acts for one of his private companies."

"I don't know, you career women meet all the interesting people," she said enviously. "Think yourself lucky that you haven't ended up like me; closeted in the house half your life, looking after a bunch of males."

"But won't you get a job when the boys are a little older?" queried Diane.

"I suppose I'll have to, Arthur's pension isn't much and the savings won't last forever; but who's going to want a forty-something widow with no qualifications?"

"Oh come on now, there must be a multitude of opportunities for someone like you. If you really want something then you'll find it. After all you've got a great personality, and you're very attractive; especially sans pinny!"

She pointed to Becky's apron and they both laughed.

"You know Diane you're a real tonic. I'm really pleased that you and Alan moved into the village

And you've got me thinking now. Maybe I will start to look for something, or take a course at home, ready for when the boys are grown. You know, just to be prepared."

Diane made a two-fingered salute.

"As we used to say in the scouts."

"Scouts!" exclaimed Becky.

Alan walked into the Audiomation store, which was packed with all kinds of vinyl records, cassette-tapes and CD's. He had a quick word with the shop assistant, who showed him to a small rack of cassettes in the back of the store. After a few minutes reading the backs of several tapes, Alan went to the cash desk and handed over the one he'd chosen, along with a ten-pound-note. The sales assistant rang-up the sale and handed Alan his purchase in a small bag.

"Thank you," said Alan. "I think this should do the trick."

The sales-assistant smiled and gave Alan his change and he left the store. As he got outside he took a look in the bag.

"Right then, let's try this out on Alan!"

The wheels of the car stopped their scrunching sound as Alan drove from the gravelled drive onto the cobbled courtyard of the farmhouse and stopped the car. And with his purchase held tightly in his hand walked up to the front door and let himself in with his key.

Diane was upstairs in the study looking over some legal papers when she heard Alan shouting from downstairs.

"I'm up here, in the study," she yelled.

Alan pounded up the stairs two at a time.

"Hi," he said," as he walked into the study, "how do you feel, any stomach cramps yet?"

"No, nothing. In fact I feel fine since Becky gave me an herbal something-or-other."

"Oh, you saw Becky today?"

"Yes, we had coffee this morning but it nearly turned into a fiasco."

"Fiasco, what fiasco?" asked Alan.

"Oh it was nothing really, I just made some comment about being in the scouts and…"

"Scouts?" blurted Alan.

"Exactly," laughed Diane, "that's just what Becky said. But I think I covered it pretty well. I told her that I was a scout leader for a while, when I was a teenager. It seemed to work."

"I won't ask how you got talking about the scouts," said Alan. "Anyway, with a bit of luck I think that we might be back in our own bodies by the morning."

"Really," said Diane excitedly, "how's that?"

Alan handed Diane the bag with the cassette-tape.

"Get your Walkman out and listen to this."

"What is it?" queried Diane.

Alan held up his hand. "Don't ask, just listen to it and then tell me what you think."

Diane looked in the bag and took out the tape.

"This," she said, holding the tape between two fingers and looking at it somewhat disdainfully, "is going to help us get our bodies back?"

"Just listen to it and then we'll talk. In the meantime, I'll make us an early dinner and then, hopefully, we can get a good night's sleep and do our stuff. Okay?"

"Okay," agreed Diane, "you're the expert."

Alan had just finished making a lasagne and green-salad for dinner when Diane walked into the kitchen. He looked at Diane and smiled.

"Well?"

"I'm not sure love. I can see why you think it might work but it's a long shot if you ask me."

"Well, it was Arthur's suggestion," said Alan.

"Oh, you didn't say you'd seen Arthur."

"Well, I didn't really see him, you see he's gone on, to the next level."

"Next level?"

"Yes, you remember? I told you about the next level, when we've finished here with our earth-lives we go on to the next level."

"Oh right, yes."

She thought for a moment and then looked dryly at Alan.

"Hang on though, didn't you say that once you've gone over to the next level you can't come back?"

"Yes, I did, but Arthur used my ID and called me to a place on the far side of the Ether…"

A far-away look temporarily cloaked his face.

"It's really beautiful," he said dreamily, then quickly snapped out of his reverie. "Anyway, that's why I didn't really see him, but he communicated with me and suggested that we use that self-improvement tape to help you to totally relax your body. It utilises a kind of self-hypnosis to get its message across."

"I gathered that from the tape's intro, and the bit I listened to did make me feel quite relaxed."

"Well, all we can do is try it," said Alan. "It's better than nothing."

"True, I'll try anything that'll get me my body back. Right, let's eat and then we can have an early night."

Diane glanced at the kitchen clock and threw her head back pulling a face.

"Oh shit."

"What," asked Alan, sounding concerned "have you got a cramp?"

Diane looked at Alan and slapped her forehead with the palm of her hand.

"No, we've forgotten dinner tonight, with Becky."

"Oh damn, you're right! Well we'll just have to call her and say that you don't feel too good. She already knows about your PMS."

"No, we can't," said Diane, "she's been working really hard preparing the meal for tonight, we have to go. We'll just have to make sure that we don't leave too late."

"You're right, come on let's get ready."

"It's alright," said Diane flashing a quick grin, "no rush, we've got an hour yet and all you have to do is shower and shave. It's us women that need all the time and I'm almost ready."

"Okay then," said Alan with a smile, "let's spend half an hour going over what we're going to do tonight, so we don't make any mistakes."

"Okay," said Diane, "I'll get the Walkman."

31

Diane, Alan, Becky and the boys were sitting around the table in Becky's dining room, having just finished their dinner. Everyone looked absolutely stuffed, as if they couldn't eat another crumb. Alan folded his napkin and placed it beside his plate.

"Oh my," he gasped, "I don't think I'll eat for a week. That really was fabulous Becky."

Becky smiled demurely.

"Thank you Alan but it's praise enough to see you leave your plate like that. It looks like it doesn't need to go in the dishwasher."

Everyone laughed and Matt looked across at Diane.

"Y' see Missis Arris," he said with a little wink, "A told y' thar our mum wer' a gud cuk."

"You were certainly right about that Matt. She's a fabulous cook."

She looked at Becky.

"In fact, remember what we were talking about this morning Becky?"

"Which particular part?" asked Becky with a frown, "not scouting!"

"No, silly," laughed Diane. "About a new vocation for you, when the boys get older."

"Oh yes," said Becky, nodding her recollection.

"Well you don't need to look for one anymore," you already have it."

"I don't understand," said Becky.

Diane looked across the table and addressed Alan:

"Would you say that we eat out more than the average couple?"

"Probably," replied Alan. "Mainly due to our jobs; and living in London for all those years changed our eating habits. You can get anything at most times of the day or night in London. Anyway, why do you ask," he said, "what are you getting at?"

"Yes, what are you on about Diane," echoed Becky?

"Well, you were saying this morning you felt you couldn't see a future for you, when the boys grew-up; and claimed that you didn't have any qualifications. Well, from what I've just seen and tasted tonight, you're a better cook than most of the chef's in the restaurants I've eaten in, and I've eaten in some of the best in the country."

"True," confirmed Alan, "very true."

Becky blushed a little at all the compliments and looked down at the table.

"Oh get away with you," she said bashfully. "It's nothing more than I've been doing all my life."

"Exactly," said Diane. "We rarely see our own abilities as skills, especially if were using them every day. We tend to take them for granted. I mean, you've got such a flair for cooking and I don't just mean the quality and taste of your food. The presentation and attention to detail that you put on here," she gestured at the table, "is equal to any of the best restaurants I know of."

Alan looked at Becky and nodded his agreement.

"She's right Becky. You have a great talent."

"Well thank you, both of you," said Beck modestly. "But I still say it's nothing special, I just enjoy it."

"Well that's a plus then," asserted Diane. "Just think how many people don't like to cook? Those people who eat to live, as opposed to those who live to eat; and even those who live to eat aren't always good cooks themselves, so they tend to eat out a lot."

"What are you saying then," said Becky looking a little perplexed, "that I should become a cook or something?"

"Not a cook Becky, a Chef!" said Diane with a grandiose gesture.

"But I couldn't do this for complete strangers," remarked Becky.

"Of course you could," said Diane encouragingly. "We were strangers not long ago."

"Oh, but that's different."

"Nonsense," chipped in Alan, "I'm sure you could do it."

"He's right Becky," continued Diane enthusiastically, "and I think that you should seriously consider the opportunity. After all, there's a lot of money in food, especially this sort of thing. Good grief woman, you could make a fortune! In fact, I'll help you set out a small business plan if you want. When you see the figures it might change your mind."

Becky seemed to warm to the idea.

"Okay then," she said excitedly, you're on! Let's work something out."

"There you go," said Diane, "that's the spirit."

Alan smiled at Diane's apt choice of words.

"Indeed," he said, "that's just the spirit that won the west, or in this case West Yorkshire. Hey, you could call it Becky's Café."

Becky laughed.

"I don't think so, there's already a famous café called Betty's, in Harrogate, it's been there for decades; and there's one in Ilkley too. They might think I was trying to poach their name."

Diane laughed at the chance irony of Becky's words.

"Very good Becky, poach, I like it. Anyway, if Betty could do it why can't Becky?"

Alan looked deliberately at his watch.

"Well, as much as I hate to break up this conglomerate talk I think we should do the washing up and then get off. We've both got to be up early for work tomorrow."

Becky got up from her seat.

"Okay but don't worry about the washing up, the boys will help me stack it in the dishwasher."

"Are you sure," asked Diane, "were more than happy to help."

"Yes," said Alan firmly, "in fact I insist that we help," and he started to collect the plates, giving Diane a little visual gee-up.

"Come on darling we'll have these shifted in a jiffy."

"Alright then," she sighed resignedly.

Everyone got up and started clearing the table; and for once, even Mark didn't grumble!

32

Back at the farmhouse later that evening, Diane was in bed adjusting her Walkman earphones as Alan came out of the bathroom.

"Don't start yet," he cried."

Diane pulled one of the earphones away from her ear.

"Sorry?" she said, cocking her head to one side.

"I said don't start yet."

"It's okay I was just getting to the right place on the tape."

"Oh, okay."

"I really hope this works love," said Diane with a sigh.

"Well it's our best shot if you ask me, so don't forget, set your alarm for four, so when you wake up, you'll have had…"

He looked at the clock, which showed ten forty-five.

"Oh, about five hours sleep. That should be plenty, and with the tape to help you, you should be able to get reasonably relaxed within ten to fifteen minutes of waking."

"Let's hope so," said Diane, who still wasn't totally convinced of the idea."

Putting the Walkman on her bedside table she snuggled down in bed. Alan got in beside her and kissed her on the cheek.

"Goodnight darling," he said tenderly, "see you soon. Oh, I almost forgot, put your alarm under your pillow, so it doesn't wake me. If I'm already out and I get woken up, it'll bring me back into my … sorry … your body, and we don't want that now, do we?"

Diane grabbed the small travel-alarm from her bedside table and put it under her pillow.

"Okay, done," she said with a yawn. "Goodnight love, sleep tight."

She kissed Alan on the cheek and reached over and turned off her bedside lamp.

It was a wonderfully clear, still night and the farmhouse and its surrounding countryside were bathed in bright, silver moonlight as a tiny speck that was a shiny communications satellite twinkled as it slowly tracked across the star-laden sky. And somewhere in the distance, on the other side of the valley, an owl hooted and then a dog-fox barked eerily, as if in response; which in turn caused a lone sheep to look up, briefly halting its near-continuous nocturnal browsing. Inside, Alan and Diane's bedroom was quite light from the brightness of the moon, which cast a sharp shadow of the window-frame on the opposite wall.

The couple was sound asleep as the alarm started to beep quietly. Diane roused groggily, reached under her pillow and switched off the alarm. Rubbing her eyes she looked over at Alan, who seemed to be fast asleep, so she very carefully reached over to the bedside table for the Walkman and placed the earphones on her head. Then, switching the machine to play, she lay back again, closing her eyes.

About ten minutes later Diane's spirit detached from Alan's body and floated up near the ceiling, rolling over to look down.

"Good," she thought, "Alan's got the earphones on. If it's going to work at all it should happen soon."

She floated down closer to the bed and noticed that the outline of her physical body was starting to blur. Then, to her great delight and sheer wonderment, Alan's spirit rose slowly but surely up from her own body. She backed away until Alan was at the same height as she was. He lay there quietly for a few moments then looked around bewilderedly.

"Hi there," said Diane excitedly, "you made it then?"

Alan laughed nervously.

"Yes," he said, "thank God, or should I say thank Arthur. That cassette-tape worked really well."

"That was an awesome sight darling," said Diane, looking back down at her body and then back at Alan's spirit-form. "You just … well … kind of appeared from within me. It was totally different from when Arthur and me pulled you out. That seemed, relatively speaking, quite natural; just like pulling you from you. But seeing you come out from me was truly remarkable."

"It felt sort of strange too," said Alan. "Just before I floated away I got this fluttering feeling in the centre of my body and then it spread out until it got to my toes and my head. Then I got this strange sensation, right between my eyes, like a tightness of the skin, a dull itch and an intense tingling all at the same time. Then I think I released from your body. Hang on, no. Just prior to that I got a funny feeling, similar to the one you get when you're on a Big Dipper, when you leave your stomach behind. Strange but not unpleasant," he concluded.

"That's different to how I remember mine; maybe it's something to do with the method," said Diane, intrigued. "Anyway, let's discuss that later, we have to go back now, the way we planned. I'll go back first and then I'll wake you up. That'll cause you to come back into your own body."

Alan looked a little disappointed at having to return so soon.

"Can't we just go for a little journey somewhere," he appealed, "seeing as I'm out now?"

"No way," said Diane adamantly. "We don't want a repeat of last time. Anyway, now you know you can get out by using the relaxation tape, you can try on your own, some other time. Alright?"

"I guess your right," he said resignedly. "Off you go."

Diane smiled warmly and touched Alan's face.

"See you in a mo darling."

She slowly floated down towards her sleeping form and at the last moment rolled over onto her back and without stopping, gently blended into the slumbering body. Alan looked on, totally amazed at the sight taking place just feet below him.

Diane awoke and looked around the bedroom, removing the earphones that Alan had placed on her head. As far as she could tell, Alan was still asleep beside her but she couldn't help looking up to where she'd last seen him, floating above the bed.

"Okay darling, it's time to come home," she said out loud as she turned over on her side and started softly kissing Alan's ear.

Nothing happened, so she leaned over and turned on the lamp.

"Come on sleepy head," she said quietly, "time to wake up."

Nothing! Alan's body was quite still and his breathing low and slow. Diane looked at him with raised eyebrows and shook his shoulder.

"Alan," she said more loudly, "come on, wake up."

Diane removed her hand and was just about to give him a real whack when she noticed his body give a little jerk and he started to move.

"Hmm, what," he groaned. "Morning already?"

He opened his eyes and blinked.

"Thank goodness," said Diane with a sigh of relief, "I thought you'd gone off and got lost again."

Alan rubbed his eyes.

"Lost," he mumbled, "what are you on about?"

Diane smiled inwardly as she watched Alan wake up. She always felt he looked at his most appealing, like a little boy, when he was half asleep; something she put down to her as yet unfulfilled maternal instinct.

"Just give yourself a minute to wake up properly," she said quietly. "Do you remember having the OOBE tonight?"

"OOBE? … Oh yes," he said, looking wide-eyed at Diane and then down at himself, prodding his torso. "Oh, wow!" he shrieked ecstatically leaping up onto his knees, "we did it. We've got our bodies back."

He leaned over and hugged Diane tightly.

"I guess you do remember," she chuckled reciprocating the hug.

He rubbed his eyes again, shaking his head in an effort to clear it.

"It's all coming back to me now. You were right; the recollection is sort of dreamlike. I remember watching you float down into your body. That was an incredibly amazing thing to behold; and then I just sort of floated there for a moment. I saw you wake up and take off the Walkman earphones and then you said something but I didn't hear properly, then you leaned over and whispered something in my ear."

"I wasn't whispering," said Diane, "I was kissing you. Trying to wake you up gently."

"Thanks for the sensitivity," he said with a warm smile. "Anyway, after that, you turned on the light and said something else but again, I couldn't quite hear. Then I saw you shake me and I heard you this time, you told me to wake up and I started to get this strange feeling, like I did over Paris, and then there was a sort of white flash and a rushing feeling and voila, I woke up."

"That's exactly what happened!" said Diane, surprised at her surprise.

She leaned over and picked up her pad and pen from the bedside table.

"I think I'll record this for posterity, or for future reference, if I decide to write that article one day."

Alan looked down at himself, patting his body.

"Don't take this the wrong way," he said, "because you've got a great body, but I'm sure glad to be back in this one."

"Likewise," said Diane. "In fact I think I'll go for a pee, just to test things out."

She jumped out of bed and headed for the bathroom.

"It'll be nice not to have to stand up and aim that little fire-hose of yours; and I won't have to wipe the rim after either."

She disappeared into the bathroom as Alan stared after her with a hurt expression on his face.

"What do you mean, little fire-hose?" he muttered in his schoolboy-lost voice.

Diane, dressed in her usual jeans and sweatshirt, was making scrambled eggs at the Aga as Alan walked in, dressed in his usual work-attire of business suit, shirt and tie. He went straight over to Diane and hugged her from behind.

"Hey there Romeo," she said coyly, "didn't you get enough of that at five o'clock this morning?"

"No ma'am," he said huskily, running his hands over Diane's breasts. "I feel like a new man. Ooh and you feel like a new woman."

"Yes, strange isn't it? Even after just a few days in your body mine feels strange to me now. It's amazing how quickly our spirit adapts to its environment."

"Well I suppose it has to doesn't it?" said Alan reflectively. "I mean, imagine how it has to adapt when it goes into an unborn baby for the first time."

"Yes, incredible," concurred Diane as she turned from the Aga with the pan of steaming eggs in her hand. "Okay, breakfast is served."

They sat at the table and started to eat, both reflecting on the last few day's experiences.

"Darling," said Diane looking up from her plate.

"Yes?" said Alan cautiously, recognising Diane's appeasing tone.

"There are some things I think I should tell you, now that we're back in our own bodies."

"What's that love," said Alan, raising his eyebrows.

"Look, don't be annoyed, I know I should have told you this earlier but I didn't want you to be preoccupied while we were planning last night; it might have made it more difficult for you to have the OOBE."

Alan raised his eyebrows again, this time a tad more severely.

"Is this bad news, something to do with work?"

"Well, I suppose indirectly it's to do with work," she said guardedly.

"Come on then, spit it out."

Diane took a long drink of her orange juice.

"You remember the lunch I had with James Alexander?"

"Yeees," said Alan, stretching out the word questioningly.

"Well, after we'd finished talking about the dream scenario, he sort of offered me … you that is … a job."

"Bloody hell," said Alan, nearly choking on his breakfast. "James Alexander, Mega-Software, offered me a job?"

"Yes. In fact, he asked me … sorry … you, to come over to his offices after the floatation, to take a look around."

Alan sat back in his chair and dropped his fork on his plate.

"Well I never," he said, grinning like a Cheshire cat.

"Oh I'm so pleased you're not angry with me," said Diane, extremely relieved.

"Angry with you?" I could kiss you. I've always wanted to represent a big corporation from the inside, but to work for such a rising company as Mega-Software; it's just … well … fantastic. If I'd wished for a career move I couldn't have done better than that."

He paused for a moment in thought then looked at Diane and his face dropped.

"Hang on a minute though," he said, slowly shaking his head. "He doesn't really know me does he?"

"What do you mean?" said Diane looking puzzled.

"Well think about it love, he offered the job to you not me. I mean, your personality in my body."

"But he doesn't know that, and anyway you've got a great personality."

Alan smiled tenderly.

"Thanks love but how do we know that he'll agree with you, once he's met me; the real me that is! I think that you should go over everything that you can remember from all the meetings with James, in fact, with everyone that you met while you were me. I've got a feeling it could be extremely worthwhile!"

33

Today was the momentous day; the day that they'd all been working towards for the past year, and everyone who'd been involved in the floatation was in the boardroom of Mega-Software. Alan and Diane; Diane having been personally invited at the insistence of James Alexander; Peter, Alan's boss, and all the team from the law-firm; including John, who was already busy chatting-up James' secretary. It was exactly four o'clock and someone at the far end of the room started to shush loudly as the business news came on a big-screen television; set up especially for the day. Everyone turned to look at the screen as the newsreader – the same one that Diane saw in the Sony shop-window during her trip to the future – started to speak. Diane put her arm around Alan's waist and gave him a little squeeze.

"Oh darling, this is so de-ja-vu; it's making the hairs on my neck stand up."

The newsreader on the screen began to speak:

"Today saw the initial public offering of Mega-Software, the Leeds based company that produces an immense range of software products, including that best-selling title Home Business Office..."

The newsreader spoke as the screen flashed up pictures of computer screens around the world running Mega's products, interspersed with internal and external shots of Mega's head-office buildings in Leeds; which elicited laughs and comments from the attendant staff as they saw themselves on the TV. The newsreader continued:

"The company's shares successfully floated on the London Stock Market this morning, with subscriptions outstripping available shares by three-to-one. The value of the shares immediately increased by fifteen percent within an hour of the commencement of trading."

More pictures flashed up on the screen, this time of the London Stock Exchange.

"Sky News was in Leeds this morning, at the Headquarters of Mega-Software, to get the reaction of its Founder and Chairman Mr. James Alexander."

The television screen flicked over to a picture of a woman reporter standing next to James on the lawns outside the Mega offices, and the assembled audience in the boardroom cheered loudly. The female reporter spoke:

"Tell me Mr Alexander, how do you feel now that the financial markets have given you such an overwhelming vote of confidence?" she asked as she put her microphone under James' chin.

"Not me," said James, "my company."

He immediately smiled at his faux pas.

"Sorry, old habits die hard, 'The Company' Mega-Software and its team of dedicated management and workers, they're the ones who made this possible and I'd just like to thank them all for..."

Another cheer emanated from the boardroom audience, and as the interview continued on the TV, James made his way through the crowd in the boardroom over to Alan and Diane.

He shook Alan's hand warmly, patting him on the back, and gave Diane a kiss on the cheek.

"I'm really pleased you could both make it."

"I wouldn't have missed it for anything," said Alan, "and thanks for inviting Diane."

"Yes, thank you James," said Diane warmly, "and congratulations, it looks like everyone in the country tried to buy into Mega-Software, several times over."

"Yes," he said quietly, leaning closer to the couple, "but would it have been as successful two weeks from now?"

"I suppose we'll only know that in two weeks time," said Alan with a smile.

"I have a sneaking suspicion that it wouldn't have been," said James. "Anyway, I take it you've had the grand tour of our meagre premises?"

"I don't think meagre is the word I'd have used but the answer's yes," said Alan. "And very impressive it is too."

"Absolutely," agreed Diane.

"It's a wonderful place," added Alan, "and your staff, so much young talent and so dedicated to you and the company."

"And have you given any more thought to our little lunchtime conversation the other week?" asked James, winking at Alan.

"Yes, lots," replied Alan, "and having discussed it with Diane here, I'd certainly like to discuss it further with you."

James looked truly thrilled at Alan's words.

"Absolutely, for sure," he said enthusiastically, "I'm delighted you feel that way. Look, do you both like rugby league?"

Diane quickly jumped in; answering the question before Alan could open his mouth:

"Oh yes, avidly," she said. "In fact we watch it whenever we can."

"Great, then you must come to Leeds this Sunday, they're playing the Halifax Blue Socks It's not common knowledge but I have a small shareholding in Leeds Rhinos."

It was Alan's turn to jump in.

"Small," he said sarcastically, "last I heard i was thirty percent."

James looked impressed.

"You do keep your ear close to the ground don' you Alan?" he said leaning over closer to the couple. "Well it'll be fifty-one percent on Friday so we'll be having another little celebration after the game on Sunday, to wet the club's head so to speak. Anyway, if you can make it I'd love for you both to come along."

"Thanks," said Alan, "we'll definitely be there."

"Yes," said Diane, I'll really look forward to that."

James looked over the heads of the crowd at someone waving to him.

"Oops, got to go, I think the local press wants me for another photo call.

I'll see you both on Sunday then, bye; and thanks again Alan, I think I owe you a great deal, no matter what the outcome in two weeks time."

James left, making his way towards a crowd gathering outside the boardroom door and Alan looked sideways at Diane.

"Avidly watch it ... whenever when we can!"

Diane smiled coyly.

"I don't suppose I'll be the only woman there now, will I," she said with a wry smile. "And anyway, you know what they say, if you can't beat 'em..."

"You know something love, those few days in my body have definitely changed you."

"Well let me put it this way," said Diane reflectively. "You can't walk in the shoes of a great man without having some insight into his soul!"

34

The main headline in the newspaper read:

"WORLD STOCK MARKETS TUMBLE".

Another, smaller article, down near the bottom of the page read:

"SHUTTLE SUCCESSFULLY DELIVERS COMMUNICATIONS SATELLITE".

Diane smiled to herself, reflecting on her little foray into outer space, then looked up from her reading as she heard a car outside.

It was two weeks on from the Mega floatation and Diane was sitting in the lounge at the farmhouse reading the 'Yorkshire Post' newspaper. She looked up again as the front door opened and Alan shouted from the lobby:

"Hi love, I'm home."

"I'm in the lounge," shouted Diane.

Alan came in, dropping his briefcase on the coffee table.

"Hi darling, have a good day?" enquired Diane, putting down her paper.

"I suppose that depends on your interpretation of good," said Alan wearily. "Of course we didn't need the TV and newspapers to tell us what happened but it was still a bit spooky watching it all unravel today."

"I know," said Diane, shaking her head, "I've just been reading all about it in the paper. It looks like it's going to be a rocky few weeks for lots of people."

"No kidding," said Alan, "I'm glad I'm not at the old firm anymore, I'd probably be handling a welter of potential meltdowns."

"You know," said Diane, "I've been thinking about the way they made you leave, the minute you handed in your resignation. It wasn't very gentlemanly was it?"

"Oh I don't know," said Alan indifferently, "it's not unusual conduct for a firm when someone like me hands in their notice out of the blue. After all I wouldn't tell the boss where I was going, so he had to assume I'd been poached by a rival firm. Still, he got a hell of a shock last week, when he called James and got put through to me. I'd have loved to have seen his face," he said with a derisive laugh.

"I'll bet he was as red as a beetroot," chortled Diane.

"Undoubtedly," agreed Alan. "I'll bet some poor sucker in the office got the backlash from that revelation. Anyway, he's had a week to get used to it now."

He sat down on the couch next to Diane.

"Oh, by the way, James said something strange to me today. It was as if we'd had a recent conversation and I wondered if he'd had it with you."

"What did he say?"

"He asked me if I'd taken his advice about today. I assumed it was something to do with the stock market crash."

"Really," said Diane quite innocently, "and what did you say?"

"I had to wing it. I said: 'I always take note of and analyse your advice very carefully James'. He just smiled at me, winked and said: 'you lawyers', and walked off laughing."

Alan looked over at Diane who had buried her head in the paper and was trying madly to stifle a laughing fit. He pulled the paper away to reveal Diane's face contorted in laughter.

"What?"

Diane couldn't stop laughing.

"What's so funny?"

"Oh I'm sorry," she said calming, "I shouldn't be laughing but I do know what James meant."

Alan looked at Diane with a frown.

"Well then?"

"At the lunch we had that day at that Italian restaurant," recounted Diane; "James said that if the markets moved as predicted in my dream, although of course at that time it was supposedly your dream, he could make a fortune; and that he was going to see his stockbroker that afternoon. Now he didn't say it directly, but I got the strong impression that he was giving me a tip; to do as he was," she said, screwing up her face in anticipation of a rocket from Alan. "So I went to a stockbroker in Leeds and made some investments," she quickly concluded.

"You what?" said Alan sternly.

"Look darling," she said with an appeasing tone, "I knew that if it had been you that had heard what he said you wouldn't do anything, because of client/lawyer confidentiality or something equally as ridiculous. But it wasn't you he told, it was me. And I didn't tell you, so you're in the clear."

"Di!" said Alan with a sigh, "I wouldn't have had a problem with client confidentiality. If you remember it was you, as me, who told the whole of our office about the impending market crash? The fact that James may have been the only one to believe you, and was prepared to back the dream with cash, is totally irrelevant."

He got up from his seat and assumed a macho pose in front of Diane, with crossed arms and legs slightly apart.

"So how much did you invest?"

"Five thousand pounds," she said wincing.

"Five grand! On what," clamoured Alan?

"Well, I asked the broker what would be the best thing to invest in if I thought the markets were going to go off by fifteen-to-twenty-percent next week."

"What did he say after he'd stopped laughing?" asked Alan with a grin.

"Actually he didn't laugh," she said indignantly. "He wasn't that sort, he was very dry. He just said: 'I'd have to advise you to go into some form of short-term futures'."

"Bloody derivatives no doubt," said Alan vehemently; good commissions and high-risk. But the broker gets paid full-whack whatever the outcome."

"Yes, that's it, futures derivatives. But they're only high risk if you don't know what's going to happen. So I bought five thousand pounds worth, which means we made about one thousand pounds profit in less than a month. Not bad eh?" she said happily.

"Do you have the purchase slip?" asked Alan quizzically.

"Yes," she said, jumping up and rummaging for the slip in her handbag.

She handed it to Alan who read it and then looked stony faced at Diane. She bit her knuckles.

"What, what's wrong?" she said nervously.

"What you actually bought, were options to buy short-term futures."

"What does that mean then, that I didn't really buy them?"

"No, you bought options-to-buy and your five grand was actually only two percent of the full amount."

He paused and looked at Diane, who looked back at him with an extremely pensive face.

"That full amount," he continued, "being two hundred and fifty thousand pounds."

Diane put her hands to her mouth.

"Oh my God. What have I done?"

"What you've unwittingly done," he said with a big grin, "is made a little short of three-hundred grand if the markets were off by the reported percentage today."

Diane's eyes grew large and she silently mouthed the words:

"Three hundred thousand pounds. Three hundred thousand pounds," she shouted, leaping at Alan and grabbing him around the neck. Alan struggled to keep his feet.

"Now hang on there young lady," he said firmly, "let me just bring you down to earth for a moment."

Diane stopped squealing and looked at Alan with a baby-faced pout.

"If the markets hadn't gone down, if they'd gone up instead, you would have had to pay the broke more than this house is worth."

"Oh," said Diane, apprehensively.

"Oh indeed. Remember one Nick Leeson o Barings Bank in Singapore."

Diane nodded in silent recall.

"Well a similar type of futures-derivatives are what put him in jail for ten years. So be warned. And I'm going to have a word with that broker and ask him what he thought he was doing selling sophisticated investments to a young woman who obviously doesn't know the difference between futures and Lottery tickets."

Diane looked down at her hands.

"Um, before you do that I think I should tell you that it was you, or should I say me as you, who bought them. And I sort of hinted that I was a corporate lawyer."

"Ah," he said nodding, "well that puts a different complexion on the matter.

"Sorry, apologised Diane.

"It's okay love, 'cause I've got something to tell you," he said to Diane, smiling from ear-to-ear.

"What?" she said, raising her eyebrows at the change of tone in Alan's voice.

"I invested some money too."

"Oh you stinker," she squealed, feigning a blow to his head. "You just put me through hell then."

"So, how much did you invest?" she said, looking at him sideways.

"Twenty grand."

"Twenty!"

"Yes and in the same sort of thing as your broker recommended."

Diane's eyes nearly popped out of her head.

"You mean you made…"

She did some quick mental calculation.

"Over one million pounds?"

"Or thereabouts," said Alan nonchalantly.

They looked at each other and burst into laughter.

"Oh my," said Diane in awe. "That's a total of around one-million-three-hundred thousand pounds."

She looked at Alan and smiled sweetly.

"Does this mean that I can have that Range Rover now?"

Alan threw a cushion at her and then leapt on her as she shrieked joyfully.

"No," he said, biting her ear, "well not just yet anyway."

He sat up to face Diane, adopting a more serious manner.

"You see I was thinking," he said, "if it hadn't been for us buying that OOBE book of Arthur's from the boys, none of this would've happened. Everything good that's happened to us since we came to Yorkshire has been as a result of that book. Your original OOBE, meeting Arthur, meeting Becky and the kids, the time travel that convolutedly got me my fabulous new job, and all this money from the investments; everything! And well, I just thought that we might use some of that money to help Becky. We could invest it, help her start up that café we were talking about."

Diane smiled but didn't speak; she just looked at Alan with a disbelieving face.

"What do you think then?" he asked.

"Oh Alan, what a wonderful thought."

She hugged him tightly.

"Let's do it," she said excitedly, "let's ring Becky right now."

Diane gazed around the room as if looking for something, or someone; then she smiled warmly.

"Arthur will be so pleased."

35

Later that evening the couple was sitting up in bed reading. Alan was looking at the notes he'd made at their meeting with Becky, who'd literally been in tears at the couple's generous offer of a fifty-fifty partnership for a new restaurant venture; Diane and Alan offering to put up all the money for the business and take care of the administration if Becky would run it on a day-to-day basis.

Diane was propped up on her pillows, looking at the commercial property advertisements in the local paper; ironically the "Telegraph and Argus", where Arthur spent so many happy years of his working life. As she turned the pages she came across a full-page advertisement for a local Sony store and looked up from the paper, stunned; as if she'd just had a revelation.

"Good God!" she cried out.

Alan looked up from his work startled.

"What, what's up?"

Diane turned to face him.

"I just had a really weird thought," she said.

"What's that then?" he asked inquisitively.

"I think that Arthur Ayres just might have engineered this whole thing!"

"What!" exclaimed Alan?

"No, listen," said Diane excitedly. "When I went on that time trip with Arthur and we went from 55BC to the future, he was the one who insisted that I chose the place and time for our next trip, right?"

"Well that's what you told me the following morning."

"And when we got to Leeds," she continued, "it was exactly thirty days in front of current earth-time, the exact day that the stock markets crashed. Today in fact."

Alan still looked a little puzzled.

"So, it was a coincidence."

"No," said Diane firmly, "it wasn't a coincidence. I just remembered something about that trip, something that I'd forgotten. It didn't seem important at the time but now I come to think about it, along with all the other little things ... yes that's it!"

"What," said Alan again, becoming more intrigued by the minute?

"When we got to Leeds that day, Arthur didn't want to come down with me, he said he had something else to do. So I went down on my own. Now you know me, the last sort of shop that I'd stop and look at would be an electrical store. But as I was just sort of cruising around I felt something pulling me, not physically pulling me, sort of steering me towards the Sony storefront. And even when I stopped, involuntarily, in front of

Sony's window display, the first thing I did was to try to move on. But I couldn't! It was like trying to drive away with the handbrake still on."

"Well, if anyone knows that feeling it's you," said Alan sarcastically.

Diane hit him across the chest with the newspaper.

"Pig, be serious for a moment will you. Now, where was I? Oh yes, I just couldn't move from the front of that store, not until the news item about the market-crash today was over. Then it was just like taking off the handbrake again, and I floated on."

"What were the other little things you mentioned?" asked Alan curiously.

Diane paused to collect her thoughts.

"Well, there was that detailed explanation that Arthur gave me about Da Vinci and Nostradamus using their OOBE's to gain information about the future; a fact that you picked up on when we discussed it. And Arthur put the doubt in my mind, as to whether or not you really believed in my OOBE's, which in turn made me even more determined for you to have an OOBE, so you really would believe. And then he came along, without being asked, and helped me get you out on your first OOBE. Then the clincher! Those pictures in my head when I was in the Mega-Software meeting at your offices. I mean, they just came flooding in, like a mini NVC. And our mix up getting back into our bodies, maybe he arranged that too. I mean, if that hadn't happened, you wouldn't have said anything at that Mega-Software meeting, would you?"

"Too true I wouldn't," agreed Alan firmly.

"There you are then, I rest my case. If the dream story hadn't come out at that meeting, none of what happened to us subsequently would have happened at all. And the news today would have been about the Mega-Software deal crashing."

Alan looked at Diane with a mystified expression and slowly shook his head. "You know love, sometimes you just amaze me. I think you could be right; I mean Arthur's pension isn't enough to see Becky and the boy's right. And he probably knew that if we got to know Becky, well especially you, that there'd be a lasting bond formed. I mean, once you'd talked to young Mat about his dad, he was fine from then on. Arthur probably knew from that moment that he could count on you and your good nature. And the rest's history as they say."

"Or not," said Diane with a laugh. "You know darling, Arthur must have really loved his family to stick around after he died, and go through all that he did for them."

She paused again in thought as something else occurred to her:

"You remember the day we moved in here, when I said I'd had a strange feeling and you put it down to a draught from one of the windows."

"Vaguely," recalled Alan.

"Well I'll bet that was Arthur, I'll bet he was around here from the moment we moved in."

She fell silent for a moment.

"It's a shame we can't tell Becky; about the OOBE's that is. She might feel a little better knowing Arthur was still looking out for her."

Alan laughed.

"Oh you could tell her alright but I think she might think twice about going into business with us if you did."

"You're right, it was just a wishful thought and I suppose that's how it'll have to stay."

She tossed the newspaper on the floor beside the bed and snuggled down, pulling the quilt around her neck.

"Gosh I feel tired all of a sudden."

Alan put his paper down and got the Walkman out of his bedside cabinet. Diane looked at him through sleepy eyes.

"Oh you're not going to listen to music are you?" she said wearily.

"No," said Alan with a chuckle. "I'm going to try to have an OOBE. I want to see if I can travel forward ten years and see how big the chain of Becky's Café's is by then."

Diane was already drifting off to sleep and smiled softly at Alan.

"Oh, that's alright then," she said drowsily.

And as Alan turned the light out and kissed her gently on the cheek, she could have sworn that she heard a faraway voice in her head. It laughed cheekily but gently:

"I knew you were a good student right from the start Diane but I didn't think you'd fathom it out that quickly. Thank you for all your help and I know you're going to have several wonderful lives."

Diane smiled to herself in that twilight zone between consciousness and sleep and didn't stir again until morning. No OOBE's to be remembered that night; at least not for one Diane Harris!

THE END?

ABOUT THE AUTHOR

Andrew Haughton was born in West Yorkshire, England, in the early nineteen fifties but had never heard of OOBE's – or for that matter showed any interest in the subject – until the early nineteen nineties. However, since then he has researched and personally experienced the OOBE phenomenon and now truly believes. He also believes that most people on earth have OOBE's, most nights, only they just don't realise it! "There have been many scientific studies undertaken on the subject," says Haughton. "Some agree that it's possible, some disagree, totally rejecting even the probability. However, for the moment, the majority of researchers seem indeterminate in their conclusions. I personally concur with the theories of the late Robert A. Monroe, who studied the subject for over thirty years and experienced and recorded innumerable personal OOBE's; and through the Monroe Institute, located in Virginia, USA, documented the experiences of hundreds of others."

Now that his Screenplay for OOBE is finished, Haughton is planning to write another two OOBE books. The next in this potential trilogy is "OOBE 2 - Coma©", centred on one of the original OOBE characters who is badly injured in an air crash and subsequently discovers what happens to ones spirit whilst in a deep coma.

Email OOBE Author Andrew E. Haughton
GetTheOOBE@aol.com

Printed in the United Kingdom
by Lightning Source UK Ltd.
98775UKS00001B/1-24